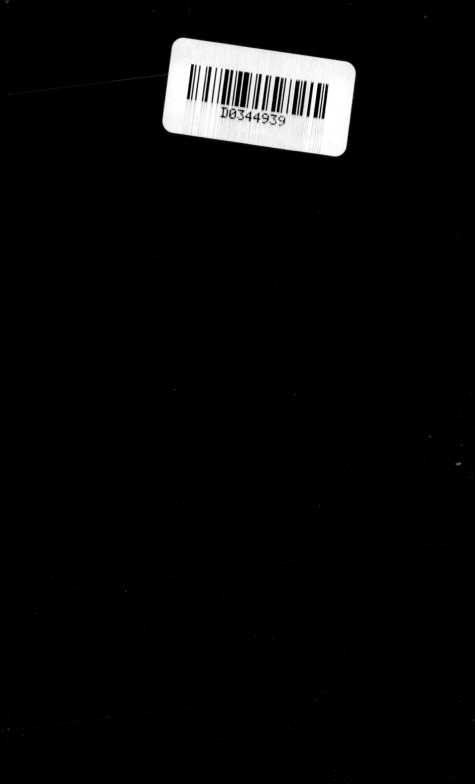

The Farmer's Daughter

Also by Jim Harrison

JIM HARRISON

The Farmer's Daughter

Grove Press
New York

Printed in the United States of America

FIRST EDITION

ISBN-13: 978-0-8021-1934-6

Grove Press

an imprint of Grove/Atlantic, Inc.

841 Broadway

New York, NY 10003

Distributed by Publishers Group West

www.groveatlantic.com

10 11 12 13 14   10 9 8 7 6 5 4 3 2 1

To Bob DeMott

Contents

The Farmer's Daughter

PART I

Chapter 1
1986

She was born peculiar, or so she thought. Her parents had put some ice in her soul, not a rare thing, and when things went well the ice seemed to melt a bit, and when things went poorly the ice enlarged. Her name was Sarah Anitra Holcomb.

She was without self-pity never having learned how to administer it. Things were as they were. A certain loneliness was an overwhelming fact of her life. Her family had moved to Montana in 1980 when she was nine years old. They felt like pioneers striking out from Findlay, Ohio, but without the young man called Brother, then eighteen and the son of her father's first marriage, who chose to stay behind but then up and joined the marines, an insult because the marines were the core of her father Frank's unhappiness. Frank had seen no combat in Vietnam but as a graduate of Purdue had been in the Competitive Strategies (all unsuccessful) Office in Saigon. His very best friend Willy, also from Findlay, had died from friendly fire in Khe Sanh. The death of Willy, a friend since childhood, was the poisonous goad that finally sent Frank out to Montana where he proposed to forget the world thirteen years after mustering out. The dissolving of the first marriage had put quite a crimp in saving a grubstake, and the second marriage and the arrival of Sarah further delayed his somewhat heroic plans. Frank was a pure ideologue and had planned a future that wouldn't include our culture and its murderous politics. As a mechanical engineering graduate of Purdue (magna cum laude), Frank was confident of making a living in Montana beyond the amount of the savings which he estimated would last three years.

In February 1980 Frank announced that they would make the big move in late April. He had just returned from Montana where he had closed a land deal for 180 acres. He made the statement with a military tinge as if saying, "We move out at dawn."

"Great! We're heading for God's country," said Frank's wife and Sarah's mother, who was nicknamed Peppy.

"There must be a hundred places in the U.S. that call themselves God's country," Frank muttered over his goulash made with super-lean beef. Peppy had been a home economics teacher when Frank met her at the Ohio State Fair where he had been manning his engineering firm's extensive display booth. One reason that he married Peppy was that his ex-wife had been an alcoholic and Peppy came from an evangelical family and didn't drink.

"I'm going to stay here and live with Grandma unless I can have a horse and dog on our ranch."

This brought dinner to a stop as Sarah's rare ultimatums always did. Her mother had never allowed her a dog because she thought of dog poop as satanic. Frank sat there waiting for his wife's lead.

"You know how I feel about dog fecal matter," Peppy said properly.

"I'll teach the dog to poop a hundred yards from the house. If we're living twenty miles from the town we need a dog to guard our chickens, cows, and horses on the ranch."

"It's not a ranch. It's a farm," Frank said irrelevantly.

"We'll think about it, sweetheart," Peppy said.

"No we won't think about it. It's a dog and a horse or I'm staying in Ohio with Grandma." Sarah's grandma was a piano teacher, a Swede who had married an Italian truck farmer, not necessarily the best ethnic mix. Every day after school Sarah stopped at her grandmother's to play the piano. She had been given her middle name, Anitra, from the composer Edvard Grieg's "Anitra's Dance" at iron-hard Grandma's insistence.

"Well, all the kids in the Montana countryside seem to have a horse and a dog," Frank offered.

"I'll pray about it," Peppy said in resignation.

Sarah had to pray with her mother every morning but she had her own eccentric versions of prayer including imaginary animals, the moon and stars, and music, horses, and dogs. Her grandmother disliked Peppy's evangelical beliefs thinking her son had traded in a drunk for a nitwit. Grandmother taught little Sarah that music was the speech of the gods while Peppy insisted that Sarah learn to play some hymns to counterbalance the sinful effects of the classics. Sarah would play the lugubrious "Old Rugged Cross" poorly because it was no more than barbed wire set to music.

Packing up was hard. Sarah wanted to take along their big backyard with its maples and oaks, its coverts of viburnum, honeysuckle, and barberry, the ornamental crab-apple trees and flowering almond, the tiny playhouse you had to crawl into, even the path out the unused back gate, and the back alley where she fed stray cats and where she walked to visit her few friends. Her best friend Maria who was a year older and prematurely pubescent absolutely guaranteed Sarah that cowboys would rape her in Montana and that she best get herself a pistol to defend herself, a matter over which Sarah spent a good deal of time brooding.

One Friday afternoon in mid-April her father showed up with a huge three-quarter-ton black pickup and a long trailer. Two neighbor men helped load the trailer and on Sunday there was a yard sale for what had to be left behind including Sarah's ancient piano. What would she do without a piano? Her parents, of course, hadn't thought of that. Her piano in a real sense was her speech, her only viable conversation with the world. Her father talked sparsely and her mother didn't listen in her busyness of figuring out what she was going to say next. Sarah stayed back in a thicket during the yard sale watching people paw over her bedroom furniture and beloved piano. So much had to be left behind to make room for Frank's tools and equipment, including a large floor tent they would live in while Frank built them a log cabin. She wept behind the honeysuckle bush when a man bought the piano for thirty bucks announcing loudly that he would tear it apart for its hardwood lumber. This man was going to murder her piano and it reminded her of when she and Maria would ride their bikes over to the Humane Society to visit the lovely dogs and pick out which ones they'd like to own should they ever be permitted a dog. Only after several trips did they learn from a brusque docent lady that most of the dogs would be euthanized because no one wanted them. They would kill the dogs like the man would kill her piano. Brushing her tears with a shirtsleeve she had the idea that children like herself were kennel dogs.

The jump from the piano to man to herself to dog wasn't difficult. Unlike most people, she knew her own story while she kept on making up a new one. She had figured out that it was the big gaps that were the problem so she tried to keep busy. Did her father love her? Off and on. Did her mother love her? She doubted it. Her mother loved the certainty of her own religion. She had only an obligatory, perfunctory love for her daughter. Peppy always reminded Sarah of that grinning, porcelain cat on the windowsill near Grandma's piano.

Chapter 2
1983

It was a far cry, as people say, from their brutally crude beginning to where they were a few years later. First of all late April is not reliably spring at an altitude of about forty-five hundred feet in Montana. That first day at noon it was thirty-five degrees with heavy sleet and a low-flying cloud bank coming up the valley from the southwest. The five miles of dirt road off the blacktop was mired in mud called gumbo from the recently melted snow still evident in the coulees leading up to the foothills of the mountains to the west.

Her father was stiff-faced grim as he coaxed the pickup along in four-wheel low and finally pulled onto a two-track near the burned-out hole where a ranch house had been. About fifty yards out in back were small corrals, an out-house, an open-faced calving shed, a small toolshed, and a small pond full of dead, brown cattails. Off in the distance a herd of about fifty elk watched the truck warily.

"What in heck are those?" Sarah asked noting that there were tears in Peppy's eyes, which that morning had glowed with hope.

"Elk," her father said, getting out of the truck and looking up the two-track to a small canyon where an ancient Studebaker proceeded toward them. That would be a man named Old Tim who had sold Frank the 180 acres, all that was left of a once sizable family ranch mostly sold to neighbors. Old Tim was seventy-one and all the family that was left. When the house had burned from an overheated woodstove pipe he had built a log cabin up the canyon on what was to be the five acres of remaining property in his name.

Sarah and Peppy watched as Frank and Tim rather quickly put up the floor tent, installing a dry sink and a potbelly stove. There was a pipe sticking up near the tent and Tim used a wrench to open a valve then walked all crouched over out to the toolshed, started a Yamaha generator, and water came out of the pipe. Frank had told them that Tim had been both a cowboy and a hunting guide and would help set up the floor tent for their home until the cabin was built.

"Don't let a boy touch you until you're eighteen," Peppy said for unknown reasons in the pickup while they watched the men work.

"Why?" Sarah asked.

"Don't get smart with me."

"I mean why would a boy touch me?" Sarah was teasing. Her friend Maria had told her boys would try to put their weenies in her which was god-awful painful. This was remote to Sarah who was staring at an old dog in Tim's truck. She abruptly opened the door. The dog snarled and Tim hurried over.

"Be careful. She don't like no one but me and some days she don't like me. Her name is Sarah."

"What kind is she?" Sarah was smiling at the dog because of the miracle of the dog having the same name.

"She's mostly an Australian shepherd cow dog mixed with something else, maybe pit bull. She thinks all this land around here is hers."

"Sarah, come," Sarah called, kneeling on the ground. The dog came and rolled over to have her tummy scratched.

Now, three years later, there was a great deal of good and bad. They were more or less at home but the bad part for Peppy was that the energy of her religion waned in isolation. She became depressed and Frank drove her to a doctor in Helena a hundred miles away where she was prescribed Valium, a popular drug among rural wives. Peppy fell into a deep lassitude and Sarah's already mediocre homeschooling failed.

For Sarah the homeschooling was the rawest item. It had been planned well ahead of their move and not shared with her. Other than for Tim's dog Sarah, which she called Rover because she didn't want to call out her own name, and her young, difficult gelding Lad, she was terribly lonely. She had joined a 4-H club, an organization for the young like Girl and Boy Scouts but devoted to all things rural including livestock and gardening, sewing, and canning.

Puberty had come unpleasantly early for Sarah and she bound her growing breasts with cloth ankle wrap. The breasts were worse than her monthlies which came in the middle of her eleventh year and for which Peppy who was no longer peppy gave her a tract on the subject for "young Christian women." It was all about the miracle of the bodily processes and in it her body was called "the temple of the Holy Spirit." This was definitely not the way she felt. Even Rover was puzzled by the odor of blood.

She was five foot ten late in her twelfth year, the tallest girl in her 4-H club. The younger, shorter boys called her "geek," her height a wound to their shorter vanity, but she was quick to stop them. When the weather was okay she would ride her rank gelding Lad six miles down the road for their once-a-month 4-H picnic meeting which was held on the ranch of the Lahren family. It was a medium-sized ranch of four thousand acres but immaculate because the Lahrens were of Norwegian descent. Sarah was miffed at her dad because he wouldn't let her raise a heifer for the county fair like many 4-H kids and she was forced to fall back on gardening.

Lad wouldn't work as a project as he was homely, also quite difficult. Rover was out of the question as when she tethered the dog at the Lahrens' she snarled at anyone who came close to Lad having added Lad and Sarah to her circle of protection. Rover would arrive at about noon at their homestead after Sarah had finished her dreary home-schooling and go back to Old Tim's by dinnertime. If she heard or sensed anything at night she'd make it down from

Tim's canyon in less than two minutes. Once on a ride Sarah had seen Rover shake an old coyote by the neck until the head separated and march around with the head as if it were a trophy.

Sarah, like nearly all young people, was alert to changes in her parents. Young people with all of their somewhat hormonal difficulties tend to want their parents to stay the same in order to avoid further problems acquiring their tenuous balance.

Frank was thriving and well ahead of his three-year deadline to make a living in Montana. He averaged twelve hours a day of work partly because he could think of nothing else to do. Back in Findlay, Ohio, he had played golf on weekends and basketball with a group of friends during the winter, diversions not available in Montana. He had erected a small pole barn in which he organized a machine shop. He put up a poster advertising his abilities fixing machinery on the bulletin board in the post office in the nearest village, twenty miles distant. Old Tim helped with advice on unfamiliar equipment like hay balers, diesel tractors, or combines to harvest wheat. This involved a lot of driving to distant ranches and Sarah often went along. Ranchers were charmed by a handsome young girl wearing greasy bib overalls helping her father. Frank's better moneymaker came from a sizable greenhouse he'd erected. He had grown up helping his truck-farmer father which he disliked but then Frank was still very knowledgeable about growing vegetables. He also had a large garden area with a high fence to defend against deer and elk. It could be covered with a mechanically unrolled cloth. At one end he had two large

fan blowers behind which there were metal wood-fire boxes
to protect his vegetables from spring and autumn frosts.
Montana was traditionally short on vegetables and twice a
week during season Frank would haul his beautiful vegetables to Missoula, Helena, and Great Falls with Sarah going along to help out and take in at a distance the pleasures
of cities. One early June when the vegetables sold high her
father stopped at a country tavern where they had hamburg-
ers and he also had a beer. The bartender said to her, "Hey,
good looking, what can I cook for you?" and her blush
burned deep into her. They detoured over to Choteau before turning south and her father drove a few miles into the
ominous Bob Marshall Wilderness. As if on order a grizzly
bear crossed the gravel road in front of them chasing an elk
fawn. In a forest clearing perhaps a hundred yards away
the big bear crushed the fawn to the earth. "Don't look,"
her father said but she watched as the fawn was rended.
He turned the truck around and there was the mother elk
standing in the bushes just off the road also watching. It
was horrible but also thrilling.

Peppy was another matter that third year. Early in the
winter when she drove Sarah to the 4-H club she met Giselle,
a single mother whose daughter Priscilla Sarah had made
friends with recently. Priscilla had loaned her Salinger's *The
Catcher in the Rye* which she read out in the shed knowing
that Peppy would take it from her. Peppy and Giselle took
to each other despite their acute differences. Giselle was
thought to have "too much life," and Peppy started going
to the village for groceries and odds and ends like chicken
feed after eleven in the morning when the tavern opened.

Giselle was the barmaid and Peppy would have an orange pop and they would talk. It was nerve-racking for an evangelical like Peppy to go into a tavern but then her family and minister were back in Ohio. Peppy liked listening to Giselle talk about her "gentlemen friends" but then one day Giselle said, "Frankly, I love to fuck," and Peppy stayed away for a lonely week. Finally she convinced herself that Giselle was helping to lift her depression and didn't that count? Peppy started to go to the once-a-week "girls' night" at Giselle's double-wide trailer where several local women would meet and drink beer, play canasta, and practice dance steps all of which was against Peppy's religion.

Sarah liked the lightening of Peppy's mood. Frank taught Sarah the sciences and Peppy literature and history from textbooks approved by her evangelical group which meant they were bowdlerized. Peppy insisted that Frank teach Sarah creationism rather than evolution but he ignored her. Sarah borrowed books from a boy in 4-H who had a clubfoot and thus was excused from the rigors of ranch labor. This was called horseback country as much of the rough-terrain pasture for cattle could only be reached by horses. The boy named Terry loaned Sarah novels by Theodore Dreiser, John Dos Passos, and Steinbeck, a volume of Henry Miller called *Sexus* he had bought in Missoula, and the poetry of Walt Whitman, a far cry from the Tennyson and Kipling her mother forced her to read. Sarah was appalled reading the Henry Miller in the cold toolshed. Why would a woman do these things? In early March her father caught on to her reading habits and installed an electric heater in the toolshed. Sarah had discovered Willa Cather and it was fun to read her without freezing her ass.

Chapter 3
1985

Age fourteen was difficult for Sarah because she was conclusively becoming a woman. There certainly was no turning back. She had become a real "looker," slang for a real pretty girl in that part of Montana, or what boys called "a first-rate piece of ass," before they actually had any idea what that meant. All of which made Sarah even more shy. When she was in the village with her mother or father adult men would look at her in an uncompromising way. At a 4-H club dance her partner pressed himself close and she could feel his hard member. When the club was having a swimming party at the Lahren ranch pond Herman, their host, tended to hang around leering. Sarah's friend Priscilla who was short but stacked and vulgarly outspoken said, "That old fuck is a lech." When Sarah and Priscilla were riding their horses and saw a quarter horse stallion mounting a mare Priscilla joked, "I'd hate to handle something that big."

Priscilla bragged that she had lost her virginity the year
before at age thirteen to a friend of her mother's but Sarah
couldn't believe that an adult man would tinker with a mere
girl.

Old Tim who was a true friend advised Sarah not to
be so withdrawn and to carry herself as if she were proud
of who she was. "Being pretty is the hand you were dealt,"
he said. In truth, Sarah was no raving beauty but simply the
handsomest girl in the area.

Early on Old Tim had shown Sarah a miniature canyon on BLM land about two miles to the north. The canyon was sheltered and south-facing so that it could be fairly
warm when it was only fifty in late April or early May or on
cool windy fall days. There was a small, trickling spring that
filled a miniature rock pool you could sit in on hot days.
Sarah thought of this beautiful canyon as her thinking place
and would ride there on Lad with Rover in tow when the
spirit called her. Her parents were confident of Rover as
a guardian. In the canyon Sarah would think religious
thoughts sometimes about Indians. Would it be easier to
be an Indian maid? Probably not. Why didn't the Bible give
a name to the virgin that was brought to King David to warm
his bones? Was screwing the original sin Adam and Eve
committed? Was Mary Magdalene beautiful? Did Jesus
ever have sexual thoughts? Sarah had a crush on Montgomery Clift who she had seen in a movie called *The Misfits* at
Giselle's house, then she found out he was dead and was sad.
Sometimes Sarah would take off all of her clothes except
her panties and lie back on a large flat-top boulder. One
afternoon Rover growled the peculiar growl she made when

Old Tim was approaching, not the outright snarl she made sensing a bear or cow. Tim didn't appear and she pretended she was asleep. If he wanted to sneak a look it was okay because she liked him. She even rolled over in case he wanted a butt view. Once when she visited his cabin and he was gone there was a lurid girlie magazine on his porch and she wondered at what age men get over this nonsense. After about fifteen minutes Tim called out, "Make yourself decent." Tim only had two cows left for his own eating beef and he would borrow his own dog back to look for a missing one. Now Tim was blushing.

"I got here a while ago and caught a peek of you. I had to take a walk and compose myself. I'm sorry."

"No crime has been committed," Sarah said and they both laughed.

"Mother told me sixty years ago to treat all females as if they were your sister. Even then I wondered how the human race could keep going."

"I'm not sure I like being an animal," she said watching Rover keep an eye on a rattlesnake on a ledge of rock about fifty feet away.

"You better get used to it," he said.

Four days before her fifteenth birthday Peppy up and left, as they say out west, as if someone abruptly got off a sofa and ran for daylight. Frank was gone to South Carolina where his son, whom Sarah called Brother, had been in an auto accident with two other drunken marines. Frank would be gone two more days and Sarah didn't call him when Peppy left. Sarah had been out riding and when she got home there was a big fancy pickup in the drive and an older man coming out of their house carrying two suitcases. Rover was unhappy about this and Sarah held her back with difficulty. Then her mother came out in her best outfit carrying her pink overnight case. She gave Sarah a perfunctory hug.

"I left you a letter on the kitchen counter. Someday you'll understand this. Maybe you'll come visit." And then she was gone.

Sarah let Rover in the house for the first time. Rover couldn't handle it and curled up just inside the doorway. Sarah thought, Now I'll get to go to school like everyone else and was quickly embarrassed by her crassness. How should I feel about my mother taking off? she wondered. She held the letter while drinking lemonade and waited for strong emotions but none arrived. "Dear daughter, I met Clyde last year at Giselle's. He was one of her many boyfriends and now he's mine to have and hold. Clyde is a bigshot rancher from up near Helena. I'm tired of working day in and day out. I'd be doing this here until I died. As the song goes, my love for Frank has died away like grass out on the lawn. I've been praying about this for months. Don't be angry about this. Love, Mom. P.S. Take care of your dad."

Sarah thought it would have been easy to say no had she been asked to go with her mother. She couldn't leave behind Rover, Old Tim, and Lad. She called Tim and he said he was sorry if she was. He said he would bring her down some dinner and keep her company. Tim and Peppy had never liked each other. In his code of the West no one should whine and complain both of which Peppy did in quantity.

When Peppy would complain to him he'd only say, "Life is hard," and walk away.

Sarah took a shower and put on a discreet shorts-and-halter outfit, all that her mother permitted. It was fair to give Tim something to look at since he was making dinner. She went out to their small sunporch where she decided to re-read Cather's *Death Comes for the Archbishop*. She had two contradictory plans for the future: she wanted to live in the austere beauty of the desert in the Southwest but she also wanted to ride in subways in New York City like in Dos Passos's *Manhattan Transfer* and the *USA* trilogy. She was sure she could manage both though it would be far easier to have a dog and a horse in New Mexico or Arizona. Her father was always reminding her that she would have to make a living and that though her reading was good for her she could make better money in the sciences. In truth she had thought this over. All the novels she read churned up her mind but it was the only way she had to learn about life outside her remote location. The sciences were pure like the desert she had never seen. When she assessed her abilities she couldn't come up with any clear triumphs except a minor one. In the summer of her first year of 4-H she had helped Mrs. Lahren bring in the remains of a picnic while the rest of the kids were playing "cowboy croquet" (you concentrate on driving someone else's ball off into the weeds). There was a crummy old upright piano in the parlor and she asked Mrs. Lahren for permission. Sarah was carried away by her first shot at a piano in nearly three years and she played Grieg, Liszt, and Chopin passionately, coming back to consciousness when the other kids

were all clapping at the windows. She cringed with embarrassment but after that she had to play for a while at
every meeting including some ragtime pieces her grandmother had taught her at which the ranch kids would
throw themselves around with freakish abandon. Her second victory, small to her, was when at age twelve she took
an obligatory test for the homeschooled demanded by the
state of Montana and though she only scored average in
the humanities and history she was rated second-year college in the sciences. It was the only time before or after
that her father was absolutely effusive with her, swinging
her around the kitchen in an energetic but clumsy dance.

Tim arrived a little late with a bouquet of wildflowers
and a pot of elk stew, her favorite dish. She had been present
when he shot the elk down by her secret canyon, crawling
behind him through the lodgepole pines until they came to
the edge of a clearing. On the far side of the clearing were a
dozen females and a bull elk with a moderate rack. Outside
hunters were always after a bull but the locals shot females
because the meat was tastier. When Tim pulled the trigger
he said, "Sorry, girl," and the elk dropped in its tracks. It
was a very cold November day and when Tim gutted the
animal she felt the warm odorous air rising up from the cav-
ity, the overripe coppery smell of the intestines.

Now she was at the counter heating up the stew and
mixing up the salad. Tim had tuned in a country station and
Patsy Cline was singing, "The Last Word in Lonesome Is
Me." She loathed the song for obvious reasons and Tim liked
it because he was old and had absorbed his condition. She
turned abruptly to see if he was looking at her and he was.

He pinkened for a moment and then pretended to be interested in something out the window. She was amused by this newfound game of sexual dance though she had few opportunities for it. Peppy hated going into the post office for fear of getting yet another dire religious letter from her parents who doubted she would remain godly in Montana. Sarah would pick up the mail, if any, and the postmaster who was in his sixties would always flirt saying things like "If only I was younger I'd take you to Denver and we'd have a high time." She wondered to what extent he meant it. Was he really hitting on a fourteen-year-old girl? What did Tim feel when he peeked through the trees and saw her sitting there in the miniature canyon in her panties? What if Montgomery Clift was still alive and asked her to take off all her clothes including her panties would she do it? Probably. Love made everything possible.

"How come you never got married?" she asked Tim.

Tim winced and his soupspoon full of stew wobbled. He looked at the ceiling as if the answer were there. Meanwhile she was wondering if old men could still "do the deed" as Priscilla called it. Once in Lahren's barn her clubfooted friend Terry had asked if he could see her breasts and she said, "No, stupid." He got tears in his eyes and it quickly occurred to her that he might not loan her any more books so she raised her T-shirt and bra for a one-second flash.

"Well, it's a dumb story. When I was nineteen my dad was working me too hard and I ran off to Wilsall north of Livingston and cowboyed for a big outfit. As bad luck would have it I fell in love with the rancher's daughter and we'd sneak off and smooch. After a few months I asked her to marry me and she said she couldn't marry anyone who wasn't going to inherit a big ranch like her dad's which was about thirty thousand acres and a quarter of that fine hay land. Since our place back home was small I knew I was out of the running. She was pissed because she had two older brothers and likely wouldn't get jack shit. I was heartbroken and went back home the next day. I decided to never marry if that's how a woman can come to the decision so I've had girlfriends but never wives. Back when I was about forty I was calf roping at the Livingston rodeo on July fourth and won a hundred bucks so I went into the Wrangler to drink it up with my old friend Bob Burns and I'll be goddamned if she wasn't standing at the bar with her husband who was an electrician for the railroad. She said she had three kids and her dad's ranch had gone under because her brothers had bought too many center pivots for irrigated hay. That's the dumb story. Now I wish I had some kids but I don't."

"That's an awful story," Sarah said, unable to continue eating for a full ten minutes, thinking that what she had heard was like a novel she was glad she hadn't read.

The next evening she cooked him the pancakes, sausage, and eggs he favored. It was warm and rainy and after dinner they sat in the living room drinking coffee with Tim putting a bit of whiskey in his. They were listening to the rain on the tin roof, a sound she loved. He was in an easy chair and she was on the sofa in a short skirt showing more than a bit of leg and wondering why she was doing so. Her father had called and said he would be home the next day.

"Thanks for teasing me," Tim said when he left. He poked her lightly in the ribs with a forefinger and laughed.

She blushed with shame when he drove away though she was glad he had told Rover to stay with her because the dark is darker when you're alone. She got out her father's pistol and holster and practiced quick draws in the hall mirror. Tim had taught her but she wasn't as fast as he was at age seventy-three. She went to bed and tried to concoct a fantasy where she was naked in bed with Montgomery Clift but with no experience she couldn't make the fantasy convincing. What worked was the two of them necking in a phone booth at night in the rain.

The next morning she was watering the plants in the greenhouse, a two-hour process, and getting ready to rototill the open garden when her father arrived to Rover's howling. The dog's fidelities were limited to Tim and Sarah and she would shy away if anyone else tried to pet her. Frank stood blank-faced in the greenhouse door. She tried to embrace him but he was stiff as an oak plank.

"Your brother's a goner, that's for sure."

"He's dead?" Her voice wobbled.

"May as well be. He and his two buddies were driving at ninety on the way back to the base with the cops chasing them. One of the buddies is dead. The car rolled about ten times. Your brother fractured arms, legs, and pelvis but most important he has severe closed-head injuries. He didn't recognize me and the doctors said he never will. He'll be like that Denison boy in town, who sits on the porch in a wheelchair drooling."

"I'm so sorry. What happens now?" She began to cry.

"Life in a V.A. hospital. How are you feeling about your mother?"

"I'm not sure what to think. I can't quite believe she went away."

"It's the same with me. She called but it didn't quite sink in. Of course I know I'm real slow emotionally. I couldn't believe these two things could happen at once."

"She wasn't too happy," Sarah suggested. "She didn't like it way out here in the country."

"She was a pain in the ass these last couple of years. When she wasn't working she was frantic and when she was working she was complaining." Tears were forming in his eyes.

"We'll figure things out." Now his body softened when she embraced him.

"We'll have to." He went outside and cranked up the rototiller. At lunch he acted as if nothing had happened.

Two days later at midmorning when he was rigging up a three-way tow hitch on the pickup, she asked him what he had in mind.

"It's your birthday and Grandma called when you were giving Lad his oats. She reminded me to get you your own vehicle on your birthday. You'll need it for school this fall."

She was nearly dizzy while she got ready, partly at the idea of her own car but also that five years of homeschooling was at an end. Perhaps in reaction to her mother she wasn't a complainer but she devoutly hoped for something fresh in her life aside from the once-a-month 4-H club meeting.

Chapter 4

"Before we visit car lots we're going to a doctor to get you a pill," Frank said halfway to Bozeman on that fair May morning.

"Dad, I don't need a pill. I've never even had a boyfriend."

"Everyone can get carried away," Frank said as if the subject was closed.

"Mom said I never could have the pill because it causes bad behavior," Sarah said idly.

"Forgive me but there were many times when your mother didn't know her ass from a hole in the ground as they used to say back in Findlay."

"I suppose that's true. Her preacher said that there should be a prison camp for all gay people in California."

The visit to the gynecologist was unpleasant though the doctor, a woman in her fifties, was quite nice and said, "You have a gorgeous body, young woman. Out in the back-country where you live you'll have to carry a pistol against cowboys."

Sarah thought the stirrups were a hundred times worse than a dentist's chair. She recovered in two hours of wandering car lots with Frank though his questions to salesmen were so thorough it made her back teeth ache. They had to double back three times before they reduced the possibilities. It came down to a choice between a red Toyota and blue Subaru, both four-wheel drive which her father thought obligatory for mud season and winter weather. Finally Frank wrote a check and hooked the Toyota up to the tow bar.

"I had planned on us having a look at the university and then a steak dinner but Old Tim wanted to bake a cake and grill an elk loin for you. I know the old fool is sweet on you. Evidently men never get over women. Back at Purdue my philosophy professor said the hardest thing for people is the unlived life."

"Dad, for God's sake, he is just my best friend." Sarah blushed over her little games which boys referred to as prick teasing. She figured that if it wasn't Tim it would be someone else but he was the only man around. Sarah wasn't mentally comfortable with the biological aspects of life. Everything comes on so fast. It was one thing to have a fantasy about the deceased Montgomery Clift which was as safe as your favorite pillow but she in no way had any desire for reality to intrude. She had developed the soul of a solitary during her homeschooling and her life had been without the dozen adolescent crushes that trail one from childhood through puberty, the terrifying lack of justice in having an infatuation with someone who hasn't quite noticed that you exist. Her taste for love was more spiritual but not the way Peppy would prate at her about how one's body was a holy temple of God. It was comically shocking that despite her beliefs Peppy had gone off and fucked a geezer rancher she had met at Giselle's. Sarah only liked to study nonhuman biology. For the time being she preferred the idea of physical love to stay bathed in mist. Just last week at 4-H club, on a warm afternoon, a Mexican man had shown up at Lahren's trailering a cutting horse stud up from Kingsville, Texas. Mr. Lahren was going to board the horse for a rich cousin from Bozeman. Both man and horse were the most beautiful creatures of their kind that Sarah had ever seen. The Mexican man was quite shy and just nodded at everyone then worked the travel kinks out of the stud in a corral. The horse was wild but everyone agreed that the Mexican sat a horse better than anyone. The boys stood back more than a bit jealous and when the man dismounted and led the horse into a box stall in the barn the girls flittered around him like fireflies with hot butts. He bowed to them all and carried his saddle and bridle toward his truck stopping at the entrance to the barn where Sarah stood having held herself back from the gaggle, looking at his chest and the muscular arm that held the saddle over his shoulder. He paused in front of her and smiled.

"What's your name?"

"Sarah," she said in a whisper because that was all she could manage.

He nodded as if he'd received an important piece of information and strode to his pickup. Meanwhile she felt a heat in her lower body almost like she might pee her pants. The girls circled her wondering what he had said but she walked out the door and watched his truck head down the road encircled by dust. She was startled by her feelings but decided she couldn't think about it at the time. It would take a trip to the canyon to figure it out.

The birthday party was subdued because everyone was tired and Priscilla couldn't come because "a certain special someone" had shown up. Frank always referred to Priscilla as "Tomcat" which Sarah didn't like but she had admitted to herself that the nickname was appropriate. She had a peculiar sense of foreboding when she saw Tim wince twice while inspecting her new used vehicle. The second time he paled crawling out from under the pickup where he'd inspected the muffler.

"She's got about a year on her," Tim said, and Sarah wondered why a muffler was a "she." "This country is hard on mufflers," he added.

The elk loin was grilled perfectly but Tim was a bit pissed that his German chocolate cake was a little lopsided. He sipped from his whiskey flask and she saw him sneak a pill with his back turned. Her father had a two-dollar bottle of Gallo burgundy and poured her a few ounces. They toasted and the men sang a horrible version of "Happy Birthday."

Twice that night Sarah had gotten up to look at her truck in the dim yard light. She fully understood that it meant freedom. Unlike Peppy, Frank never tried to control her. There was always the example of his younger sister Rebecca who had been wild in her youth but now was an important astronomer on the faculty of the University of Arizona in Tucson. Rebecca had only visited them a couple of times because she loathed Peppy and the whole idea of Sarah's homeschooling.

In the morning Sarah confronted her father.

"What's wrong with Tim?" In the night she'd recalled that she'd first noticed that Tim was in pain a few weeks before when he took her to the county seat in his old Studebaker so she could get a learner's driving permit. He had stumbled in a cafe when they'd stopped for a hamburger and when he'd caught himself at the table's edge he'd lost his color.

"He's feeling poorly." Frank was listening to the weather and livestock report without interest.

"I figured that. I want to know why?"

"He didn't want you to know anything on your birthday. Well, you know he was gone two days last week. He was at the V.A. hospital in Great Falls. There are five kinds of prostate cancer. Three aren't so bad and two are real bad. He's got one of the real bad ones. These old cowboys are used to putting up with pain and he waited too long for any possible treatment. It's spread around, you know, metastasized."

Sarah began to sob and Frank came over and put his hands on her shoulders. Frank couldn't think of a thing to say about an obviously fatal illness.

When Sarah went outside to start her morning's work in the greenhouse and the open garden she barely noticed her red pickup. The lump in her throat was overwhelming. She kept on walking up toward Tim's cabin meeting Rover, who looked distressed, halfway. Tim was dozing in his rocker on the porch facing east toward the rising sun. There was water and a bottle of pills on a small table beside him. She was questioning herself whether anyone had a religion to deal with this. Peppy had browbeaten her with her own evangelical religion but she had followed her father's example and not much had stuck. Her father had taught her astronomy all too well setting up his Questar in the nighttime yard. Sarah could not imagine that people like God and Jesus shaped like humans could invent the billions of galaxies. She meant the gray-bearded God sitting on a throne behind a gate and the Jesus perpetually on a cross with blood leaking from his hands and feet. The invisible Holy Spirit made more sense. Someone had to invent horses, dogs, and birds. She thought she sensed a spirit of some sort in certain creatures or places but was unsure about humans who according to her history books had a grim and murderous record. As she was sitting there beside the sleeping Tim her mind whirled with the immensity of it all, and then it winnowed down into the inevitable self-pity. How can I lose the only man I love in my life except my dad? Her loneliness was as big as the landscape.

Tim awoke and she took his hand.

"I suppose you've been told?"

"Yes."

"It feels like I'm sitting on a spike or a hot rock. I figured it would go away."

"I'm so sorry."

They drove up to their miniature canyon with her at the wheel of the Studebaker and Rover between them ever alert for threat. It was a warm morning and she reminded herself to be wary for rattlesnakes. She helped him up onto her flattish boulder.

"I hate these goddamned pills. They make me woozy as a bottle of whiskey but they said the cancer is traveling up my spine."

She cradled him with his head and shoulders on her lap and the braless nipple of a breast beneath her T-shirt grazing his nose.

"You got my heart sounding like a beehive. I suspect this is how I started."

"There has to be a chance."

"That isn't what I was told. Three score and ten is what they call it."

They went up to the canyon for nearly another month until he couldn't walk and then she would visit his cabin. Several times he called her Charlotte, the name of his first love over near Livingston, and they would laugh. A hospice woman came from the county seat during the day. She and Tim had known each other in childhood and didn't like each other. Sarah would referee their spats.

"In first grade she was always beating on me," Tim said.

"You and the other boys peed on my dog. You were the one I could catch," Laverne said. She was about seventy, quite religious, and an expert on cancer care having nursed her husband and sister through their deaths, the husband with a brain tumor, and the sister pancreatic. She had a sense of humor and after praying on her knees beside Tim's bed she'd say, "Here's God's answer to pain," and give him a shot of morphine. At night Sarah gave Tim a shot which

was illegal but Laverne would say, "I don't give a shit about
the law." She carried a six-shooter in her purse and while
driving she'd shoot out the window of her car at marmots,
coyotes, crows, whatever. To her knowledge she had never
hit anything.

Sarah slept on a cot near Tim's bed. Sometimes she'd
read to him from old Zane Grey novels which she didn't care
for, and sometimes she'd play old-time country music like
Marty Robbins, Merle Haggard, and George Jones which
she also didn't like preferring Pink Floyd and the Grateful
Dead or classical music.

What kept her going was her four hours of work with
her father in the gardens every morning. Counting the different lettuces they were raising twenty-three kinds of vegetables, some of them exotic for Montana but they sold well
to the university people in Missoula. When they first raised
arugula and radicchio to fulfill a demand Sarah and her
father were suspicious of the flavors but shrugged off their
own tastes. Japanese eggplant was also a mystery. It was
the spirit of repetition in gardening that soothed a person.
She'd finish work, eat a little lunch, doze in the hammock
for fifteen minutes, then head up to Tim's.

The deathwatch was forty-nine days but Tim was dead
a couple weeks before he died. Well beyond consciousness it
was hard for a body to let go. Sarah that evening kept putting her face to his to see if he was still breathing and finally
near midnight he wasn't. She actually thought she saw his
spirit rise and float out the open front door over Rover's head
who turned to look at her. She shivered and looked around
at the cabin which was homemade and crude but beautiful

to her. There was a woodstove and then a propane heater which was used when the weather got to its coldest. There were two rifles and a shotgun in a cabinet but the only thing of beauty was a wood chest that doubled as a coffee table. When he was still conscious he told her that the cabin was hers, also about three thousand dollars in a tobacco tin at the bottom of the trunk. The eighty grand that Frank had paid for the land was going to a county fund for the poor and indigent. That last conscious day he had reached out with his left hand, the only one that worked, and touched her breast.

"I don't want to be impolite but that's the finest breast I've ever seen," he whispered.

"Thank you." She stood and curtsied and they both smiled. After that moment he was pretty much incoherent.

Two days later at the small funeral at the canyon's mouth Sarah strewed Tim's ashes on the rocks for the rain to wash away as he had requested. Tim had fashioned himself an agnostic ("I don't really know anything for sure except horses, cows, and dogs") so there was no preacher, just a half dozen old cowboys, a few townspeople, Laverne, and Frank and Sarah. For lunch after the funeral on Tim's porch Sarah had made a ham-and-potato salad. The old cowboys drank whiskey and water with their lunch except for one who had taken the pledge. Two took off their hats and their foreheads were so white compared to their brown, wizened faces. Listening she learned that at one time Tim had been the best fistfighter in the county which didn't jibe with the gentle old man she had known.

The next two days she struggled to prepare her 4-H club vegetable display for the upcoming county fair and rodeo. She had burned up body and mind in her long vigil and felt generally out of contact except with the steering wheel of her truck. Her father was no help because he spent so much time on the phone with his ex-wife about whether or not to pull the plug on Brother who was now unconscious with his brain damage and severe pneumonia. Frank's ex-wife had been in AA for three years and had flipped back into booze with the injury to her son. Frank kept saying to Sarah that her half brother was a "vegetable" which made Sarah feel odd about her 4-H display exhibit.

Luckily she felt secure in her truck because when she got up past Lahren's ranch, normally the range of her world, she felt a little eerie outside her circumscribed Eden. Her father had joined a co-op of a half dozen other growers so that there would be far fewer trips to Great Falls, Helena, and Missoula with the members taking turns on the marketing chores. She mostly drove for two days, stopping now and then to sleep on a two-track leading into the mountains. Once a cowboy on horseback stopped to see if she was okay and Rover went crazy. He was fairly handsome but her senses were dead as a doornail. She even visited the regional high school up near the county seat. It was sprawling and modern, actually crummy-looking she thought, and it was hard to imagine attending it in a month or so. Rover, who was enjoying these drives because dogs are also susceptible to boredom, stared at the high school with incomprehension. Rover had seen nothing of the outside world what with Tim always leaving her behind to look after the cabin. On the way home Sarah stopped at the fairgrounds to watch them set up the Ferris wheel and merry-go-round. Men were practicing calf roping and people were pulling in with trailers. She absolutely counted on the fair and rodeo to lift her spirits.

PART II

Chapter 5

On the second and last night of the fair and rodeo the worst possible thing happened to Sarah short of fatal illness and death of which she was recently all too familiar.

She had been sleepwalking since the fair began and was angry at Lad during the "best-groomed horse" event because he misbehaved having developed a hatred for another horse. He was on a lead but advanced on the other horse with his ears laid back and clacking his teeth. It is not largely known that horses, like people, can develop instant hatreds. The judges asked her to get Lad out of the arena for which she needed the help of a cowboy, an embarrassment in itself. Winning the top blue ribbon for her vegetables helped though this was muted by the fact that the competition was dismal.

A good thing happened after the Lad mud bath when the cowboy who helped her said that Lad had probably been gelded late and thought he was still a fighting stud. She was still half in tears and eating a lukewarm hot dog when two girls approached. She had met the tall, rawboned girl with her father up at Tim's two years before. The short one was feisty and pissed off after winning third in the barrel racing. The girls knew that Sarah was coming to their regional high school in the fall and wanted to know if she wanted to join their hunting club. There were two girls now and Sarah would make three. They could hunt elk near Sarah's place and antelope five hours east near Forsyth where the tall girl, Marcia, had an uncle who owned a big ranch with plenty of antelope. Marcia herself had shot three since she was twelve and also a cow elk over near Lincoln. Sarah confessed that though she had gone hunting a dozen times with Tim she had yet to pull the trigger on an animal. Before doing so Tim wanted her to be able to fire five shots within a five-inch pattern at a hundred yards with either his .270 or .30-06. The girls agreed with this and said that there was plenty of time to practice before hunting season.

This meeting gave Sarah an expansive but brief relief from her sleepwalking mood which affects anyone who has experienced the recent death of a beloved. She had no one to turn to because her friend Priscilla was a pleasant nitwit and her father had emotional limitations. His own son was near death and he was flying back to South Carolina in a day but he couldn't say a single thing about Tim or Brother.

She put the irritable Lad away in the horse barn with hay and water but no oats. It occurred to her that Lad had misbehaved in part because he wasn't used to being around a crowd which only reminded her of her own stunted access to people. On the way to the 4-H heifer barn where the 4-H club camped out her mind flared in anger at the whole idea of homeschooling and that she had been a puppet of her parents' daffy ideas that though you had to live within the culture you could minimize the bad effects by staying as remote as possible. Now she found herself quite happy that Peppy had run off with the rich rancher because finally she could join the human race.

In the box stall she and Priscilla had as a camping spot Sarah lay down on her sleeping bag spread on fresh alfalfa which had a sweet, haunting odor. Priscilla had been sent home by their leader Mrs. Lahren to get some different clothes to replace her very short short-shorts. "Young woman, your ass flaps are sticking out!" she said and everyone laughed. Sarah was thinking that everyone touches each other and hugs but she had mostly just petted Rover. She slid a hand in Priscilla's pack feeling the usual condoms and then she reached what she wanted, a small rack of two-ounce shooters of Kahlúa. Sarah didn't care for whiskey or beer but she liked the coffee-chocolate flavor of Kahlúa. Priscilla would ride to the liquor store in the county seat with her mother when she restocked the village tavern. While Giselle was choosing stock Priscilla would go into the walk-in cooler with the geeky clerk who was in his midthirties and let him suck her breasts for a minute in exchange for a dozen Kahlúa shooters. When she heard the story Sarah had said, "You're so biological," and Priscilla had answered, "What the fuck is that supposed to mean?"

Sarah lay splayed on her back listening to the Grateful Dead on her tape deck wondering how a tiny bottle of

booze could make you feel that much better. She slept for
two hours until dinnertime.

In a hall in the middle of the fairgrounds they had their
annual beef barbecue. Outside there were a number of steer
halves roasting on wood-fired grills. There were at least five
hundred diners who drank beer and gorged on the meat.
Whiskey was banned on the fairgrounds but most men carried their own bottles anyway. When dinner was over all
the tables were pushed off to the side and a country band
that had traveled over three hundred miles from Billings
began setting up their equipment. Mrs. Lahren had insisted
that Sarah do the warm-up for the band on an upright piano.
Sarah had snuck off to the toilet to have another Kahlúa
which she downed in a single gulp feeling her body suffused
with warmth. Nearly all of the young people would have
preferred a rock band but ranchers controlled the fair and
at least Sarah's ragtime and boogie-woogie was a compromise. She didn't have to look to play and she exchanged
glances with the country band fiddler who was plugging in
amplifiers. Priscilla had told her all about the band. The fiddler who was big and mean-looking was in his twenties and
hauled horses for his living with his partner, the bass player,
because they couldn't quite make it as a full-time band. They
had taken fifth place in calf roping that day and were too
erratic to be really good. She also knew that the fiddler's
name was Karl and he hailed originally from Meeteetse,
Wyoming.

She played a half-hour set to everyone's delight until
the end when she snuck in a little Mendelssohn and Karl
moved forward and played along with her beautifully to her

surprise. Afterward he bowed to her in mock lust or maybe it wasn't mock. She was jangled and exhausted and couldn't wait to get out of there to have her third wonder-working Kahlúa.

"How old are you, cutie?" Karl said grabbing her arm way too tight.

"I'm fifteen, sir." She always called older men sir.

"Fifteen will get you twenty," Karl laughed and turned away.

Sarah had heard this before and knew it meant that if a man fooled with a fifteen-year-old girl he could do prison time at Deer Lodge though this was less likely out in the country than in the city. She felt curiously flattered that someone might want her though nearly every man did but she wasn't conscious of it. It was different anyway from the day before when a hideous, dirty creep setting up the merry-go-round told her that he wanted to go down on her, an act she had heard about but did not yet comprehend.

After her drink in the dark and looking back at the yellow square of light made by the big open door of the dance hall she was overwhelmed by loneliness for Tim because the band was playing Bob Wills's "San Antonio Rose" which was Tim's favorite. She swallowed a sob and hurried to her campsite in the heifer barn, confused that the drink had made her forlorn rather than relaxed. Her bookish friend Terry had given her the novel *Light in August* and she had just begun the book but felt like the girl Lena standing on the side of the dirt road. She paused outside the barn to try to vomit up the last drink but couldn't do it. She got in her sleeping bag and slept the sleep of the dead. In the middle

of the night for a moment she heard Priscilla on the other side
of the box stall with a boy but drifted back to sleep remembering back in Findlay one summer day when Brother had
taught her to roller-skate.

At first light she was up and had saddled Lad. Her
intention was to school him after his naughtiness. On the
way out of the fairgrounds she paused seeing Karl the fiddler sleeping facedown in the dirt under a cottonwood near
a travel trailer. She wondered how someone could get so
wiped out on whatever, likely a combination, that he would
collapse facedown in the dirt unable to make himself comfortable as an ordinary pig would. Tim had told her that such
people are unhappy in their skin which was simple enough.

She rode in new country which exhilarated her, even
letting Lad chase a jackrabbit on a sagebrush flat, something
he had learned from Rover. It was a deliriously cool early
morning on a day that was to be hot and she was amazed at
the way the weather could change the mood. She turned up
a two-track that led into a forested mountainside listening
to the profusion of birds. It was all perfect except for a slight
ball of fuzz in her head so she got off Lad and led him up
the mountainside to see if her exertion would pump out the
remains of alcohol. She thought of the old gossip she had
heard before they left Findlay how the police had found her
father's first alcoholic wife naked in a public park at midnight with some teenage boys.

Her spirits were fairly high when she got back to the
fairgrounds a couple hours later noting that Karl was still
facedown under the cottonwood but his partner, the bass
player, was drinking a morning beer on the trailer steps. This

was the last day of the fair and they were breaking down the vegetable exhibits to avoid spoilage. Sarah gave her display to a woman who lived down the road near their home with her hired-hand husband and four children in a rickety pole barn.

She ran into her new acquaintances, Marcia and Noreen from the girls' hunting club, and the three of them drove over to a stream a few miles away and went swimming. Marcia had a boom box that worked off the cigarette lighter, a couple of six-packs on ice, and some baloney sandwiches, a regular Montana picnic. It was very hot and Sarah came off the wagon she had decided on that morning and kept up with the other two girls in the beer drinking. They sang along with Jagger's "Honky Tonk Women" while skinny-dipping. They finished the beer and went back to the fairgrounds where a local bluegrass band was playing. Sarah danced with a half dozen cowboys insistently pushing their hands off her bottom. She also had a few sips from whiskey bottles she didn't need. Karl showed up not completely revived from whatever he had done the night before, his eyes cold and glittery. He was an amazingly good dancer but they became tired and went over to her camp spot to rest with Priscilla and the bass player who she seemed not to like. Everyone else was outside in the gathering dark waiting for the fireworks. Karl got fresh and despite his size she was able to push him away. The bass player was in the dimly lit corner of the box stall making drinks from his shoulder satchel. Sarah said she only wanted water and he drew some from a corner faucet. They toasted the first of the fireworks glowing through the dirty window. Within a minute Sarah was floating down a black hole which in her unconscious delirium she thought of as one of the uncovered abandoned mines in the area. One of the nicknames of ketamine is actually "black hole." Karl had gotten the drug from a veterinarian to help subdue rank horses for hauling. A minute quantity and you could fuck any resistant girl. He couldn't get a hard-on because of his drugs and alcohol but he thought a piece of ass is a piece of ass whatever happened. Going down is going down and is better than nothing. He actually chewed. He and the bass player made short work, as it were, then packed up and headed back to Billings.

Sarah woke up with a headache and nausea a few hours later, her shirt pushed up to her neck and her jeans and panties twisted around her ankles. Priscilla was crying in the corner her chest covered with vomit. Sarah pulled on her clothes and took out the big jackknife Priscilla kept for protection. It had begun to rain as she walked toward Karl's trailer with the blade open. She was without doubt that she would kill him but the truck and trailer were gone. Her vagina felt raw and ached and her breasts mauled.

Chapter 6

She ran in the early mornings, never having run much before. It relieved her mind. Rover and Lad ran with her though Rover was obnoxious and forced Lad to run behind them in an orderly fashion.

She bought an upright piano for seven hundred bucks with some of Tim's cash. Her father was upset that she had bought a piano without his permission and she asked why. "I don't know," he said. He wearied of her hours of playing so she had a group of 4-H boys move the piano up to Tim's porch where it would stay until the late summer and early fall weather turned bad. There was a porch light for when she played in the dark but she only used the light when playing a piece she didn't know well or learning a new one. Other than this she preferred to play in the dark where the music would envelope her pleasantly in the soft arms of the night.

The piano and running were the only things that lessened the intensity of the ache in her heart and mind. The first few days she couldn't figure out the soreness of her pubis and then it occurred to her that Karl must have been chewing on her vulva. She checked in the mirror and saw that her hymen was intact and noted that many hairs had been uprooted. The last image she could remember before the ketamine totally hit was that Karl had forced her knees back against her chest and was fiddling with his large but limp penis, his face looked strangled. She planned without afflatus on shooting him one day but only when she could get away with it. She had no intention of further damaging her own life. Her gun club friend Marcia had a .22-250 she used for shooting prairie dogs which she could hit at four hundred yards. When the bullet hit the prairie dog's head it was called "red mist." She imagined the impact on Karl's head with satisfaction. If he would do that to a girl he plainly deserved to die.

By the time school started she and Priscilla had drifted apart perhaps understandably because the shared pain was unbearable. Priscilla took to drinking in the mornings and her mother Giselle had to enter her in an alcohol rehabilitation clinic for teenagers in Helena. Sarah's burgeoning friendship with Marcia helped. In lieu of the oncoming hunting season the three of them, Sarah, Marcia, and Marcia's diminutive friend Noreen, who was moment by moment pissed off, would go out to the rifle range twice a week to practice. There was something mindlessly cleansing about shooting at a target that was an outline of a deer at varying distances from one hundred to three hundred yards.

Her other friend was the bookish young man with a clubfoot, Terry. For obvious reasons she no longer was interested in distinctly male writers and began reading Jane Austen, Emily Brontë, and Katherine Anne Porter but also the more modern Margaret Atwood and Alice Munro. She had long since decided that if she were to endure her secret she would have to summon up all her resources. She deviously joined the Bible Club. She knew all of the evangelical lingo from her mother Peppy but the sole reason was to throw off her scent for all of the high school boys. They quickly believed that she was "real religious" and that none of them was going to get close to her body. Her distance irritated them so they snubbed her.

There were certain friendship problems because Terry was infatuated with Sarah, and Marcia who was a half a foot taller than Terry was infatuated with him. Her affection seemed odd to Sarah but Marcia said that her dad and three brothers were "blowhard jerk-offs" and Terry was a gentleman. Marcia also said that she knew that all the young cowboys that bird-dogged her only did so because her dad had the biggest and best ranch in the county. Montana most certainly wasn't the land of opportunity and if a young man or young woman attached themselves to a big ranch they shot up the social scale.

What bothered Sarah most was that her personality began to develop in fixed ways. She had lost her whimsy she thought, and her imagination was dullish except when it was carried away by music and even then it wasn't as expansive as before the rape. One Sunday afternoon on a lovely Indian summer day she ran up to her secret canyon

with Lad and Rover in tow, sat down on a boulder, and
wept. This was the first time she had wept since the event
some ninety days before and as she cried she felt her insides
convulse over the ugliness in people. She wondered how she
could possibly accommodate what had happened to her life.
She had no choice but to live around it. Rover was upset
with her weeping and pranced around as if to coax her out
of it. She spoke sharply to the dog which she never did and
Rover sulked away and settled under a juniper. She yelled,
"Goddamn God," and ran as fast as she could on a steep trail
up the mountain until she was sure her hurt would burst
and then she would be done with it.

She began inevitably to look at males as another species. And not that she could summon up any special admiration for women. Her mother, for instance. She would get
postcards from Peppy that were relentlessly inane. "It looks
like Clyde and me are going to shop for a condo in Maui"
or "The governor came to dinner and I was proud as punch
to be sitting at the table with this great Republican." Peppy
was a virtual parody of a nitwit but then perhaps she was
better than nothing because Sarah's father was bitterly
lonely.

Sarah took to rating men and few could pass through
the eye of her cultural needle. Of course there was her
hyperliterate pal Terry and her biology teacher, an eager
young recent graduate of Montana State University in
Bozeman. His enthusiasm for botany, chemistry, and biology was infective for even his simplest-minded students
of which there were many. She knew that he had a fresh
eye for her but that was merely a fact of life and didn't mean

he was a rapist. And then there was her taciturn father who was an acceptable taciturn father.

One Saturday she went over to Terry's for lunch. The pump shed and kitchen were normal but the rest of the house was rather grand as if transplanted from New England. His father and brother were away for the fall cattle sale but Terry wanted her to meet his mother. Her name was Tessa and she came from Duxbury, Massachusetts, had gone to Smith College, and had met Terry's father who was a wrangler at a dude ranch she had visited with her parents. Sarah had heard the gossip that it was her money that thirty years ago had bought the present ranch, a wedding gift from her father.

It was the library that dumbfounded Sarah. There were thousands of books, floor to ceiling, and a moving ladder to get at the upper shelves. She misted her eyes so that all the muted-colored book jackets looked like a landscape painting. Tessa never attended any school or 4-H functions so Sarah heard her voice and its rather alien eastern accent as if she were from a foreign country. She had seen her from a distance jumping a horse over a wooden corral fence in an English saddle which was breathtaking. As Sarah stood in the library Tessa rattled on while Terry was off in a corner looking embarrassed and pretending to search for something. Tessa's voice was slightly slurred like Priscilla's mother Giselle when she was taking tranqs to get over a boyfriend. "Excuse my vulgarity but Montana is a dick place and my response is reading but then it was also my peculiar response in Massachusetts." She held out her hands as if helpless and Sarah reflected that maybe all the women she knew talked the same way because they had the same things to say. "I spend a month a year in San Francisco with my sister and a month in Boston just to keep tuned to the actual world. Out here it's all staring at cow's asses. I know Terry never gives you any poetry to read because around this country deep feelings are an embarrassment."

When Sarah left her head was a knot of pleasant confusion. In this remote part of Montana it was easy to forget there were all kinds of people that you only knew from reading or listening to NPR. She hadn't been able to relate to television since her childhood *Sesame Street, Lassie,* and *Walt Disney.* When she left the lunch which had been comically dismal she carried Wallace Stevens's *Harmonium* and Hart Crane's *The Bridge.* Tessa had told her that she was welcome to use the library when she wished and that way she wouldn't be guided by Terry's taste. Terry, for instance, loathed Jane Austen. The next day, Sunday, she would go riding with Tessa who wanted to show her a spring creek at the back of their ranch. When Terry walked her out to her truck he apologized for his mother's eccentricities saying she drank too much wine and took too many pills. This irritated Sarah who said she thought his mother was fine. He became downcast so she gave his hand a squeeze.

Sarah knew that her main struggle had to be against a specific dullness that kept creeping into her mind which she knew was an incipient depression. The good thing about meeting Tessa was that it opened up ways to be like her rarely seen aunt Rebecca who was an astronomer in Arizona. She knew at fifteen that if there was a place for her in the world she would have to determine it as opposed to certain characters in fiction and Tessa whose place was determined by their family's wealth. Of the thirteen girls in her class only three hoped to go to college and four wanted to be stewardesses because they wanted to travel. The other six wanted to marry and stay right where they were.

Chapter 7

"You've been so quiet. What are you thinking about?" Tessa asked.

"Shooting someone," Sarah said blankly before she could catch herself.

"We've all killed others in our minds," Tessa laughed, "but they don't serve wine in American prisons. How horrid."

They sat down on a shelf rock near the spring and watched small brook trout swim lazily around the pool. She had left Rover at home and a ride without Rover didn't seem right. Tessa was prattling about how Sarah should go east to college to a place like Smith and she was sure scholarships were available. Sarah, meanwhile, was thinking she couldn't go anywhere to college without her dog and horse. She also thought that she would shoot Karl during hunting season when gunshots wouldn't be out of the ordinary.

Things began to come in a rush a few days before the antelope-hunting trip. Terry desperately wanted to go along and the girls couldn't make up their minds. Sarah and her father Frank were called in for a meeting with the school principal and the guidance counselor who both felt the school was holding Sarah back. They had never had a student like her and proposed to graduate her the following spring. She would be sixteen the following summer and that was likely old enough to go off to college.

They were in the principal's office and the man shoved a term paper across the desk. The principal was a pleasant man but was a bachelor with a singsongy voice and many of the high school boys joked that he might be "light in his loafers." The term paper had emerged from the usual banal high school assignment but Sarah's, "Why I Intend to Become a Metallurgist Rather Than a Novelist," was certainly one of a kind locally. Frank looked at it hastily noting with approval his daughter's excitement about the nature of metals got from his own beginning textbook on metallurgy from Purdue and also her quote from Bell's *Men of Mathematics*. He quickly passed over the material about becoming a novelist because he never read fiction and even nonfiction could sink him into a rage. Caputo's *A Rumor of War* was one of the main reasons he moved from Findlay to Montana, the thought of his boyhood friend dying in vain in Vietnam driving him close to the edge. Sarah wrote that she loved reading novels because the emotional lives of characters "supplanted" her concern for her own. Many days she felt unable to carry the weight of her own life and it was wonderful to take refuge in books. She couldn't become a novelist like her friend Terry intended because every day is the end of life as we know it and she needed the solidity of the sciences to endure it.

The guidance counselor said that Sarah might need counseling for this melancholy way of thinking and the principal said, "Nonsense." The room was cool with a November wind rattling the windows but Sarah felt hollow with sweat rising on her forehead. She had finally made it into public school and now they were bent on getting rid of her. The rule of thumb of older people was to relentlessly manipulate those who were younger. The other day the homely guidance counselor who was in her thirties and thin on top and heavy on the bottom had said to her that it was "hard to be pretty and smart" because "you got it all." Sarah didn't bother asking this woman to explain because she disliked her generally patronizing attitude.

On the drive home Frank mused aloud that though he loved Montana because it felt like the 1950s it could be a little difficult for a young person to get ready for the real world unless they were going to stay in Montana. Then he mentioned that a woman was coming to visit him and said he hoped Sarah wouldn't mind. Of course she minded but why say so? One more discordant item in her mental stew pot would scarcely help but then right now in her father's truck she was rehearsing the venison meat loaf she was cooking for dinner. Marcia was coming over for dinner to make last-minute plans for the antelope-hunting trip. Sarah's feeling of hollowness had entered her head and looking at her father she wondered if he had those empty cold spaces in his mind full of metallic question marks or was his mind full and smooth?

The woman was there when they arrived. She was standing in a business suit looking in the door of the greenhouse. Her dad had said her name was Lolly and she was a third cousin by marriage, of Italian parentage, and in the truck-farm business. She had flown into Missoula and rented a car and Sarah noted she was clearly pissed off tiptoeing through the muddy yard on rather short legs. Lolly and her father passionately embraced and Sarah felt oddly pleased for him. He and Peppy had often been at odds but she knew that hadn't included their sexuality from the night noises.

When they were introduced Lolly gave Sarah the hyperappraising look a shorter person often gives to a taller but she was smiling. Frank poured himself and Lolly drinks and they disappeared into the bedroom.

While putting baking potatoes in the oven and mixing the venison meat loaf Sarah was thinking about how puzzled Wallace Stevens's poems made her feel but then the feeling of solution always gave her something to think about that she had never thought of before. At that point she recalled a troublesome dream from the night before just as it occurred to her that she had to keep expanding her life so that her trauma would grow smaller and smaller. In the dream she was teaching the handsome Mexican cowboy who had trailered the horse up to Lahren's ranch how to ride. She caught him as he got off and he slid roughly down her body. It was a good feeling in the dream but when she half-awoke she was close to nausea. She had turned on the light and read a Hart Crane poem that sounded good but was incomprehensible. Terry had told her that Hart Crane had committed suicide, an option that she thought about herself, but then Tim had asked her if she ever had a baby to call it Tim even if it was a girl.

The dinner didn't go so well for an absurd reason. Lolly said the stewed tomatoes were "wonderful" because Sarah used fresh thyme and plenty of garlic but then Lolly thought the beef in the meat loaf tasted "peculiar." Sarah told her it was ground venison plus one-third pork and Lolly rushed to the toilet and spit it up. Marcia laughed loudly and Sarah frowned at her. Lolly came back to the table with tears in her eyes and apologized because *Bambi* was her favorite childhood book and movie. Marcia continued to giggle and ate like a horse. She was a big girl and did the work of a man. Except for the ritual of Sunday dinner their meals were ample and hurried. Marcia was talking about waking up at dawn and seeing a coyote out in the pasture chasing after a ewe with a bad leg.

"I somersaulted that son of a bitch with my .280 right out my bedroom window," Marcia said.

Frank explained what she had said to Lolly who said, "Oh my goodness."

To give her father privacy the girls drove up to Tim's cabin and started a fire in the woodstove. Sarah had drained the pipes for winter but still used the cabin for general solace. She would talk to Tim as if he were in the kitchen making the chicken-fried steaks she loved.

In the last light of the early November evening Sarah threw out cracked corn for her magpies, a quarrelsome but playful member of the Corvidae family. As a child in the second grade in Ohio she was fascinated with birds and Peppy would take her for walks in wooded acres so she could try to identify them. Peppy didn't know the names of any birds except "robin" but declared that they were "God's choir."

They went over their trip list and Marcia announced that irritable Noreen, the other member of the hunting club, couldn't come along because her mom had to start chemo, so she had invited Terry. Marcia hoped Sarah wouldn't mind and Sarah didn't say anything because it was a done deal. She just hoped that Terry wouldn't whine too much about the world in general, a habit that could drive anyone batty. And then Marcia said something that appalled Sarah to the effect that she intended to try to seduce Terry. She blushed which she never did. Sarah said that since she knew that Marcia was infatuated with Terry and since he was also horny as a toad maybe she could bring him to her side with sex. "Why not?" said Sarah, embarrassed.

When Marcia left Sarah decided to stay at the cabin for the night. Rover was pleased and they sat before the hot woodstove listening to the cold, blustery November wind. She thought of Tim but her mind was insufficient to imagine raising a son or daughter named Tim. Right now the first step, making love to someone, seemed forever out of the question. If anyone could be her patron saint it was Tim. A number of times she had been reminded that Tim would wish her to kill Karl—not, certainly, herself.

Rover growled but Sarah suspected it was the little bear she had seen her playing with from a distance. The bear was a year and a half and had likely been pushed away by its mother in favor of new cubs. She had heard of dogs and coyotes playing but never a dog and a bear. Rover was so relentlessly mean and protective that she wondered why she had made an exception for a little bear.

Having read so many stories and novels it unnerved her that she, in essence, was writing her own story day by day. Drifting toward sleep she recalled going with Terry to Priscilla's birthday party because Giselle had called to say that Priscilla was depressed and drinking too much and needed company. Giselle had a fancy satellite TV hookup a rich boyfriend had given her for her double-wide house trailer. Way up the valley at Sarah's house their TV reception was hopelessly fuzzy but Frank would sit there on Sunday watching pro football especially if it was the Cleveland Browns. It was Labor Day weekend and Terry was watching U.S. Open tennis and talking about Thomas Wolfe, the novelist. They had both enjoyed *Look Homeward, Angel* but less so the other novels by Wolfe which Terry pointed out were mostly the writer talking about himself. Sarah began to say something then stopped when the screen showed the New York City skyline which she found totally unimaginable, then she said that not much happened in Wolfe's life except writing so that's what he had to write about. Why was it that a big terrible thing had to happen in her otherwise uneventful life? Was it fate or chance? She couldn't free herself to believe in fate or destiny. Such concepts were for the important and famous people the camera showed at the U.S. Open. In bad novels lots of stuff happened but in the good ones this was far less so. She asked Terry if it upset him to watch tennis when he couldn't play it, meaning his clubfoot prevented his playing such games. "No, life has set me aside as an observer," he said.

Chapter 8

They left before daylight and reached Livingston in four hours with four more hours to go for their destination whereupon the police closed I-90 because the snowstorm had grown in force and the wind was so high between Livingston and Big Timber that a semi had tipped over. They rather nervously checked into a room at the Murray Hotel that had two double beds. Terry in particular was giddy opening his suitcase and showed the girls six bottles of fine French wine he had swiped from his mother's cellar. It wasn't quite noon and they agreed it was a little early for wine. Marcia called her uncle over past Forsyth to say they'd be delayed, and then they abandoned the sack of baloney sandwiches they were going to eat for lunch and went across the street to Martin's Cafe. After lunch Marcia winked at Sarah so Sarah went off to Sax & Fryer's to look at the new books for sale and Marcia virtually led Terry back to the

hotel. Sarah thought that to be on the safe side she'd give
Marcia an hour to manage her seduction.

It occurred to her that this was a good time to do some
research on Meeteetse and hard thinking on how to exter-
minate Karl. Pop goes the muskmelon, she thought, or she
could aim lower since she clearly remembered what the big
exit wound of a .30-06 looked like on an elk that Tim shot a
half mile from his cabin. The elk was so large it took two
trips to get it back to the cabin in the dark on a packhorse,
at which point Tim fried up part of the delicious liver with
onions. Sarah had read how many people these days were
squeamish about hunting but where she lived it was merely
a fact of life.

She spoke at length with the proprietor of the bookstore who was kindly and rather handsome. He knew a lot
about the country south of Cody and said the main fact of
Meeteetse was the huge Pitchfork Ranch. His cousin cowboyed there. Sarah flushed because this man reminded her
of Tim and was not at all repellent. As a future murderer
she lost some caution and asked about the Burkhardt spread
because that was Karl's last name. He said, "Those people
are rapscallions," and she said she was unsure what that
meant and he answered, "Real rough people." The father
was a mean old goat, one of the boys was in prison in Deer
Lodge for repeated assaults, one was an itinerant musician
who had done time for selling coke and meth, and one was
fine having left with the mother years ago for Boise. When
the man was curious about why she wanted to know Sarah
said a friend of hers had gotten mixed up with the musician
and it was unpleasant. "I bet it was," the man said, then he

pointed out the public library down the street where she might find solid information about that area of Wyoming. She bought the new novel of a regional writer named Thomas McGuane whom Terry was very fond of but she had found a bit abrasive.

The snow seemed to be lifting but the fierce wind continued from the northwest so that she raised a hand to protect her eyes while walking to the library. Karl had it coming, that's for sure, she thought. Shooting him would be a public service. The point was to make certain that she got away with it.

The library was grand and a librarian helpful and she soon had a stack of books about Wyoming on the table before her but then she drifted. Even so, once in a while she had a microsecond glimmer that she might be insane. Conjoined to this was the brief flash from her unconscious of a physical memory of the hairs of her pubis being uprooted. If there's a God why can't we control our minds? she thought. She'd talked to Terry about this and he had read some Oriental literature and quoted, "How can the mind control the mind?" This boggled her. In her weakest moments she found herself wishing she had an actual mother to talk to. Or anyone she could trust like Tim.

She ended up sitting at the library table for a couple of hours and wished her area had such a library. She even studied topographical maps of the location of the Burkhardt ranch which included two-tracks to get on and make a good departure. She would have to call first to make sure he was there and not on the road playing music. Perhaps for relief her mind flittered away in a comic reverie of the little boy who'd lived next door in Findlay when she was seven. He was homely with buckteeth and people would yell at him when he walked around the neighborhood picking flowers which he would pass to her through the fence between their yards. Sometimes she would press her cheek to the fence and he would kiss it. Maybe that was love at its best she thought.

On the way back to the hotel the snow had stopped and the wind had subsided. She overheard in front of the post office that the interstate had been reopened which meant that they could reach Marcia's uncle's ranch well before midnight. She stood outside their room door listening for signs of life, looking down the dark hall toward the south where a window squared the waning but glistening light off the snow-covered Absaroka Mountains. Her skin prickled with the beauty of it and she walked down the hall seeing the winter sun palpably losing its power. She couldn't imagine a life without mountains and thought that whatever happens to me I'm lucky to live inside beauty.

She heard muttering when she knocked on the door and when she opened it Terry was asleep but Marcia was smiling beside him. She laughed and gave Sarah the thumbs-up sign. There was a slight animal smell to the room and Sarah opened the window to the cold air then brewed a pot in the coffeemaker on the dresser. She sat down and pulled a book about the human genome out of her duffel thinking that someday they might find evil in the genes of certain people. She noticed that Terry and Marcia had finished a bottle of wine with the peculiar name of Échézeaux and thought she would take the first stint driving.

Chapter 9

Marcia's uncle Lester woke them in the bunkhouse at five A.M. by hammering at the door and yelling, "Off your ass and on your feet." He was far more jovial than Marcia's father and even larger. They had made it to the ranch at ten-thirty in the evening because the snow had given out by Custer which was east of Billings. When they reached Lester's his wife Lena, who couldn't speak because of a stroke, served them a pinto-bean-and-short-rib stew and now at short of six in the morning Sarah was looking at a chicken-fried steak with cream gravy, fried eggs, and potatoes. No wonder these people are so big she thought but in truth they were rangy rather than fat.

Terry had drunk another bottle of wine in the truck and refused to get up. Sarah had pushed him and Marcia off into a small corner bedroom of the bunkhouse to soften the sound effects of love. She slept in a small daybed by the woodstove which she fed several times in the night during which she dreamt of hunting mule deer with Tim and her butt was cold because she had forgotten to put on her blue jeans and was only wearing hunter-orange panties. She questioned what this might mean and decided on nothing.

Lester drove her and Marcia on a lumpy two-track a couple of miles toward the back of the ranch near a series of small buttes overlooking the Yellowstone River. He dropped them off a mile apart and said he would check on them at noon. Sarah sat down near a juniper bush and watched the landscape to the east slowly reveal itself, the moon set and Venus disappear. The sun rose reddishly and streaks of cirrus clouds meant it would likely be a windy day. She cradled the .30-06 across her knees pleased that she had brought a small space blanket along to sit on, a buffer against the frozen earth. Way to the north she could see Lester's alfalfa fields and to the east there were thousands of flat acres of wheatland that reminded her of Willa Cather. She meant to visit Nebraska someday because of Cather but she intended to visit a lot of places and had been nowhere to speak of except western Montana. Sitting there glassing the landscape with her binoculars for antelope she felt a sharp pang of loneliness beneath her breastbone. Who did she know? She recalled a few childhood friends from six years ago. Her grandmother who was her piano teacher was insensate in a rest home. Priscilla had drifted away. Terry was pretty much buried alive in his own mind. Marcia had felt the mating call early as do many country girls in Montana where the passage between girl and woman is a short voyage. Her solid friends were the spirit of Tim and books.

At about nine-thirty she heard a rifle shot off to the northeast and suspected Marcia had scored. Sarah glassed a group of about fifteen antelope running toward the south that unfortunately would not be coming close to her. The wind rose and she backed into the juniper bush for shelter looking down at a jackrabbit skull and part of its skeleton. After a while during which she gutted the animal Marcia was visible heading toward Sarah alternately carrying the antelope for a hundred yards then dragging it a hundred yards. That was true Marcia, Sarah thought. How many fifteen-year-old girls can carry a hundred-pound antelope? She knew that at her family's request Marcia had shot a young doe favored for its tender and delicious meat, including the liver and heart. Readily available elk and venison were one thing in their area but not antelope.

Marcia dragged her antelope up the hill to Sarah's juniper then laughed at herself for doing so because Lester was coming by with the pickup at noon. Marcia backed into the juniper and Sarah could feel the heat of her exertion off her body. Marcia splashed water from her canteen and washed the dry blood off her hands saying that the "girl" had only required a fifty-yard shot. They chatted for a while with Marcia talking comically about Terry and her losing their virginity at the hotel, then Marcia tapped her on the shoulder and pointed. There upwind about two hundred yards to the west a young male antelope was picking its way along a thicket of buck brush at the bottom of a butte.

Marcia had Sarah use her shoulder as a rest and Sarah chose a neck shot. The antelope bucked straight up like a horse then landed on its side. "You blew that sucker out of his shoes," Marcia said. Sarah immediately thought, I shot one mammal and I can shoot another. It was unpleasant when she gutted the animal and the steamy rank-smelling heat of the innards rose against her face in the cold air.

Chapter 10

Of course Lolly screamed in the morning when she discovered the antelope hanging in the pump shed off the back door of the house. When Sarah reached home in the middle of the night Frank got up and congratulated her and before going to bed Sarah moved the three empty suitcases Lolly had put in the corner of her room. Imagine that bitch using my room for storage, Sarah thought. At Frank's urging Sarah moved the carcass up to Tim's, adjusting the propane to forty degrees, a good hanging temperature for both beef and wild game. She'd wait a week before butchering and wrapping it for the freezer. Rover was enthused when she fried up the slices of heart and shared it.

They had taken an extra day getting home because Terry wanted to see the confluence of the Yellowstone and Missouri rivers up between Sydney and Williston, a beautiful and historically significant place. Sarah, however, was distracted by the idea that she would have to make a trial run into Karl's territory. She couldn't just go in cold and do the deed. There was also a nagging sense that she shouldn't have identified the idea of shooting Karl with having shot the antelope. She was a good student of history and knew that humans find it altogether too easy to shoot one another, but then sanity fled too easily and when they drove home on Route 2 across the top of Montana and stopped at a diner at Wolf Point there was a trace of Karl's odor of yogurt, breath mints, and cow shit and she again felt murderous. Only fifteen minutes later out in the parking lot she saw a group of local Anishinabe Indians getting out of an ancient car and thought that of all Americans along with the blacks they were the people with the right to shoot people. She stood there in the cold wind hoping that at some point soon her brain would stop being a shuddering elevator.

The winter started out difficult but resolved itself in purposeful physical exhaustion. One morning a week before Christmas Lolly had said to her, "If you hang out with horses and dogs you're going to smell like horses and dogs." This was at breakfast and Sarah answered, "I like the smell of horses and dogs better than I like the smell of people." Lolly huffed off into the bedroom and Frank gave Sarah a lecture on civility which she thought was unwarranted. She went on a hard ride in the snow on Lad and Rover caught and ate a whole jackrabbit leaving a big smear of blood on the snow. When she got back to the house she packed up essentials, including frozen packages of antelope, and moved up to Tim's where she played the piano for hours. She wept briefly then figured weeping wouldn't help one little bit. She thought of the damage people do to each other, sometimes incalculable, and then there was the damage you could do to yourself by toughening up. While she was playing the piano it occurred to her that the least tough woman in the world, Emily Dickinson, was one of her favorite poets. Despite this she felt she had no choice but to become prematurely older and austere. She would live in this cabin like a cloistered nun and then finally leave town and try to find another life.

When school started again she joined the volleyball team to spend more time with Marcia and being tall she quickly learned how to spike the ball with brutal speed and to feel the tranquillity of exhaustion. She joined the track team and ran the eight hundred meters or half mile. Beginning in February the track team worked out in a wealthy rancher's horse arena which was larger than the school gymnasium. The girls' team ran in circles on a mixture of sawdust and dirt for an hour each day. They ran as fast as possible to keep warm because the arena wasn't heated. Sarah liked it but not as much as running outdoors. The good part was that in the first ten minutes of running you would rehearse your mental problems and after the ten minutes all of the problems would drift away. She quit her Bible Club sham which anyway no longer fooled the older boys who badgered her. One day while she was talking with Marcia in the school hall the goofy son of the local Baptist minister passed her a note that read, "Can you take seven inches?" Sarah passed the note to Marcia who slugged the boy knocking him to the floor.

Sarah got up at five A.M. and studied and read. She then fed Rover and Lad and took Rover for a short walk. Unlike

at her home down the hill Rover would come into the cabin
and he slept at the end of the bed which kept Sarah's feet
warm. For protection against the unknown she kept Tim's
pistol under her pillow. Frank had helped her build a shed
for Lad next to Tim's porch. Hay was expensive but Terry
would swipe it from his dad in pickup loads and haul it over
with Marcia. Terry and Marcia were Sarah's only social life
except for an occasional weekend visit to Terry's mother
Tessa to borrow books. Tessa had Sarah reading George
Eliot, Henry James, and Stendhal. She liked Stendhal but
the others were too claustrophobic.

One Sunday afternoon while she was playing Schubert
Frank came up to make peace and offer a compromise. He
said that Lolly thought she had driven Sarah out of the house
and Sarah said, "She did." Frank asked if for his sake Sarah
would have dinner with them at least twice a week and Sarah
said yes mostly because she was tired of cooking all of her
own meals. Then Frank entered an area that startled her.
He had been talking to his sister Rebecca down in Tucson
about their family problems and Rebecca had sent a ticket
for Sarah to come down for a visit and see if she might like
to attend the University of Arizona. At first Sarah said no
because she had intended to use spring vacation to do a
reconnaissance on Karl over in Meeteetse. She changed her
mind and said she would visit her aunt because she wanted
to ride on a plane and she could always skip school when
the snow melted and it would be easier to investigate Karl's
environs.

PART III

Chapter 11
1986

Frank and Lolly drove her all the way to Bozeman which was three hours because Lolly wanted to shop for things unavailable in Butte. At the airport Sarah's mind was a whirling dither and she seemed unable to take a full breath. Unlike in her home area the cars pulling up to the entry were new models and clean and shinier and inside many men wore suits and ties and had the general appearance of being rich though she knew that was unlikely to be true. These men were fresh-faced while the big ranchers back home might own thousands of acres of land and several thousand cows but were weathered and battered by their life in the elements.

Once in her window seat Sarah found herself humming a song taught to her by Frank's old father Antonio who had died when she was five. She remembered his wrinkled face next to hers on the piano stool as they sang together, "Off we go into the wild blue yonder, flying high into the sky . . ."

She had loved this old man who always seemed to be laughing compared to her father Frank.

The takeoff is shocking indeed for one who has never been on a plane but then she was quickly enmeshed in the somewhat cryptic design of the landscape below remembering a line in a poem, "Where the water goes is how the earth is shaped." The man in the trim suit next to her was reading the *Wall Street Journal* and the smell of his aftershave was so strong it was enough to gag a maggot. She idly wondered how anyone could sleep with a man who smelled like that. For inscrutable reasons the mountains below her called the Spanish Peaks reminded her of Terry's teasing to the effect that she was far too austere and prematurely old. She knew that this was also true before her attack and her consequent decision to kill Karl. Terry would mockingly say that she had "her lid screwed on too tight" and that she was a bit of an ideologue like her father. After that contretemps she wept on the way home in her pickup, lamely trying to excuse the obvious truth by the fact that Terry was drinking too much. She had gone down in their wine cellar when his mother was visiting Boston and she questioned why on earth anyone would want that much wine. There must have been thousands of bottles but then Terry said that Tessa averaged two bottles of wine a day.

The plane ride was causing other unexpected thoughts as it does to many people, a free-floating anecdotage. On the way back from antelope hunting on Route 2 they had turned south on Interstate 15 in Shelby, then stopped in Great Falls for something to eat. Terry had been drinking wine and insisted that they try to get into a strip club he'd noticed. Occasionally Terry had the snotty boldness and sense of entitlement of a rich kid. He sent Sarah and Marcia ahead of him through the door. They made it but the bouncer wouldn't let Terry in. In the brief moment she was in the club Sarah saw a pretty stripper rubbing a patron's face into her pubis while the patron's friend cheered. The sight so shocked her that it was a minute before she would flee. Outside Marcia laughingly told Terry what they had seen and he was angry having missed it. In the spring as a practical joke Terry had given Sarah a very naughty Erskine Caldwell novel which had itemized such behavior and once in Missoula when she and her dad were having lunch with other vegetable growers an old Italian at the table said that he wanted to kiss the waitress's pretty ass. Frank spoke sharply to him but he hadn't noticed Sarah and apologized. Sarah was reading Laurence Sterne's *Tristram Shandy* at lunch and pretended she hadn't heard him to save him from embarrassment. It was clear to her on the plane that Karl wasn't the only animalistic man and obviously there were women taking part. Suddenly she questioned whether shooting Karl would make things even but after a pause thought that it would.

After a brief layover and changing planes to a bigger jet in Salt Lake City, Sarah was thinking that though there was a lot of anti-Mormon prejudice in the West they certainly lived in a grand place. One day in the future she hoped to ride Lad around in the Escalante area of southern Utah. After only a couple of hours of her trip everything seemed brand-new and she was forgetting where she was from. Montana might be huge but it was also confining. Now, finally, the world was opening its windows for her. She had memorized an Emily Dickinson sentence that was *au point,* "To live is so startling it leaves little time for anything else." When her family had come west five and a half years before and crossing South Dakota she had looked over her father's shoulder and had seen the dark, immense shapes of the Black Hills in the distance she had decided not to believe her eyes. To a flatlander from Ohio the first mountains are mentally not quite acceptable.

Now in the Tucson airport with her aunt Rebecca approaching she was back in a slow-motion dreamscape. Rebecca shook her hand and hugged her and looked down at Sarah's hands which were calloused and there was a raw spot from a rope burn she got from helping Marcia pull a calf.

"You've been working, I see," Rebecca laughed.

"Well, I work in the garden, split wood, and the other day we pulled a difficult calf." Sarah was embarrassed because Rebecca's hands were soft and smooth compared to her own which were the hands of a workingman. They'd had to pull hard or they would have lost both cow and calf and when the calf came out suddenly she and Marcia had fallen backward. It all reminded her of mouthy Terry saying that nearly everyone in their area except the big ranch owners were actually peasants in the old European sense. They weren't called peasants because it was a democracy but that was what most locals were.

Rebecca had a four-wheel drive with the same name as Sarah's dog and explained she needed it to get up the steep grade to Kitts Peak Observatory on the occasional icy nights. They drove nearly an hour to the southeast of Tucson to the crossroads village of Sonoita. When Rebecca stopped at a corner store to get cigarettes Sarah heard two dark men in ranchwear speaking Spanish outside their pickup and decided she was in a foreign country. She didn't know that there was a local saying that all of the territory south of Interstate 10 was mostly Mexico.

Rebecca had a pleasant, sprawling adobe house on ten acres. There were two large Labs she called Mutt and Jeff in a kennel that were drooling nitwits when released. It took Sarah a while to comprehend the house which was built to welcome the outside rather than to keep it at bay. There was an inside, roofless patio with a fair-sized cottonwood growing in it. Sarah wandered around, then unpacked her clothes while Rebecca started dinner. The Labs sniffed her luggage and asked with looks, "Where is the girl dog?" By looking outside her bedroom and through the patio she noticed a small grand piano in a sunroom which delighted her. On the wall by the door there was a small map on which Rebecca had scrawled "you are here" pinpointing Sonoita and the surrounding mountain ranges, the Rincons to the far north, the Whetstones and Mustangs to the east, the Patagonias and the Santa Ritas to the west. To the south forty miles was all of Mexico. What a place to ride a horse, she thought.

At dinner Rebecca made a proposal that at first angered Sarah because of her uncommunicative father. Frank and Rebecca had been talking and there was the idea that if Sarah would go to the University of Arizona Rebecca would finance it because Sarah could also house-sit. Rebecca was going to be spending a lot of time in Chile with a consortium

of astronomers designing a new observatory facility. Sarah
mellowed with a glass of wine and was startled when
Rebecca said how much she disliked Lolly. "Lolly was always wicked and she and Frank were fooling with each
other when they were only thirteen and now she's got him.
With women my brother is lame. I don't see how you stand
her." Sarah told her that she had moved up the hill and was
living alone with Rover and that she had rigged Lad's corral so he could look in the window. She asked if she could
bring them and Rebecca said of course and that half the
people in Sonoita had horses in their yards.

That settled that and Montana began to drift away. The
sense of an idyll was broken in the middle of the moonlit
night. She was trying to sleep facing east but the moon was
enormous and not looking particularly friendly. She got up
and drew the curtains but they were thin and only slightly
diffused the light and actually made the moon look larger.
Her life had been comparatively uneventful and now it was
too eventful. In the dark she could perceive that what we
have is the life of the mind and now it was whirling and
humming like an old-fashioned top that you pumped. These
so-called big decisions like coming to Arizona were essentially out of her control and had been made for her by Frank
and Rebecca. Of course she could refuse but what were her
options? She could wait for news of a full scholarship to
Missoula or Bozeman. The principal had said there was a
good chance but she had the feeling that she had painted
herself into a corner in Montana. And maybe if she headed
south the image of Karl would fade. And her disordered
mind had its own sound effects. Wherever she drove with

Marcia she was forced to listen to Patsy Cline and Merle Haggard on the eight-track tape deck. In the nighttime she could hear Cline's clear voice singing, "I Fall to Pieces" and "The Last Word in Lonesome Is Me" and some Haggard line to the effect that the singer had turned twenty-one in prison doing life without parole. Terry was always saying that our bodies were our prisons. What if she spent her life in a real prison for shooting Karl?

One of Rebecca's Labs, she couldn't tell which, came into the bedroom, jumped onto the bed, and curled up next to her hip. Putting a hand on his chest and feeling his heartbeat calmed her as it did with Rover. She began to sleep fitfully but then after midnight when the moon had moved away from her window she awoke sobbing and screaming and the dog began barking. She was having a nightmare where Karl was eating her bare left foot and leg and the white bones were sticking out. He was moving upward in huge ripping bites. Rebecca came running and turned on the overhead light. Sarah was now weeping and thrashing around on the bed with her eyes wide open but not seeing. Rebecca dragged her off the bed into an upright position and walked her up and down the room until she recovered true consciousness but, doubting that it would work quickly enough, led Sarah from room to room in the house turning on the lights as they went, backing out of the darkish but moonlit patio when Sarah stiffened.

It was the piano that worked and perhaps the sunburst color of the walls and the many potted desert plants. Rebecca put Sarah on the piano stool and asked her to play some Schumann.

"Schumann's too scary. I only play him in the daylight," Sarah said, beginning to play Schubert. She played at least an hour by which time Rebecca and the dogs were asleep on the sofa. Sarah put an afghan throw over Rebecca thinking that she wished Rebecca were her mother but then it was too late to have a mother.

At midmorning they drove to the Desert Museum. For an hour Sarah was startled enough by the flora and fauna to forget everything else but what she was seeing and thinking which was that maybe game biology or botany might be better to study than the safety of dry, cold metallurgy.

Rebecca had to teach a seminar about the mathematics of astronomy so Sarah wandered around the U of A campus thrilled at the number of Asian, black, and Latin students she saw after being raised in ethnically monochromatic Montana. The buildings were intimidatingly big and grand and she questioned why they needed such expensive buildings to learn. She walked sleepily up to a noodle shop on Campbell and ate a bowl of duck soup which would have been better with the wild mallards Tim used to shoot. After the nightmare and the piano she had only dozed with the bed lamp on rather than chancing the continuation of the nightmare. She read some from Hemingway's *Islands in the Stream* and didn't much care about the story but loved the descriptions of the Gulf Stream. She couldn't fathom why Terry was so fond of Hemingway when she would rather read Faulkner or Steinbeck or dozens of others. Some books crossed her teenage intemperance. She wondered why the heroine of *Madame Bovary* didn't shoot herself or take a boat to America.

On the way back to Rebecca's office she saw a big ungainly boy who reminded her of Karl. It occurred to her that if she got caught for shooting Karl she wouldn't get to identify all of those bizarre desert plants she'd seen near the museum. This contrasted bleakly with the fresh urgency of shooting him after the vividness of the nightmare.

Back at Rebecca's in the late afternoon she slept for several hours waking at twilight to hear a number of voices in the distance and the piano playing Stravinsky quite well. She had awakened with confused thoughts of normalcy, the perhaps imagined normalcy seen in other people. There was a family story about Rebecca's marriage which had lasted only a week. Her hot-tempered young husband had hit her after they returned from their five-day honeymoon in New York City. He had wanted to go to Miami. She immediately went to the police with her black eye and pressed charges. The parents of both families tried to talk her out of the divorce or annulment, Sarah had forgotten which. They said the husband deserved another chance to which she replied, "No one deserves to hit me even once." Rebecca was thought to be eccentric in the old neighborhood because after the parting with the wife beater she went on to get a PhD at MIT, a far reach for a girl with a truck-farmer father.

Sarah thought about the story in the shower looking down at her rough hands which didn't go with her smooth and supple body. What was the point in being attractive? With the shower off she could hear a beautifully done Villa-Lobos piece. She hurriedly dressed and met three of Rebecca's friends in the kitchen, two male astronomers and a female artist, but was in a rush to get to the pianist who

turned out to be an exchange professor in botany, a Mexican about thirty-five from Guadalajara named Alfredo. He
had a soft, lilting, accented voice and seemed to be gay, she
thought, which certainly was the last thing that mattered to
her. He began teaching her a four-hand piece (Schubert's
Fantasy in F Minor) and they played for nearly three hours
breaking briefly for dinner. This was the first man in her
life that thoroughly captivated her short of Montgomery
Clift in *The Misfits*. That night, not surprisingly, she heard
Schubert in her dreams. Alfredo had to teach in the morning but would come out in the afternoon to take a walk and
play the piano. He was bringing some botany books and said
that if she studied them hard, he would get her into an advanced course of his in the fall. She was crestfallen when
he said he would be in Tucson only one more year.

The next morning at breakfast Rebecca teased her a
little which wasn't welcome. Sarah alternated between feeling dreamy and antsy. She wanted to ask Rebecca about
Alfredo but was too timid.

"Do you have a boyfriend?"

"Not really, just a friend who is a boy." She found herself telling Rebecca about her friendship with old Tim and
then Terry and Marcia. All the other boys in school were
nitwits and she had never felt romantic about Terry.

"Alfredo's a little old for you," Rebecca teased. "I think
he's in his late thirties. He was married once and I know he
has a daughter but I'm unsure about his sexual taste."

The blood rushed to Sarah's face and she pretended to
be interested in a bird that had landed in the pyracantha tree
and was singing beautifully.

"That's a canyon wren. It's my favorite song," Rebecca said.

Rebecca had to go in to the university so Sarah took the dogs for a walk in the hills and sparse forest at the end of the road. She was immersed in something her dour history teacher had said about how certain minorities like blacks and Indians didn't have much in the way of political empathy for each other. Soon she was lost in a long arroyo and fearful that she wouldn't make it back for Alfredo's arrival. A strong cool wind from the north came up and the dogs ran off chasing a jackrabbit. There was a lump of despair in her throat but then the dogs returned and she said, "Let's go home," like she did with Rover when she was lost. The dogs turned in what she thought was an unlikely direction but they were right as Rover always was.

Alfredo brought her a large bouquet of cut flowers and she was a little dizzy looking for a vase. He put the flowers on the piano and they began working on four-hand compositions of Mozart's and then Fauré's. They broke for sandwiches and coffee and he asked her to tell him about her life. She did so and he said, "It's time for you to get out of there." He said the same had been true about himself. His family and their relatives were prosperous farmers about fifty miles from Guadalajara but all he'd wanted to do was play the piano so his parents had sent him off to Juilliard in New York City when he was sixteen. At Juilliard it was finally determined that his hands were too small for him to become a top-notch pianist. His only other interest was plants so he went to Cornell and "froze his ass" for eight years until he had a PhD in botany. He had been married for a couple of years to a rich, spoiled landowner's daughter but they had divorced. He had a thirteen-year-old daughter who went to a private boarding school in Los Angeles.

They were both melancholy about their stories and then he suddenly laughed and played a mocking version of the dirgelike "Volga Boatmen," and quoted a line of Lorca's in Spanish translating it as "I want to sleep the dream of apples far from the tumult of cemeteries."

"Let's take a walk. I have to give an evening speech to old-lady cactus gardeners and I'd rather stay here."

They walked with the dogs for a half hour and he named the wild flora they were seeing then said good-bye at the car. When he smiled he reminded her of the Mexican cowboy who had brought the horse to the Lahren ranch.

"Rebecca said you weren't sure. Will I see you in the fall?"

"If you want to."

"You're too young to say that." He shook a finger at her.

"No I'm not. I'm older than you in most ways," she laughed.

She watched him drive off with a palpable tremor, clear evidence to her that she was acting crazy and should dampen her own spirits. Inside she looked at the three botany textbooks he'd left behind for her. Inside one the bookplate was a small reproduction of Botticelli's *The Birth of Venus* and underneath he had written, "Dear Sarah, So good to meet you," which, though it said nothing, she grasped to her being.

Chapter 12

The descent into Bozeman was tummy-clenching with high winds causing the plane to pitch and shudder, and the view out the tiny window blinded by snow. Sarah liked the irony that it was April Fools' Day and the Montana weather was cooperating with the calendar. She was hoping to do her reconnaissance of Meeteetse in a few days but the weather would have to clear for the long drive. She was enervated because her sleep had been unkind to her. She hadn't actually seen Karl in her dreams but his presence was as malevolent as the coldest wind in the world. He was hiding in the forest behind Tim's cabin and was going to shoot and eat both Rover and Lad. She couldn't find the cartridges for her .30-06 and she knew she had bought three boxes with twenty shells in each in preparation for her trip to Meeteetse. At the hardware store she had envisioned the exit wound along Karl's spine as looking like a red basketball. As the plane taxied she was disturbed that Alfredo hadn't even touched so much as her hand.

Marcia was there waiting for her having volunteered for the chore. She was a babbling brook and Sarah struggled to keep up with what she was saying. Priscilla had OD'd on her mother Giselle's tranqs and was at a care facility in Helena. Marcia's speech had always been colorful and was especially so with her obsessive interest in all things sexual. She said that "that bubble-butted whippet sophomore Karen" who ran the hundred on the track team had told her minister's wife that her uncle, the town banker, had been "tinkering" with her since she was ten and the minister's wife had told the sheriff who had tried to hush it up but failed. No one knew what was going to happen but everyone in the county knew the story.

There were a lot of semis collected along the shoulder at the bottom of Butte Pass in the drifting snow and it took Marcia a full half hour to get over the top in low-range four-wheel drive. They talked to a state cop at the interchange of Interstates 90 and 15 and decided to head south for thirty miles in the gathering dark and spend the night in Melrose where the weather wasn't supposed to be quite as violent. They checked into a cabin at the Sportsman's Lodge and Marcia revealed a fifth of schnapps she had swiped from her dad's workshop. Her dad was always sure that it was one of her two brothers who did the deed. Marcia had a stiff drink and Sarah a small one and then Marcia began laughing and told her that Terry had arranged a mirror in his bedroom so he could watch them making love but Marcia had ruined it by laughing. She was so much taller than Terry and also outweighed him. She told Sarah that it looked in the mirror like some big Catholic priest was raping a little altar boy. Sarah found the image terribly ugly but Marcia continued laughing and said, "I might have to pick on someone my own size."

They walked a hundred yards in the blowing snow to a bar and restaurant that actually had a hitching post for horses in the front. The place was owned by a second cousin of Marcia's and was filled with cowboys, ranchers, and townspeople who all appreciated the moisture the snow was bringing which would help the spring grass after a fairly dry winter. Wet, heavy snow in April translated into weight gain for cattle on which the economy of the area depended.

Sarah was lost in her peculiar inner space so Marcia ordered her chicken-fried steak in creamy gravy and real mashed potatoes. Sarah could only deal with a third of the massive portion but Marcia finished it in a trice. The lovely waitress Nicole told Sarah that the two of them could be related. They had the same olive skin and light brown hair. Sarah was distracted by a memory of singing a song with her grandpa with the line, "If I had the wings of an angel over these prison walls I would fly," which reflected on the idea that if she got caught shooting Karl she might never see Alfredo again. When her grandpa taught her the song at the piano she was only five and didn't yet know what the word "prison" meant. When he'd died of a heart attack in his commercial truck garden she had looked at him in his casket at the funeral home and had sung in a whisper, "Wake up, sleepyhead."

Dawn was bright and clear but with slushy roads. They made it home by noon and Lolly told her that a man named Alfredo had called and left a number. Sarah was breathless until she got up to the cabin and could return the call though first she had to deal with the hyperexcited Rover and Lad who was screaming his horsey scream of welcome. Terry had house-sat and she could smell the slight fetor of his four nights of coupling with Marcia but didn't have time to be disgusted. She got Alfredo on the second ring.

"I saw the Weather Channel and was worried about you in the storm."

"We made it okay but we had to stop for the night." There was a long pause.

"Say something. I don't know what to say," he said.

"I miss you." This took courage.

"I miss you but this is crazy and maybe it's wrong." His voice was a little weak.

"I asked Rebecca and she said I'd be legal in Arizona on my sixteenth birthday this summer." Rebecca had been startled that evening when Sarah asked but looked it up on the computer.

"I think we should take this slowly."

"If you like. We can always play the piano."

"We'll figure this out by the fall. We can write letters. I'll start one when we hang up."

"Me too," she said.

She saddled up Lad and with Rover in the lead rode up to the canyon, her thoughts drifting. If only Tim were alive he would certainly shoot Karl for her. Probably Marcia would too. Maybe such attitudes were in the landscape.

Montana was too large and there was vertigo in the land-scape with no apparent peripheries. Boys left the school property to fistfight at noon down behind the grain eleva-tor, and men fistfought at night in the tavern parking lot though Giselle had joked that fighting was showing a de-cline in Montana with the advent of marijuana. Some called a joint a "peacemaker," the old name for a Colt revolver.

When she got back to the cabin she called the school principal and said she would miss school for a few days because she had to go to Denver to visit a sick aunt. He said, "Fine," and that she should probably be teaching rather than studying anyway. His comment only served to remind her how abnormal her life had been. She had grown tired of teachers telling her that she was "gifted" or "exceptional" when all that she had ever wanted was to be normal and be around other young people more often than 4-H meetings.

She cleaned her .30-06 though it didn't need it and packed her duffel with outdoor wear and the three boxes of cartridges. She studied both her road and her topo maps of Karl's area suddenly worried about who would take care of Rover and Lad if she got caught. Certainly not her dad or Lolly. She thought about affection, or what the popular culture called love, which she had only recently experi-enced. You couldn't count Montgomery Clift. This emo-tion was often inchoate as music that startles us then regains its melodic shape. When she cleaned the lenses of her binoculars she knew that the rhythm of her affection for Alfredo was all in the music they played together be-cause they didn't actually know each other. Peppy as an evangelical was always verbally assaulting the Catholic saints as "blasphemous" but now in the night Sarah wished she knew how to voice a prayer to Saint Tim whose spirit she tried to sense hovering in the roof beams of the cabin.

She left at five A.M. after vomiting up her breakfast cheese sandwich and coffee. Lad was difficult to load into the horse trailer not wanting to move at the early hour but she needed him because it was three miles according to her topo map from the county road over the hills to the small dirt road that led to Karl's place which originally had been owned by the famed "Indian killer" Thadeus Markin according to a book in the Livingston library.

Her stomach felt full of acrid ice cubes as she drove slowly on the blacktop trying to avoid the nearly invisible black ice she caught in her headlights. She figured that the drive to Meeteetse was eight hours and she had left so early to get a few hours of April daylight when she arrived. It would have been far shorter to drive through Yellowstone Park but the roads weren't open yet because of the snow so she was forced to take the same route as to the antelope hunt only following 310 south in Laurel toward Powell, Wyoming. She pretended she was only going to look things over but knew very well that if the opportunity was there she'd pull the trigger.

By midmorning her spirit had lightened and she felt righteous. Aside from her own vengeance she was on a mission to save other girls. Who knew but Karl and his friend how many victims there had been? She and Priscilla had never talked about what had happened to them but once when she was drunk in the evening after school had started Priscilla had tried to joke by saying that her ass had hurt for a week. Sarah deduced that this meant she had been sodomized which sounded worse than getting hairs torn out.

When she stopped for gas and food at a creepy McDonald's in Livingston she sorted through her eight-tracks because Vivaldi, Scarlatti, and Mahler weren't working. She found Hank Williams's *24 Greatest Hits* which Marcia had left in the truck months before. Williams's hard and mournful voice was more in keeping with her mission.

By the time she reached Cody and made the turn toward Meeteetse she was nearly asleep at the wheel and the strong coffee in her thermos wasn't working. She was drowsily amused by the idea that murder required physical training and good sleeping habits. She knew that the last time she had looked at the clock last night it was three A.M. and she had gotten up before five. If you intend to murder someone you need more than two hours of sleep. The fatigue gave her minimum control over her mind, the mystery of which boggled her to the point that she intended to read up on the brain. The merest thought of Alfredo gave her cold feet for her mission to the point that three times on the trip she had nearly turned around. And she was forced to admit the fact that shooting Karl didn't mean her nightmares about him would end. She struggled to divert herself by thinking about cartridges. There was a carton of old 220-grain Silvertip cartridges in Tim's cabin. Marcia would use those for elk but would drop back to the 165-grain factory loads for deer or antelope. Marcia's whole family went elk hunting, even her feminine mother whose strongest swear word was "gosh." They took four elk and a number of deer every year and though they were partial to beef they ate wild meat

half the time like old Tim. Marcia was saving for a heavy
Sako target rifle after hearing that a man north of Butte had
shot a deer at seven hundred yards with his rifle but then
he had been a sniper in Vietnam. You could pop a skull and
the victim would be dead before the noise caught up.

She was parked dozing on the main street of Meeteetse
at four and when she woke in fifteen minutes there was
Karl's big pickup parked in front of the tavern in a twisted
version of luck. She drove around the corner to use a pay
phone in case he might recognize her out the tavern window. She called his home and got Karl's dad letting him
know she'd be dropping off a horse at the front gate at eight
the next morning. He told her to bring the horse down to
the corral near the hay shed and she said no because she was
hauling a real big rig from Sheridan and had to deliver seven
more horses in Casper. He said okay and then said, "Who
are you?" and she answered, "I'm one of Karl's hot young
chicks from Billings." The man cackled.

She went into a grocery store and bought bread, baloney, and a can of beans which she would eat cold not wanting to chance a campfire. She drove off northeast on a county
road along the Greybull River, then a few hundred yards
up a log road to conceal her truck and horse trailer. Rover
was pissed when Sarah left her in the truck and saddled up
Lad to reconnoiter, putting her loaded rifle in the saddle
scabbard just in case. It was an easy ride up and over the
hill but the steep descent was slow. She wended her way
through a patch of boulders and loblolly pines and then she
could see the gate to Karl Burkhardt's place, a drive leading to a small ranch house about a mile distant. She found a

boulder that would make a perfect rest for her rifle to ensure accuracy. She decided to load up with 220-grain Silvertips for what gun magazines referred to as "knockdown" power.

She made it back to her truck just before dark and Rover acted as if she had been gone for days. She fed Lad some hay and shared her can of beans and boloney sandwiches, both of which were barely edible. Even Rover wasn't enthused. Rover had loathed Peppy but Lolly was fine because she offered little tidbits of Reggio Parmesan as dog treats.

Of course it was the longest night of her life, longer than the night of her uprooted short hairs and the ketamine-and-alcohol swoon which had made her feel like her brain was vomiting. She had intended to sleep on the ground but it was pretty cold and she had forgotten the air mattress for her sleeping bag so she curled up in the bag on the front seat using Rover as a pillow. She read one of Alfredo's botany texts with a penlight wishing she had brought along something more appropriate like one of the Elmore Leonard murder mysteries that Terry's mother had turned her on to. She slept fitfully waking at midnight with a start because her mind was playing loud symphonic music that she had never heard before. This had happened twice before in her life and it made her think she might become a composer. This time in the pickup the music was loud and discordant and derivative of Stravinsky. It was strange enough to frighten her and she looked up through the windshield at the density of the stars of the Milky Way. She questioned whether this music would prevent her from shooting Karl. She would ask her glum history teacher if those wretched Nazi generals loved classical music or did Mozart prevent murder?

At first light she woke from a delightful dream of her walk with Alfredo. He was explaining to her the mysterious life of a pyracantha bush that was almost solid with berries. After a hard frost the berries would ferment and the birds eating the berries would get drunk. At the exact moment he said this a canyon wren began singing nearby and she shivered at the beauty of its voice.

She ate half a sandwich and drank cold coffee then saddled up Lad while Rover examined their surroundings for threats. Rover didn't want to be left behind and refused to get back into the truck. She flopped down in the frosty grass and Sarah had to lift her ninety-pound body back into the truck which made her cold back twinge. "You miserable bitch," Sarah said.

She reached her destination a little after seven and tethered Lad several hundred yards back in the trees. She sat beside the boulder letting the early-morning sun warm her cold hands and face and body. At about a quarter to eight Karl drove his pickup up the driveway towing an ancient slat-sided open trailer most often used for hauling a bull or pigs. He pulled the truck in sideways with the trailer near the gate. She watched through the Leupold scope as he got out and leaned against the hood with a cup of steaming coffee. He limped badly when he opened the gate and she hoped he hurt. She squeezed off three rounds blasting out the truck's windshield and the two near-side tires in case he tried to escape. Karl started screeching and struggled to get in the near-side truck door. She put a bullet near the handle and he crawled quickly back to get behind the trailer. Another bullet shattered a low wood slat of the trailer into splinters.

She slowly reloaded wondering why she was teasing him rather than shooting him. Now the crosshairs of the scope were directly on his forehead and eyes peeking through the slats of the trailer. This was the money shot but she couldn't do it, seeing again the antelope arching upward. Instead she shot twice a foot or two on each side of his head. He tried to run for it so she shot once in front of him and once on each side. Now he was screaming and sobbing and groveled in a shallow irrigation ditch. When she reloaded this time she finally realized she wasn't going to shoot him and possibly end her own life in misery. For good measure she fired five rounds around him in the ditch noting afterward that he was now playing dead. She reloaded a last time and scrambled up the hill. Before she entered the trees she fired two more rounds into the truck to make sure he stayed in the ditch for a long while.

She was soon back in her truck with the horse loaded and heading down the country road but about fifteen minutes later she was weeping and confused because she couldn't find the road to Cody. She tried to turn at too sharp an angle and the horse trailer bound up against the back of the pickup and she couldn't move it. Now she would have to get out and unhitch the trailer and start over. She leaned her head against the steering wheel sniffling and cursing and then Rover began to bark and roar. A county deputy had pulled up, gotten out of his squad car, and had stooped to look at where the trailer had bound up against the back bumper of the truck. The deputy was an older man with gray muttonchops and a big tummy. Sarah rolled down her window halfway struggling with Rover who was snarling.

"You're a girl!" the deputy said.

"Yes, I am. I tried to turn too sharp. I drove too long in the night and pulled off on the side road when I got sleepy. Then I hid my rig when I heard a lot of shooting because it's not hunting season, is it?"

"No. There's this guy over east of here. We think he shot up his pickup for insurance. He's three payments behind so it was going to get repoed anyway. He's a longtime chiseler. He's got enemies so maybe someone was shooting at him but who gives a shit."

He helped her detach the trailer and swing it around so she could hitch up properly and gave her directions to Cody. They shook hands.

"You're a handsome girl. Be careful," he said.

She was damp with the sweat of fear as she drove off though she knew she was home free. She ate most of an enormous breakfast in Cody and had her coffee thermos filled. To celebrate she bought Rover biscuits and sausage to go, her favorite food.

Chapter 13

She had made it home just before dark, stoked the wood-stove, and slept a dozen hours getting to school a little late. The principal asked after her sick aunt in Denver and Sarah for want of an answer said, "She died," and walked off down the hall. She had had a thin slice of a nightmare about Karl but the leaden aftereffects weren't there when she awoke. Lolly had left a piece of fine lasagna in her refrigerator which she'd shared with Rover for breakfast after which she'd sung the dog part of the Hank Williams song about Kaw-Liga, the wooden Indian. When she sang to Rover the dog squirmed with pleasure.

She began a letter to Alfredo in geometry class which was childish compared to what her father had taught her years before, and continued in chemistry class (her father had hung up a poster of the periodic table when she was ten). At the school lunch of fetid Spanish rice she sat as usual with

Terry and Marcia. They wondered where she had been the two previous days and she would only say "camping out up the canyon."

After school it was the first day of outdoor track practice though the weather was cloudy and in the midthirties. She was delighted to put on her sweat suit and after a few laps on the cinder track she and Marcia vaulted one fence and then another and ran down a long pasture with two little bull calves running along beside them for no apparent reason with their quite exhausted mothers following up in the rear.

When she got home she begged off having dinner with Frank and Lolly saying she wasn't feeling well. She picked up a letter from Peppy and Lolly gave her a container of veal stew in case she got hungry which she already was. The letter from Peppy was typically inane but she cautioned herself remembering that Frank had said that Peppy had done well in academic subjects but the nature of her family had closed all of the windows to the world.

Sarah spent a long evening intermittently working on her letter to Alfredo and reading in the three botanical texts he had given her. She liked best *The Biology of Horticulture* but *Introductory Plant Biology* was also fascinating. It all seemed quite exotic compared to her life above the forty-fifth parallel where bird and flora species are slim indeed compared to farther south.

The letter was hard going. By late evening she had five pages which she thought was too long and edited it down to three by midnight. She was amused by the irony of saying, "Not much is happening around here except for the long wait for true spring." Not much, that is, if you exclude shooting a carton of cartridges at a rapist.

Some of what she wrote intrigued her in the act of writing what she actually thought. "I so wish that I were on the piano seat with you feeling the notes of Schubert in my body." Or, "Staying with Rebecca was to enter an entirely new world which makes me wonder how many hundreds of worlds there are to which I have only gained entry by reading?" Or, "Whatever happens I feel much better about life having met you."

After she turned off the lights and put her hand on Rover's chest to get the calming sense of a heartbeat she worried that she might be delusional like her mother Peppy. Peppy had said in her note that she had called Giselle who told her that Frank had found "another." She was grieved because she thought that one day she might return to her loving family. This had momentarily stunned Sarah and so did the statement "Older men aren't very affectionate."

Her hand actually trembled when she dropped the letter in the mail slot the next day. It was nine days before she got an answer which was like nine days in a dentist's chair but then she had had so little experience writing and receiving letters she didn't know what to expect. Meanwhile she and Marcia were running five miles every late afternoon and in the evening she was playing the piano for so long that Rover would beg to go outside.

When Alfredo's letter finally came she drove up to the canyon to read it. He was profuse in his apologies. His daughter had been kicked out of private school in Los Angeles for smoking pot and her mother was in Italy. It had taken him nearly a week to find another school that would accept her. He asked Sarah's forgiveness for sharing such "grim" news. After that he was quite romantic saying how much he missed her and that it seemed impossible to fall in love in two days but it had happened. Did she think that it was mostly the piano? A thought that had actually occurred to her but then time would certainly tell. His father was a "large-scale" farmer and neither rich nor poor. His family had sacrificed with no complaint to put him through Juilliard and then Cornell but he had graduated summa cum laude and gradu-ate school had been on ample fellowships. He finished by saying that he wished that they were in each other's arms which made Sarah feel faint. On a silly impulse she smelled the letter and then looked down at her feet where the first shoots of green grass were emerging on the south-facing side of the canyon.

Chapter 14

After the slowness of letters they began talking on the phone every other day and he sent her many new pieces of music to learn. Frank confronted her with the phone bill and she untypically fell apart and then admitted she was in love with a professor. He just as untypically laughed, gave her a hug, and said he had wondered when she would find someone to care about. She was irked at dinner one night when Lolly told her that she was fifteen going on thirty-five. She said she was nearly sixteen and went outside and stood in a May shower until she cooled off.

Luck arrived in the last, slow-motion, dreary days of school. Rebecca wrote to say she had to go to Chile in July for her observatory work and was there any chance that Sarah could come early? Sarah began packing the day after graduation. Alfredo offered to fly up to Montana and drive

down to Arizona with her. He felt that it was proper for him
to meet her father.

It was three days short of her sixteenth birthday when
Alfredo arrived. Lolly decided to cook an elaborate Italian
dinner and Marcia and Terry were invited. The Bozeman
airport had a better connection and Sarah was tremulous
during the three-hour drive. Alfredo had said that before
the summer ended they had to fly to Guadalajara to meet
his parents. Rebecca had agreed to go along as a chaperone
or duenna or his parents would have been scandalized. In
Bozeman the plane was a half hour late and when Alfredo
came down the long stairway from the boarding area they
kissed for the first time.

Out in the sunny parking lot his eyes swept past three
mountain ranges to the east and south still with snow on
their peaks, the Bridgers, the Gallatins, and the Spanish
Peaks. They held hands near her pickup.

"We don't know what we're doing or do we?" she said
shyly.

"Well, we have our music and it seems to be spreading
through us, doesn't it?"

"Yes," she said, terribly certain of herself.

Brown Dog Redux

PART I

Brown Dog drifted away thinking of the village in the forest where the red-haired girl lived. When she had served them pie and coffee at a diner and a chocolate milk and cookie for Berry he had teased her by saying, "Cat got your tongue," when she didn't respond to his flirting. She had gestured to her mouth indicating that she was mute and when he hid his face in his hands in embarrassment she had come around the counter and patted his head and laughed the soundless laugh of a mute.

Now he was waiting for Deidre in a very expensive coffee shop in downtown Toronto in which he felt quite uncomfortable. He was nursing a three-buck cup of Americano, more than a six-pack of beer back in Escanaba where in some places a cup of coffee was still a quarter. He much preferred the diner with the red-haired mute girl up near Gamebridge where a kindly social worker had taken him and Berry for a Sunday ride in early March so that they finally could have their first trip out of the city in months. They had a fine walk on a snowmobile trail through a forest while Berry had run far and wide as fast as a deer over the top of the crusty snow. Berry's legs were getting longer and when they visited nearly every day the lovely winter ravines in Toronto she'd run far ahead of him.

Now it was early April and he was getting an insufferable case of spring fever. The proprietor of the coffee shop, a big strong woman, was staring at him as if he was a vagrant. He avoided her glance by eagerly looking out the front window hoping to see Deidre, though his errant mind was back at Moody Bible Institute in Chicago thirty years before where in a dark hallway there was a painting called *Ruth Amid the Alien Corn*. At the onset the painting irritated him because it was obviously wheat, not corn. Ruth, however, was lovely and fine-breasted looking into the somber distance with teary eyes. Once while he was looking at the painting one of his devout teachers, Miss Aldrich, had happened along and explained that Ruth had been exiled and was terribly homesick thus the wheat or corn was *"alien."* *Brown Dog in Alien Toronto* didn't have a ring to it but it was on the money.

Finally Deidre appeared at the window and waved to him. Brown Dog was startled because she was talking to a man he recognized as her husband. They had all met two weeks before at the Homeless Ball, a fund-raiser for the indigent. The man, Bob by name, had a peculiar shape what with being thin from the waist up with a silvery goatee, and quite large down below with a big ass that even now forced the tail of his tweed sport coat out at a sharp angle. The question was, why was he here? He sat himself down at a table twenty feet or so away and glared at B.D. with the usual sullenness of a cuckold.

Meanwhile Deidre sat down all flash and bustle with the usual merry smile and began to unwrap her ten-foot scarf. When she ordered her double-decaf soy-milk latte with a pinch of sassafras pollen, B.D. momentarily forgot the glowering husband thinking that he would get stuck with the bill which would equal a good bottle of whiskey. The coffee fetish that was sweeping North America left him restless and puzzled. Like his uncle Delmore, B.D. would often use the same grounds for two pots.

Brown Dog was wise enough to understand that the presence of Bob meant that their two-week affair with a mere four couplings was over. He wasn't really listening to Deidre as his mind rehearsed the four: once in his room while Berry was at speech therapy, twice in a modest hotel, and once in a snow cave he and Berry had carved into a hillside in the Lower Don Parkland. They screwed while Berry was running in the distance. The snow cave had been awkward because B.D. had to back in first and then Deirdre backed partway in and pulled down her trousers. There was very little room to maneuver and she was a big strong girl so that he was driven breathlessly into the narrow back wall of the cave freezing his own bare ass.

"Are you listening?" She waved a hand in front of his face. "I was saying that I think I must have taken an extra Zoloft by mistake. Bob made me a gin fizz before putting his salmon soufflé in the oven. Suddenly I became dizzy and weepy and just plain spilled the beans. Of course Bob was outraged and wanted the details. He thought it was strange that I was fucking a proletarian which is his professor language for a workingman. Anyway, we had it out and when we were finished the soufflé was ready to eat, an odd coincidence, don't you think? You could use a shower."

"I've been shoveling snow since seven this morning so I worked up quite a sweat in nine hours." There had been a few inches of dusty snow and B.D. had wandered the streets of a wealthy neighborhood near the curling club. He would shake a little cowbell and those who wanted their walks cleaned would come to their front doors. This system had worked well the entire winter and he had made enough money to support himself and Berry in their ample-sized room in an old Victorian mansion in an area gone to decay.

"I have the distinct feeling you're not listening to me," said Deidre in a huff.

"You're saying that our love is not meant to be," B.D. said seeing a wonderful piece of ass disappear into the usual marital void. He could feel her heat across the table. She was a real burner and in the ice cave he had marveled at the heat her bare butt had generated during its strenuous whack-whack-whack. She seemed fit as a fiddle though she claimed to have allergies to peanuts, dairy products, and latex so that she carried nonlatex condoms for emergencies in a secret compartment in her purse. One afternoon they were at a sports bar watching football and he had eaten free peanuts while she went to the potty and when she came out she shrieked, "You could kill me." If he so much as touched her arm, with peanut oil on a finger he could kill her, or so she said. His uncle Delmore was always watching the Perry Mason repeats on television at lunchtime and this peanut thing seemed like a good plot though B.D. regarded Perry as one of the most boring fucks in Christendom.

Suddenly Bob was at the edge of their table and B.D. slid his chair back in case the dickhead made a move. "You cad," Bob said, grabbed his wife's arm, and then in a miraculous act grabbed the check for the Americano and the double-decaf soy-milk mocha latte with a pinch of sassafras pollen (two bucks extra). Despite being called a cad which he thought might be an old-timey swear word B.D.'s heart soared when Bob picked up the check which meant that he and Berry could eat out rather than cooking something in the electric fry pan in the room. How could he be a cad when it was Deidre who'd instigated the affair after they had fox-trotted in a dark corner at the Homeless Ball and she had been delighted when his wanger got stiff as a rolling pin?

On the way out of the coffee shop he discovered that someone had stolen the snow shovel he had left tilted against the building near the doorway. Maybe this was a good omen, a sign that it was time to somehow leave Canada? The blade was made out of plastic anyhow and didn't make the old-fashioned grating noise on cement. After Deidre had slumped forward steaming in the snow cave she had said, "It's so primeval," and B.D. had began quoting Longfellow's "Evangeline." "This is the forest primeval. The murmuring pines and the hemlocks . . ." As a high school teacher Deidre had been impressed but then B.D. told her the story of how in third grade he and five other skins, three mixed and two purebloods, had been forced to memorize the first pages of

the poem for the school Thanksgiving program but on stage
his friend David Four Feet had made loud farting noises
instead. The assembly fell apart, laughing hysterically, and
the teachers and principal ran around slapping as many students as possible. David Four Feet was severely crippled
and got away with murder because none of the teachers
wanted to beat up on a cripple. Since B.D. was David's best
friend he offered an alternative for their anger.

B.D. waited outside the lobby door until Berry's speech
therapist appeared with Berry leaping down the last flight
of stairs crouched like a monkey. The therapist was terribly skinny and B.D. had the fantasy of fattening her up to
a proper size. There was the old joke of getting bone splinters while screwing a skinny girl. He doubted that this was
an actual danger but it was easy to see that this young
woman was about thirty pounds on the light side. He
thanked her profusely even though Berry hadn't learned
a single word. Berry was his stepdaughter and the victim
of fetal alcohol syndrome due to her mother's voluminous
drinking of schnapps during pregnancy.

They made the long twilight walk to Yitz's Delicatessen with growing hunger. More than ever before Brown
Dog felt on the lam. Five months before, their entry into the
safety of Toronto had been nearly jubilant. Their contact,
Dr. Krider, who was a Jewish dermatologist, had taken
them to lunch at Yitz's and B.D. had eaten two corned
tongue sandwiches plus a plate of beef brisket for dessert
while Berry had matzoh ball soup and two servings of herring during which she made her perfect gull cries as she
always did when eating fish. The other noontime diners were

startled but many of them applauded the accuracy of Berry's
gull language. Dr. Krider for reasons of historical and political sympathies was an ancillary member of the Red
Underground, a loose-knit group of activists on both sides
of the border and extending nominally to native groups in
Mexico. In recent years any action had been made complicated by Homeland Security to whom even AARP and
the Daughters of the American Revolution were suspect.
Dr. Krider had found them their pleasant room and had
B.D. memorize his phone number in case he was short of
sustenance money. B.D. had assured the good doctor that
he had always been able to make a living which was less than
accurate as this often meant the forty bucks he could make
cutting two cords of firewood which he would stretch out
for a week of simple food and a couple of six-packs in
Delmore's drafty trailer. The escape from Michigan into
Canada had been occasioned by the state authorities' impending placement of Berry in a home for the youthful
mentally disabled in Lansing. B.D. and Delmore had made
the eight-hour drive south from the Upper Peninsula to
Lansing only to discover that the home and the school in
which Berry would be stored was profoundly ugly and surrounded by acres of cement, an alien material, and thus the
escape plan was made. Gretchen, B.D.'s beloved Sapphic
social worker, had driven them over to Paradise on Whitefish Bay where they had boarded a native fishing boat, a fast
craft that was sometimes used to smuggle cigarettes into
Canada where they were eight bucks a pack. In the coastal
town of Wawa they were met by a kindly, plump middle-
aged Ojibway who was traveling to visit a daughter and

drove them the two days to Toronto in her ancient pickup. The woman named Corva had drunk diet supplement drinks all the way and B.D. and Berry had subsisted on boloney and white bread because Corva had been forbidden by the Red Underground to stop for anything but gas. Since they were used to eating well on venison and trout and illegal moose and the recipes from B.D.'s sole printed volume, *Dad's Own Cookbook,* they were famished when they reached Toronto, and Yitz's was their appointed meeting place. It wasn't until they passed the Toronto city limits that Corva turned to him and asked, "Are you a terrorizer?" and B.D. replied, "Not that I know of." The few members of the Red Underground he had met in Wawa were terse and rather fierce and it had been hard to feel what Dr. Krider had called "solidarity." Dr. Krider had said to him, "The weather has beaten the shit out of you," and B.D. had replied that he had always preferred the outside to the inside. It was so pleasant to walk in big storms in any season and take shelter in a thicket in the lee of the wind. Once he and Gretchen had taken Berry for a beach walk and a violent thunderstorm from the south on Lake Michigan had approached very quickly so that they took shelter in a dogwood thicket. Berry had what Gretchen called "behavioral issues" and kept running around in the storm despite Gretchen calling out to her. Lightning struck very close to their thicket and in the cold and wet Gretchen came into his arms for a moment. She said, "How can you get a hard-on during a lightning strike, you goofy asshole?" and he didn't have an answer though it was likely her slight lilac scent mixed with the flowering dogwood plus her shimmering wet body, the thought of which drove him sexually batty.

Now the air was warmish in a breeze from the south in the twilight and walking through a small park Berry incited a male robin to anger by making competitive male calls. B.D. held up his hand to protect them from the shrieking bird and said, "Please, Berry, your dad is thinking," which was not at all a pleasant process. As they neared the delicatessen, he remembered two rather ominous things. In their good-byes Corva had said, "Don't hurt no innocent people. You're with a rough bunch." And Dr. Krider had told him, "Since you entered Canada illegally you'll have to leave Canada illegally. You don't have any papers so you're limited to odd jobs." The latter part of the admonition didn't mean much because all he had ever done was odd jobs except for cutting pulp for Uncle Delmore, a job abbreviated when a falling tree bucked back from the spring in its branches and busted up his kneecap.

This hard thinking made B.D. hungry so he ordered both a corned tongue and a brisket sandwich plus a plate of herring and potato salad for Berry. Berry refrained from her gull calls waiting for this old man to enter wearing his Jewish black beanie. They would spend a few minutes across a table from each other exchanging different birdcalls. The old man was some kind of retired scientist and tricked Berry by doing a few birdcalls from a foreign country which at first puzzled her but then made her laugh. B.D. watched them at play pondering the obvious seventy years' difference in their ages. He wondered where the word "Yitz" came from because he associated it with one of the best things in life, good food. It wasn't like one of those Michigan diners with a barrel of generic gravy out back connected by a hydraulic hose to the minimal kitchen which heated up grub from a vast industrial food complex named Sexton. B.D. could imagine the actual factory with cows lined up at a back door waiting patiently to become the patented meat loaf and their nether parts stewed into the barrels of gravy.

It was at three A.M. that his destiny changed. He awoke with an insufferable pain in his lower unit accompanied by a dream in which he had been kicked in the balls by a cowboy as he had been so many years before in Montana. As life would have it things suddenly began to happen. Since he was moaning when he turned the light on, Berry was hovering over him and started singing one of her verbless songs. Her words were not quite words but were always pleasant.

He couldn't stand up straight but managed to slink down the stairs and drop Berry off with Gert, the landlady, a horrid old crone who, however, adored Berry for playing by the hour with her two nasty Jack Russell terriers. The dogs loathed everyone including their owner but liked Berry whom they perhaps regarded as an intermediate species.

Luckily the closest hospital was a scant five blocks away and B.D. trotted through the night bent over from the waist in the manner of a Navajo tracker. He tripped over a couple of curbs with his eyes closed in pain soaking himself in a puddle from yesterday's slush. It was not in his nature to be fearful and he had anyway guessed a kidney stone as the grandfather who'd raised him experienced a kidney stone about once a year whereupon he would take to bed

with a fifth of whiskey which he quickly drank. Grandpa
would howl, roar, and bellow in drunken rage and then after
a few hours of this would fall asleep and on waking act fit
as a fiddle.

The emergency room was fairly crowded and B.D. was
out of luck because he didn't have a Canadian health card
with a photo ID. He also made a mistake by acting manly
despite the pain which made his eyes roll back in his head.
This faux manliness was typical of some men in the Great
North who pull their own bad teeth with the aid of whiskey and grip-lock pliers. He was slumped in a chair in a far
corner pondering his lack of options when a diminutive
young woman in a gray dress and white hat stooped beside
him. She had been near the front desk and had overheard
his ID problem and asked him if he knew a private doctor.
He said no but then remembered his Red Underground
contact Dr. Krider who was a skin doctor. He had written
Dr. Krider's number on the back side of a photo he had
begged off Gretchen, hoping for a nude though he knew it
was unlikely. Instead he got a photo of Gretchen on the
beach in a two-piece blue bathing suit, a towel wrapped
partly around her hips, but clearly showing her slightly pro-
tuberant belly button. This photo and his Michigan driver's
license and an old brass paper clip to hold cash were the sole
contents of his pockets except for a lucky Petoskey stone
with its pattern of ancient invertebrates. Unlike most of the
rest of us except the homeless, B.D. had no Social Security
card, draft registration card, credit or insurance cards.

Despite her miniature size Nora, his immediate savior,
drove a large Plymouth station wagon, sitting on a stack of

cushions to see out the windshield. B.D. slumped on the seat beside her, tilting sideways until his head rested against her thigh. Despite the near delirium of his pain he was always one to take advantage of any possible physical contact with a woman. He looked up at the passing streetlights determining that Nora's scent was wild violets. Another surge of pain prevented him from trying to turn over so he could be face-down on her lap, since his teens a favorite position.

When Nora pulled to a stop at Dr. Krider's home an immense man appeared and carried B.D. inside the house, impressive B.D. thought since he weighed one-ninety. He also noted that he was in the posh neighborhood of his snow shoveling. The huge man lowered him to a sofa at which point B.D. could see that he was an Indian with a pock-marked face and a bushy ponytail. Dr. Krider poked and probed B.D.'s lower stomach and bladder, determined that he had a sizable kidney stone, and administered a shot of painkilling Demerol. Nora had retrieved a warm washcloth and had bathed B.D.'s face and now he had it buried in her neck, a vantage point from which he could see down under her blouse to a single peach-shaped breast. Krider had pushed up his shirt and pulled down his trousers and as the Demerol slowly took effect B.D. was embarrassed that he was wearing wildly colored Hawaiian underpants which Gretchen had sent him for Christmas as a joke. He was also chagrined that the peek at Nora's titty had given him a boner.

"I can't believe that a man passing a kidney stone is tumescent," Dr. Krider chuckled, "but then I've seen gee-zers in hospitals minutes from death still trying to pat a nurse's ass."

Nora blushed and snapped B.D.'s dick with a forefinger, wilting it. This was a well-known nurse's trick to control excitable patients.

"Nora! That was unkind," Dr. Krider said. "Surely a penis isn't a threatening object to you?"

"Bitch!" said Charles Eats Horses, the big Indian who was a Lakota.

"You could make it up to me later," B.D. squeaked in his drug trance as Nora rushed from the room in tears.

B.D. dozed for a few minutes then lapsed back into pain. The stone was making its determined way down his urethra, propelled by satanic forces. He flapped his hands wildly in the air as does a dying grouse its wings. He crooned a song of pain which resembled Berry's verbless melodies. In short, he flopped and writhed. Dr. Krider gave him another quick shot and Charles Eats Horses put on a CD of Mozart's *Jupiter* Symphony. Charles had heard his oldest sister die giving birth in a remote shack on the Rosebud Reservation and the savagery of B.D.'s personal sound track was close to home. B.D. himself was sure that he was giving birth to an unadorned concrete block and if a river had been available he would have gladly rolled into it in a fatal winter swim.

Finally the stone emerged, rough-hewn and the size of a smallish marble.

"I'll have this set in a ring for you," Nora joked washing away a splotch of blood.

"Will I ever love again?" B.D. croaked.

"It might be a few days," Krider said, yawning.

B.D. fell asleep wonderfully without pain for the first time in half a dozen hours. Dr. Krider and Charles went back to bed and Nora settled in at the far end of B.D.'s sofa with an afghan throw after covering him with a duvet. To be sure this man's penis was decidedly more ample than her boyfriend's. He wrote book reviews and everything else in the catchall category for the Toronto *Globe and Mail* and she felt lucky indeed that he was a compulsive oralist who also sang in an Episcopalian choir. Only last week he had started singing "A Mighty Fortress Is Our God" while going down on her. A former boyfriend with an XXL wanger had caused her discomfort and she had dropped him like a spoon when the smoke alarm goes off. As her eyes closed she tried to erase the vision of the half dozen silly-looking penises of her past in favor of a cinnamon sticky bun at the airport. The mind can become so tiresome when it comes to sex and the man at the far end of the capacious sofa mystified her until she remembered the louts up on Manitoulin Island when at thirteen she had gone to the cabin of a friend's parents. She and her friend had been sunbathing on the cabin's deck and a mixed-blood had brought a cord of wood in a battered pickup and when stacking the wood had said, "How about a blow job, cuties?" They were shocked but then laughed when her girlfriend replied "Beat it, jerk-off." The man had swarthy good looks but at the time she couldn't imagine herself ever following through on such a request.

B.D. slept for an hour or so waking at the first peek of dawn through an east window when he felt the toes of his right foot touch what was obviously smooth skin toward Nora's end of the sofa. He was instantly alert enough to be cautious, squinting in the dim light and noting her soft feminine snore and answering with his fake snore to show her if she awoke that anything was an accident of sleep. The drugs had worn off and his hardening dick was painful but then one must be brave. The hurt reminded him of his early teens when he and his friend David Four Feet who was crippled and walked like a crab would have off-the-cuff masturbation contests and on the way to school would mysteriously yell, "Four times," "Five times," or less. B.D.'s record was seven and it had caused the kind of pain similar to the passing of the kidney stone.

Now he moved his toes lower until he encountered the magic area and it felt like his big toe was touching a mouse under a thin handkerchief. He snored louder in a proclamation of innocence. Dare he wiggle his toes to offer her pleasure? he wondered. She stopped snoring and pushed her vulva against his talented toes. From the other room a clock alarm rang. She stopped moving but he didn't, his destination now dampish. They heard Dr. Krider's padding feet in the hallway and she moved well back into her corner of the sofa. His friend David Four Feet used to say, "Drat it, foiled again," when one of their pranks went awry. B.D. never gave time much thought but it occurred to him that if Krider's clock had delayed itself ten minutes she could have been slowly spinning on his weenie like a second hand. Time is a bitch, he thought, his right toes feeling absurdly lonely. He continued to fake sleep until he dropped off listening to Nora and Dr. Krider talk. She said something about visiting Berry to tell her that her daddy was okay.

When he woke again there was only Eats Horses offering a breakfast tray of a bowl of oatmeal pleasingly piled with sausage links to counter the banality of oats. B.D. was still morose about his lost opportunity with Nora and the obvious healing power of a good fuck. Now that the white people were gone Eats Horses dispensed with the Indianness of his speech, the peculiar way our characters offer people what they expect.

"We have to get out of Dodge pronto," Eats Horses said.

"Why?" B.D.'s first thought was, Why leave an area with such fine pork sausage?

"We're both illegal and Dr. Krider is too valuable to the movement. He could be busted for harboring illegals. We have to leave Canada."

"I can't figure out how," B.D. said. "Trout season starts in two weeks and here I am high and dry." He had finished the sausage and now the oatmeal looked real ugly.

"Fuck your trout season. First you trade in illegal shipwreck artifacts, then you try to sell a frozen body, then you violently raid an archaeological site. You become a phony Chip activist and befriend a convict named Lone Marten. You steal a bearskin from a fancy home in L.A. You smuggle your stepchild out of Michigan in defiance of state laws. A criminal like yourself is no help to us."

"How do you know all this shit?" B.D. was appalled.

"Until a year ago I was a cop in Rapid City and when you got here I had a buddy on the force check your rap sheet. You're poison. That's why we never got in touch with you. I quit being a cop and went into the house-painting business with my cousin but we were going to paint a shed and got caught with seven gallons of red paint and Homeland Security entered the picture. For years the Lakota have been threatening to give those presidents on Mount Rushmore a dose of blood-red paint. We'd bought ours in Denver to escape the hassle. The paint store in Denver must have tipped the cops off. Anyway I was accused of plotting a terrorist act but after a month in jail the ACLU bailed me out. I made my way here but now I have to leave. Your uncle Delmore made a contribution to the movement so the leadership instructed me to take you and your stepdaughter along."

"Were you, in fact, going to paint a shed?" B.D. was suddenly thinking of Delmore watching the Perry Mason reruns and thus he asked a Perry-type question.

"None of your business," Eats Horses said.

"How come you're called Eats Horses?"

"Many years ago in the time of my grandparents the rez got cheated out of its government-allotment food and people were dying of starvation so some started eating their horses."

"Why go back if we're only going to get arrested?" B.D. was horrified at the idea of jail having been there a number of times. He'd also heard that you could no longer take Tabasco with you to jail so how could he eat jail food?

"I have a new identity and I think Krider is arranging one for you. I'm going to be security and a bouncer at a strip club in Lincoln, Nebraska. I got a poet friend Trevino Brings Plenty who says, 'Alive in America is all we are.'"

Eats Horses lapsed into a melancholy silence and B.D. joined him. They were clearly homesick men on the run.

"When I was a kid I told my grandpa who raised me that I wanted to be a wild Indian when I grow up and he said, 'If you do keep it under your hat.' I guess I'm only about half anyway."

"I'm three-quarters and that doesn't make it easier. If my brain was white my ass would only be in a different kind of sling. A white friend got his house foreclosed and I said, 'At least I don't have a house.'" Charles Eats Horses laughed hard so B.D. joined him while thinking of the five-hundred-buck trailer he had lived in with Berry before escaping to Canada.

The phone rang and it was Nora. She was sending a cab for B.D. because she had to be at work in an hour or so. Berry was fine and playing with the terriers. A letter had come from someone named Gretchen.

While B.D. dressed he thought how dramatic life had become. He had never ridden in a cab and there was a letter from his beloved Gretchen whom he hadn't heard from since Christmas. He dressed hastily still feeling spongy from the drugs, the railroad spike in his bladder having become a thumbtack. While waiting at the door Eats Horses told him to get packed up as they would be leaving in a few days and B.D. replied that since they owned practically nothing he could pack in minutes.

It was a fine glittery late morning with a specific warmth in the sun not felt since the autumn before. In the cab B.D. had a rare sense of prosperity sniffing the air which had that new-car smell. The driver was from far-off India and was nearly as small as Nora. They didn't understand each other but that was fine. The driver pointed up through the windshield and said, "Sun," and B.D. said, "You got that right."

Up in the fourth-floor room Nora was kneeling side-ways on a kitchen chair, her body halfway out the window, watching Berry far below leading the terriers around with grocery string for leashes. B.D. couldn't help but make contact with Nora's jutting butt which she wiggled a bit.

"I feel bad about snapping your weenie so go ahead if you wish. I have a boyfriend so I'll pretend it's an out-of-body experience."

He felt like the luckiest man in the world as he lifted her skirt. Her rump was so pretty his skin tingled. There was a song he should be singing but he couldn't think of what one. He pulled down her delicate panties and planted a big wet kiss on target and then stood remembering that in his narcotic haze early in the morning Nora had drawn a small vial of blood while Dr. Krider watched.

"Why?" he had asked.

"To check your PSA, your prostate."

"You don't have one," he'd said, a little smug in this rare piece of knowledge.

"I've got other stuff," she'd laughed.

"I'm aware of that," he had said dreamily.

B.D. liked this kind of confab, this banter or repartee, a word he didn't know, because it meant the world was going along okay. Now he began to do his job admirably, staring down at the sacred mystery and beauty of female physiognomy, trying to divert his enthusiasm so he wouldn't come too quickly. His mind started singing a song they sang in fourth grade, "A Spanish cavalier stood in his retreat and on his guitar played a tune, dear." The kids sang this loudly though the meaning of "Spanish cavalier" was in question.

Nora began to furiously rotate her butt counterclockwise and that was that. B.D. was in no way prepared for the pain caused by his urethra so abraded by the kidney stone. He yowled and fell backward on his ass, the passage of the sperm raising the image of the hot liquid lead Grandpa poured into molds to make fishing sinkers.

"I could have told you the last part wouldn't be fun but I was looking out for number one," Nora said, looking down at him with a merry smile.

"I forgive you," he said, jumping up at hearing Berry climb the stairs. He recalled a magazine article in the office of his ex-lover the dentist, Dr. Brenda Schwartz, that said, "No gain without pain." "I just pray we get another chance."

"This was a one-shot deal, kiddo." Nora let Berry in the door and embraced her, then left.

The blues descended lower than his sore dick with Nora's departure. Never in his life had he been attracted to a small woman and the idea that it was a "one-shot deal" left him bereft. He was nearly irritable with Berry which was unthinkable. When she had nothing else to do she would jump straight up and down in place and in the year this habit had begun she had acquired the ability to jump astoundingly high. "Too bad she'll never make a living out of her jumping and birdcalls," Uncle Delmore had said.

B.D. took a large package of pork steak from the mini-fridge and decided to cook it all in his outsized electric fry pan. Once the pork began to brown he opened Gretchen's letter with a bit of dread. Delmore maintained that no one in the United States complained as much as those who'd graduated from college and that sure was true of Gretchen.

Despite her beauty and good job as a social worker she was often lower than a snake's ass, B.D. thought. Once a week she'd drive all the seventy miles up to Marquette just like Brenda the dentist to see a psychoanalyst. Brenda went for what she called her "eating disorder" and she had wept hysterically when B.D. had said, "You're fine, you just eat too much." Gretchen on the other hand was lithe and beautiful but beginning with her Christmas letter she'd said she was discovering in therapy that she was sexless and it was driving her batty. After college she had discarded men as "horrid" and B.D. remembered poignantly her nitwittish young woman friend who had discarded Gretchen. Once when he and Gretchen had had a couple of drinks in her kitchen he had asked about the mechanics of Sapphic lovemaking and she only said, "You're disgusting." Now in her early thirties Gretchen was thinking about having a baby and was seriously considering B.D. as a sperm donor. He was proud as a peacock but couldn't understand why she would refuse him the pleasure of slipping it in for a minute rather than an artificial method.

While chopping a head of garlic to add to the pork steak, B.D. meditated on the letter. Gretchen's analyst had said that her sexless nature was "rare but not unheard of." Once when they had taken Berry swimming Gretchen had fallen asleep on her huge flowery beach towel and B.D. had slowly studied her body from the vantage point of an inch distance trying to memorize it for recall on cold winter nights. She had awakened and looked down under her sunglasses and thought he was on the verge of probing her pubis with his nose.

"What are you doing?" she'd shrieked.

"I'm memorizing your body for cold winter nights. Turn over because I'm missing the butt side."

"You asshole," she'd said, raising her foot and pushing him away. Her soft warm insole against his neck was one of his most cherished memories.

Berry nudged him to remind him not to burn the garlic. She used to like burned garlic but now she wanted it softened. They ate the entire pan of pork steak with a loaf of the French bread he bought daily from a bakery down the street, the likes of which was unavailable in Michigan's Upper Peninsula. The bread was so delicious it mystified him. They were always passing stupid laws, why not make it a law that this sort of bread be available everywhere in America?

B.D. began to doze in his chair from his long uncomfortable night and full stomach. Berry was making a variety of birdsongs and he knew she was begging for an afternoon walk. She also made a couple of guttural mutters, a struggle for the "b" consonant that might mean she was on the verge of saying "bird" after nearly four months of speech therapy. Berry loved the teacher which led B.D. to the obvious fact that Berry at age ten needed a mother and the sadder fact that her own birth mother would be in prison a couple more years for, among other things, biting a thumb off a cop when a group of malcontents had raided an archaeological site. The therapist had pointed out that Berry hadn't felt an urgency toward speech since B.D. was basically her only current human reality and they communicated perfectly well. B.D. had nervously confessed that he had whisked Berry

out of Michigan rather than subject her to a state school and
the therapist had said Berry would still need "socialization"
with kids her own age in some community. B.D. had
thought of moving her over to the Sault Sainte Marie Tribe
of Chippewa Indians rez near Sault Sainte Marie but he
was persona non grata in the Soo area for reasons of past
misdemeanors.

He dozed for a few minutes while she brushed his hair
and brought him his coat, and then they headed out for the
Lower Don Parkland. Outside, B.D. wasn't sure of reality
because the long night of pain and narcotics made the
world uncommonly glittery and vivid. There was also a
brisk southwest wind and suddenly the temperature was in
the low seventies. It was Saturday afternoon and the streets
were full of nearly frantic walkers trying to shake off the
lint and cobwebs of a long winter. Younger people, say
under twenty, were moving into dance steps as they walked
and kids were jumping up and down a bit envious of Berry's
jumping power. It all reminded B.D. in his floating body of
those musical comedies from the forties that Uncle Delmore
loved on television. Delmore's highest admiration was saved
for Fred Astaire. He would say, "Just think if Fred had
learned Indian dance steps and showed up at the Escanaba
Powwow!" B.D. admitted it would be quite a show. Delmore
also loved Gene Kelly who could run up a wall, do a flip,
and land on his feet. It would be fun to do that in a tavern,
B.D. thought when he saw the movie.

When they reached the area Berry ran up the gully to
their snow cave. B.D. followed slowly noting that the snow
and ice had collapsed part of the cave and if he had been in

there with Deidre when it happened they might have been suffocated or, more likely, he would have pulled an Incredible Hulk move and burst upward through the snow and ice saving his true love. Only she wasn't much of a true love. She and her turd husband were going to a place called Cancún to renew their vows. At least Nora, who had also removed herself from the list of possibles, wouldn't die if she touched a peanut butter sandwich. Nora had said she was a gymnast in high school and could move her butt like a paint mixer in a hardware store.

B.D. sat on a big rock while Berry called in groups of crows, not a difficult thing to learn to do as the Corvidae are curious about why humans might wish to talk to them. What's the motive? they wonder. Soon enough, though, Berry had attracted a massive number of crows and a group of bird-watchers, those cranky coup counters known as twitchers to the Brits and some Canadians, made their way up the gully and scared the birds away. Birds have finely honed memories for people and they were familiar with Berry from the dozens of trips into this part of the Lower Don Parkland. Berry was irked and crawled into what was left of the cave.

As B.D. dozed in the sun his half-dream thoughts turned to Deidre's heat source. A thousand Deidres making love in a gymnasium would melt candles. He opened his eyes to the departing birds not knowing that their raucous cries were his Canadian swan song. In his view far too much had been happening and he craved the nothingness of the Upper Peninsula, a feeling he shared with the ancient Chinese that the best life was an uneventful one.

They walked. And walked and walked. Because of his tough night B.D.'s feet were marshmallows which nonetheless dragged him along. Berry teased the bird-watchers along the paths by hiding in thickets and making the calls of dozens of northern songbirds that had not yet arrived from their winter journey south. A man with thousand-dollar binoculars told B.D. that Berry could be a "valuable resource" and B.D. agreed, lost in his diffuse homesickness for brook trout creeks and the glories of snowmelt time when the forest rivers raged along overflowing their banks, and bear fed happily on the frozen carcasses of deer that had died of starvation, and icebergs bobbed merrily in Lake Superior on huge waves often carrying ravens picking in the ice for entombed fish. On this afternoon Toronto seemed vividly beautiful, a characteristic in the perceptions of those who had endured extreme pain and survived it. The world, simply enough, became as beautiful as it does to many children waking on a summer morning.

By late afternoon Berry had shown no signs of tiring while B.D. was barely shuffling along. He saw a young man taking a Tums and asked for one.

"My fried pork lunch is backing up on me," B.D. said, explaining himself.

"I had pizza with too many red pepper flakes," the young man said in a strange accent. They spoke for a few moments and it turned out that he was a country boy from near Sligo in Ireland. B.D. had been amazed by how many of the foreign-born he had met in Toronto and had often wished he had recorded the nationalities in his memory book which, of course, he didn't own. Geography had been his best subject in high school but he had found to his dismay in Toronto that someone had changed many of the names of countries in Africa after they gained their independence.

He was asleep on his feet by the time they reached Yitz's for supper. He settled for a bowl of beef borscht while Berry had three orders of herring and a serving of French fries which she ate at a back table with the children of a couple of waitresses who were kind to her. B.D. in his semi– dream state was thinking that it was only ten days from trout opener in Michigan which seemed so fatally far away. The first week of the season he often visited a daffy hermit north of Shingleton who was a fine angler but had some peculiar ideas. One of the theories the hermit mourned over was that there was a hidden planet in our solar system that contained an even million species of birds but we would never be al- lowed to visit them because of our bad behavior as earth- lings. The hermit painted watercolors of these birds and one that B.D. especially liked was a huge purple bird with an orange beak that had three sets of wings. Who was to say it didn't exist? B.D. had never cared for the naysayers of the world of which there were far too many.

They took a cab home after they proved to the driver that B.D. had the estimated ten-buck fare. Berry was fright- ened of the driver who was angry over the war in Iraq and decidedly anti-U.S. B.D. was helpless to say anything but "It's not my fault."

B.D. fell asleep in his clothes while Berry danced for an hour or so to country music which she did every evening. He drifted off to Patsy Cline singing "The Last Word in Lonesome Is Me." It was a full seven hours but seemed only moments when there was an alarming knock on the door, startling because it was the first time there was a knock at the door in their five months of residence. B.D. heard Nora's voice and his heart took flight as he turned on the lamp. She had obviously returned for more of the same and in his pleasant drowsing head he had a vision of her delightful paint shaker doing its sacred job. But no, when Berry opened the door it was not only Nora but Charles Eats Horses and a sturdy Indian woman in her fifties who wore a business suit and was introduced as the Director.

"We move out at dawn," said Eats Horses. "I heard that line in a movie once and always liked it." Eats Horses was wearing a leather jacket with beaded lightning bolts and looked ominous. Berry who was wary of strangers went to him and took his hand. He picked her up. "We're going home."

Nora and the Director helped them in their hasty packing. B.D. was miffed when they said there wasn't room for his big, used electric fry pan which had set him back five bucks. The Director also shook her head no when he tried to put the last remaining beer from the fridge in his jacket saying that no alcohol was allowed on the "tour bus." B.D. was confused and picked up Gretchen's letter and sniffed it for signs of life feeling an ever more insistent tug of homesickness. Nighttime wasn't his time for clear thinking. In troubled times B.D. tended to cut way back on alcohol to avoid feeding the fire of chaos but at the moment he felt the need for a double whiskey because Nora was sniffling at the door and bounteous tears were falling.

"You poor redskins. I love you."

"I can't be more than half. I'm just a mongrel," B.D. said, embarrassed.

"My great-grandmother was married to a Jewish peddler in Rapid City in 1912. There aren't hardly any Lakotas with a streak of Jew," Eats Horses joked.

"I'm a mean-minded, ass-whipping pureblood," the Director said, embracing Nora.

It took only minutes to arrive at the arena parking lot a dozen blocks away. B.D. was irritated because the Director beat him to the front seat where he had fully intended to feign sleep and let his head fall onto Nora's lap.

The tour bus was an immense affair with THUNDERSKINS painted in large red letters on the side surrounded by yellow lightning bolts, all on the black metal skin of the bus which was lit up like Times Square and ready to go. The Director explained that the Thunderskins was a Lakota rock-and-roll group with only two more stops on a month-and-a-half tour, one in Thunder Bay, on the north shore of Lake Superior, and the last in Winnipeg, after which they would head south to Rapid City and Pine Ridge to drop everyone off, "everyone" being the usual assortment of roadies and soundmen, both skins and whites who were now outside drinking from pints and perhaps dragging at joints before entering the bus where the Director manned the door like a guard dog. The four stars of the band would fly on a plane to Thunder Bay and the Director explained to B.D. that the plane wouldn't work for him and Berry and Eats Horses because of the tight security at all airports. B.D. noticed that the small crowd of employees all nodded to Eats Horses and then averted their eyes.

"They think I might be a *wicasa wakan* but I'm not," Eats Horses whispered to B.D. who was even more confused not knowing that *wicasa wakan* meant medicine man, often a somewhat frightening person like a *brujo* in Mexico.

Eats Horses took over the door frisking while the Director showed B.D. and Berry to a small compartment at the back of the bus across the aisle from her own. There were two cots, an easy chair, a miniature toilet, and a window looking into the night. Before B.D. fell back to sleep after a cheese sandwich and two cups of strong coffee he wondered how so obvious a bus was going to smuggle himself and Berry back into the United States. He was diverted by seeing Nora drive away and how when they'd kissed good-bye she had rudely pushed his hand off her ass when only yesterday at high noon she had allowed him to grip her hip bones like a vise. Berry was sitting on her cot looking frightened and B.D. held her hand but the Director came back and got Berry saying she needed some mothering. B.D. fell asleep to the wheezing of the big diesel engine beneath him as the bus moved north on Highway 400 toward the landscape he called home, dense forests of pine, hemlock, tamarack, and aspen surrounding great swamps and small lakes that had wonderful fringes of reeds and lily pads. There were creeks, beaver ponds, and small rivers where B.D. would always find complete solace in trout fishing. He was observant of the multiple torments people seemed to have daily and felt lucky that he could resolve his own problems with a couple of beers and a half dozen hours of trout fishing and if a female crossed his path whether fat or thin, older or younger, it was a testament that heaven was on earth rather than somewhere up in the remote and hostile sky.

B.D. had a head-and-chest cold, an infirmity he only experienced every five years or so and which he blamed on his kidney stone exhaustion. He slept most of the day and a half it took to reach Thunder Bay, waking now and then to study the passing Lake Superior Provincial Park south of Wawa and the Pukaskwa National Park farther north along the lake. There were an unimaginable number of creeks descending from the deep green forested hills down to Lake Superior which tingled his skin despite the irritation of coughing and blowing his nose. He felt much better the second morning when they had stopped at a bar and restaurant and with several of the crew had drunk his meal in the form of three double whiskeys with beer chasers, a surefire cold remedy. Two of the Lakota crew members not realizing that B.D. was local to the other side of Lake Superior warned him that they were in "enemy territory," the land of the Ojibway, the dreaded Anishinabe who had driven the Sioux out of the northern Midwest.

B.D. had never been more than vaguely aware of rock and roll and was ill-prepared for the spectacle that would meet him in Thunder Bay. He knew it mostly as the music heard in bars favored by young people in Escanaba and Marquette but then he had never owned a record player in its varied forms and had certainly never fed a jukebox with any of his sparse beer money. He couldn't recall understanding a single lyric of this music except "You can't always get what you want" which he viewed as the dominant fact of life. He was back asleep from his liquid lunch when the tour bus pulled into the arena parking lot. He awakened to an oceanic roar and screech that reminded him of a ninety-knot storm on Lake Superior hitting the village of Grand Marais. In the bright afternoon light out of the window thousands of young people, mostly girls, were jumping straight up and down in the manner of Berry and screaming, "Thunderskins, Thunderskins, Thunderskins!" Within minutes of leaving the bus it occurred to him that he should have taken up a musical instrument, say a guitar, when he was young and learned how to sing. The Director had put a small laminated card around his neck reading "Backstage Crew" and the frantic girls stared at him like kids looking at a gorgeous ice cream cone on a hot day. He felt a little embarrassed, actually unpleasant at this sense of power, quite uncomfortable over the way he was encircled by the most attractive females looking at him imploringly. He had always had more than a touch of claustrophobia and recalled his panic at nineteen when he had been caught up in a big Labor Day parade in Chicago and had run for it a few blocks down to Lake Michigan where he could breathe freely. When looking at the *Tribune* the next day he had figured out that there were many more people involved in the parade than lived in the entirety of the Upper Peninsula. Now it occurred to him that one girl was enough but thousands screaming like banshees made you crave a thicket.

"Hey, B.D., they just want a fucking backstage pass," one of the Lakota crew yelled at him, noting his puzzlement.

B.D. made himself busy helping the crew unload the sound equipment, then when he found he was getting in the way drifted off toward the waterfront to get back in touch with Lake Superior which would likely calm his rattled brain. He was pleased to find Charles Eats Horses down near a pier sitting on a park bench.

"This water reminds me of the sea of grass in the Sand Hills of Nebraska south of Pine Ridge."

"If I had a good boat I could head straight south to the Keweenaw Peninsula and be fairly close to home but then I don't have a good boat and storms come up real sudden."

Eats Horses explained to him that Berry would be staying in a nice hotel with the Director who had to watch the rock stars carefully. One of them was her son and he was crazy as a weasel in heat. B.D. felt mildly jealous about Berry but since he had grown up without a mother himself he figured Berry needed the company of a female. Looking out over the water toward his homeland he felt his homesickness become as palpable as a lump of coal in his throat.

PART II

Dawn in Thunder Bay. The two A.M. announced departure of the tour bus was delayed by a snowstorm but by dawn the wind had shifted to the south and the snow turned into an eerie thunderstorm so that Brown Dog peeking out the bus window was startled by a lightning strike glowing off white drifts in the parking lot. He had a somewhat less than terminal hangover and could easily see the dangers of life without the immediate responsibility of looking after Berry. It was quite literally a "blast from the past" what with B.D. not having had a hangover in his five months in Canada, certainly the longest period since age fourteen when he and David Four Feet had swiped a case of Mogen David wine from a truck being unloaded in an alley behind a supermarket in Escanaba. The aftermath had been a prolonged puke-a-thon in the secret hut they had built beside a creek outside of town.

B.D. lay there in his bus compartment watching the
rain that had begun to lift so that he could see far out into
Lake Superior to the water beyond the shelf ice. He diverted
himself from the memory of last night's mud bath by pondering the soul of water. He had meant for a couple of years
to enter a public library and look up "water" in an encyclo-
pedia but doubted that any information would include the
mysteries of water that he so highly valued. Life could kick
you in the ass brutally hard and a day spent fishing a creek
or a river and you forgot the kick. Now, however, with no
fishing in sight he could vividly remember the wonderful
whitefish sandwich in the bar, and then meeting the two girls
in their late teens who had spotted his "Backstage Crew"
badge. The concert was sold out and they had no tickets.
He was sitting there with a Lakota nicknamed Turnip who
thought the girls "skaggy" but B.D.'s mouth was watering
though one of the girls was a tad chubby and one very thin.
B.D. thought that if you put the two together the weight
issue averaged out. Playing the big shot he got them in a side
door of the concert which was far too loud for him to endure and the flashing lights were grotesque. Berry was up
on stage jumping straight up and down batting at a tambourine and looking very happy. The girls jotted down their
address and phone number and said they'd see B.D. at their
apartment after the concert. He left feeling smug about his
worldliness. Back at the bar after having more drinks and
playing pool with Turnip, who looked a bit like a turnip, he
saw that the streets were filling up with the concertgoers so
it was time to make a move. Unfortunately after walking
around in the snowstorm and stopping at another tavern

B.D. gave the slip of paper to a bartender who said there
was no Violet Street in Thunder Bay and what's more the
phone number only had six digits. Turnip thought this very
funny while B.D. was morose.

"I bet they're backstage with the stars. We could check
it out. Those guys get more ass than a public toilet seat,"
Turnip said.

B.D. waded through the snow to his lonely bed with
the honest thought that women in general were as devious
as he was.

When they reached Winnipeg early the next afternoon
he was having an upsetting discussion with the Director
about Berry and couldn't quite separate the conference
from a wild series of dreams he had just had during a nap.
He had confused the roar of the bus engine with that of
a female bear he used to feed his extra fish when he was
reroofing a deer cabin. He had cut twenty-two cords of
hardwood to get through the winter and when April came
and the bear emerged from hibernation she was right back
there near the kitchen window howling for food. Tim, a
commercial fisherman, had given him a twenty-pound lake
trout no one had wanted so he cut off a three-pound slab
for dinner and tossed the rest to the bear who ate it in a
trice then took a long nap in the patch of sunlight out by
the pump house. One night when he heard a wolf howling
down in the river delta the bear had roared back. She was
simply the most pissed-off bear he had ever come across
so he named her Gretchen.

"What are you going to do when Berry hits puberty in
the next year or two?" the Director asked.

"The court appointed me to look after her," he answered irrelevantly. He was still caught up in the dream where he was down on the edge of the forest on the Kingston Plains and he and Berry were chasing two coyote pups who dove down into their dens under a white pine stump and Berry suddenly became as little as the pups and followed them which was impossible.

"What are you going to do when she reaches puberty?" the Director persisted. "I talked to your uncle Delmore on my cell and he's obviously senile. He said he contacted Guam on his ham radio. What the fuck is that supposed to mean? I talked to your friend the social worker Gretchen. She lives twenty miles away in Escanaba and only sees you two on weekends if then."

"Berry would have died at the school. It's all cement around there." B.D. was becoming irritated with the Director and wished he knew how to retreat to his dream state where when Berry came back out of the coyote den they had driven to his favorite cabin and fried up a skillet of venison.

"What I'm saying is that you got your head up your ass. Time moves on. Berry is going to be nicely shaped. What are you going to do when boys and men come after her for sex?"

"Kick their asses real good." B.D. felt a surge of anger that accompanied the beginning of a headache. The Director reminded him of an interrogation with the school principal he and David Four Feet had undergone in the seventh grade when they had thrown chunks of foul-smelling Limburger cheese into the fan attached to the oil furnace in the school basement. All of the girls in the school had run screeching into the street while the boys had merely walked out to show that they were manly enough to handle a truly bad smell.

"Well, I have a friend in Rapid City who runs a tribal program for kids with fetal alcohol syndrome and when we get there she's going to look at Berry."

They were both diverted by the bus pulling into the arena parking lot in Winnipeg. There were even more hysterical fans than there had been in Thunder Bay. It was a mystery to B.D. because this horde of fans must know that the stars were arriving by plane. It reminded him from way back when, of a geek kid in the eighth grade who claimed that his cousin in California had seen the Disney star Annette Funicello in the nude. Boys would gather around the geek to hear the story over and over. This was about as close as anyone in Escanaba was ever going to get to the exciting life of show business. B.D. figured that to these thousands of fans the Thunderskins bus without the stars was better than nothing.

In truth he found the noise of the fans repellent. The only loud sound he liked was a storm on Lake Superior when monster waves would come crashing over the pier in Grand Marais or Marquette. He also liked the sounds of crickets and birds, and a hard rain in the forest in the summer with the wind blowing through billions of leaves.

The Director stood up to leave and B.D. shook her hand hoping that she would believe his heart was in the right place in regard to Berry. She gave him a hug and he held her as tightly as possible. A spontaneous hug from a woman always filled him with the immediate promise of life. Sure enough his pecker began to rise and she pushed him away laughing.

"I'm fifty-nine and it's been quite a while since anyone got a hard-on over me."

"My friendship is there for the taking." B.D. wanted to say something proper far from the usual "Let's fuck." In truth she was more than ample and most would think her dumpy but he craved to get at her big smooth butt. She escaped all atwitter and he turned to see female fans staring in the window and he thought if the window would only open he could pop it in that brunette's chops making sure to avoid her big droopy nose ring.

The ride through western Manitoba into eastern Saskatchewan had increased his homesickness to a quiet frenzy. Creeks, rivers, and lakes were everywhere in the forested landscapes. To a lifelong fisherman even a large mud puddle presents a remote possibility and the water he saw was overwhelming. Once when the bus slowed for a logging truck hauling pulp to make paper he saw an American redstart in a white pine, a wildly colored bird that he often saw near his favorite stretch of the Middle Branch of the Escanaba near Gwinn and seeing the bird enabled him to smell the river and the forest in that area which tingled his skin.

In Winnipeg the Director checked B.D. and Berry into a room that adjoined her own in a fancy hotel which added a different kind of tingle as B.D. assumed that at some point he might be able to pull off a quick one with the Director. He had hoped to take Berry to the zoo but by the time they got settled in and had a room service bite

it was midafternoon and Berry and the Director had to go
to a rehearsal. This was the last stop on the Thunderskins'
tour and they wanted to go out in a firestorm at the huge
sold-out arena. Berry beat on her tambourine every waking hour but B.D. found it oddly pleasant since she did it so
well which made him wonder about the intricacy of the
rhythms she heard in her limited brain. Once in high school
he had driven with a couple of pureblood friends way up to
a powwow in Baraga and was amazed at how good it felt to
dance for hours and hours, a state of being carried away that
reminded him of the pleasure of being half-drunk rather
than fully drunk.

While the Director and Berry were getting ready two
of the stars dropped by but as with his other brief encoun-
ters their eyes passed over him as if he didn't exist. B.D.
figured this was what happened when you were around far
too many people like when he had gone to Chicago at nineteen or more recently in Toronto. The only way people got
along was by largely ignoring each other, a far cry from the
Upper Peninsula where if you avoided the downtowns of
Escanaba and Marquette you were never surrounded by
people and on the rare occasion he saw another human in
the backcountry he always hid until they passed from sight.

At present he was sick to death of people and decided
to stay as far as possible from the music folks. He set off on
a long walk mostly enjoying the vast railroad yards because
there were no high buildings around to block out the late-
afternoon sun though there was the troubling question of
who could keep track of so many trains? He was somewhat
disappointed that the fabled Red River wasn't red and when

headed back to the hotel he saw in the distance Charles Eats Horses enter a building he followed. It turned out to be an art museum with a large display of Inuit work. He was pleased with himself that he remembered that the Inuits lived up in the Arctic and were what most people thought were Eskimos. He noticed that when Eats Horses passed an attendant several rooms ahead she averted her eyes. She was, however, friendly to him and he took her short, round figure to be Inuit.

"Were you born in an igloo?" he asked.

"Were you born in a tepee?" she joked. Her smile was so glowing he felt the usual tremor. He wanted to tell her something interesting but she turned away to explain some whalebone and walrus-tusk carvings to some elegant old ladies. The art was so striking to B.D. that he felt hollow in his head and chest and he did not hear Eats Horses walk up behind him.

"I just knew you were an art lover," Eats Horses said, half seriously.

"I heard it's all in the wrist," B.D. answered, a little embarrassed at the strength of his emotions.

Eats Horses put a heavy hand on B.D.'s shoulder. "I want you to listen carefully about Berry. I know kids like her and they don't turn out well."

"Yes, sir. All I know is that she has to walk in the woods every day." He squeezed his eyes shut so tightly that he felt a little dizzy and when he opened them to regain his balance Eats Horses was gone. B.D. doubted that Eats Horses was the ex-cop and house painter he said he was. Once over near Iron Mountain back near a beaver dam in the woods

B.D. had run into this Crane Clan Midewiwin guy that he had seen years before at the Baraga powwow. It was generally thought that this man flew around at night and ate whole raw fish. The man was pleasant enough but when he reached under a submerged stump and caught a brook trout with a single hand B.D. had left the area.

On the walk back to the hotel he rejected the idea of the five double whiskeys he felt a need for and instead stopped at a diner for a fried T-bone. The Director had passed on a gift envelope from Dr. Krider with five hundred bucks in twenties which B.D. figured was the third-highest amount of money he had ever possessed. If you have five hundred bucks a ten-dollar fried T-bone seems less of a luxury. The meat was only fair but the potatoes were pretty good with ketchup. The waitress was a sullen, bony young woman who never met his eyes. It seemed to him that young women were getting more sullen every year for undisclosed reasons, all the more cause to keep the Director in mind as a possible target if Berry went to sleep. Grandpa had the theory that you should never go after a female with a bad father because they're always pissed off. However mediocre the meal was B.D. figured it was better than the catered backstage buffet before the concert which, though it was free, featured food he didn't recognize. Once Gretchen had served him a tofu burger that tasted like the algae that formed pond scum. Gretchen had mentioned dozens of times how awful her father was and also that an older cousin had tinkered with her pussy when she was eleven. There seemed to be no end to the problems that could arise in life. When he was eleven there was a neighbor girl who would show you her butt for a nickel but if you tried to touch it she'd smack the shit out of you. He'd heard that now she was a school principal up in Houghton.

Back in the hotel room he recognized that the quivery feeling was due to the idea that if things went well he would be back in the United States of America, more exactly North Dakota, in less than eighteen hours. He opened the minibar where he'd seen the Director take out cans of orange juice for herself and Berry. This was the first minibar of his life and he was amazed at the rack of top-shelf shooters on display. He went "Eeny meeny miney moe" and took out a small bottle of Mexican tequila which went down easy as pie. He snooped in the Director's room and saw a rather large pair of undies she had washed out and hung up to dry on a towel rack. He felt a twinge of lust which he knew couldn't be resolved. He sat down with the clicker and shooters of Johnnie Walker and Absolut vodka noting a sign on the television that first-run and adult movies were available at twelve dollars a crack which seemed outrageously expensive but then when would he ever stay in a fancy hotel again? Even the glasses were glass rather than cellophane-wrapped plastic. He was never allowed to touch the clicker for Uncle Delmore's satellite television so he was very wary about its operation and it took some time to get it working. It was easy to reject *Teenage Sluts on the Loose in Hollywood* as porn made him feel silly and he had never regarded sex as a spectator sport. You simply had to be there with the raw meat on the floor as they used to say. The slightest peek up Gretchen's summer skirt would set him churning but neither film nor the Playmate of the Month did the job. Un-

fortunately he selected a film called *Pan's Labyrinth* because
of the unknowable mystery of the title. It took a total of ten
shooters to get through the film and he was frequently either frightened or in tears. He assumed that the film was a
true story and he thought of the little girl as Berry and he
was the satyr trying to help her get through life. By the time
the film ended he was drunk with a tear-wet face. If this
could happen in the world it was no wonder that he craved
to live in a cabin back in the woods. He had done poorly in
world history in high school but was aware of the twentieth
century as a worldwide charnel house. His teacher who was
a Democrat from the working-class east side of Escanaba had
told the students that there were at least ten million Indians when we got off the boat and only three hundred thousand left by 1900. Now in the hotel room, however, the fact
that this evil Spaniard had murdered the little girl, the Berry
equivalent, sent a sob through his system and he finished
his last shooter, arranged the bottles in a circle, and fell
asleep in his chair.

He awoke at four A.M. to pee and in the bleary toilet
mirror he saw that there was a note pinned to his chest. It
was from the Director and only said, "Shame on you." Soon
after daylight Berry and the Director were having room service in the other room when he came fully awake and examined his mind for vital signs. Berry came in and kissed his
forehead and headed into the bathroom with her armload of
rubber snakes which she always played with in the tub. On
this morning the two-headed cobra didn't look good to B.D.

"Are you up for it, Lone Ranger?" the Director asked
standing in the doorway of her room.

"Come to think of it I am," said B.D. squirming slowly out of the easy chair. During even minor league hangovers sudden movements cause sudden pain, the physical equivalent of a blowing fuse.

They had to arrange themselves near a dresser to keep an eye out the nearly closed door of Berry's bathroom. The Director's butt was large indeed but as marvelously smooth as B.D. had hoped for. In his not limited experience Indian women had the smoothest butts though this was a Lakota, the ancient enemy of B.D.'s half-Chippewa blood. Let there be peace in the valley he thought. The only drawback was the mirror over the dresser. He certainly didn't want to see himself what with being the least narcissistic of all modern males. The Director let out a few muffled yelps and he hissed, "Sssh" and then it was over and a sharp pain descended into his noggin from the heavens.

He pulled up his trousers and quickly moved to the room service table for some lukewarm coffee, cold sausage, and sodden toast.

"It's so like a man to go from fucking to eating in a split second," the Director giggled, rearranging her clothes.

"What was I supposed to do?" B.D. said with a full mouth.

"You're supposed to say 'Thank-you ma'am' and give me a heartfelt kiss."

B.D. swallowed a mouthful of food, choked a little, and gave her a passionate heartfelt kiss, dipping her as one does a woman on a dance floor. Lucky for her he was strong.

Shortly after noon the tour bus followed by the equipment semi turned off on a gravel road south of Boissevain.

The moves were well planned and the crew unloaded two big ceremonial drums and hoisted them onto the long luggage rack on top of the tour bus. The Director took the tambourine away from Berry and B.D., Berry, and Eats Horses went up the ladder and Eats Horses got under one drum and B.D. and Berry under the other. Two crew members beat tentatively on each drum with Lakota wails and laughter. For some reason Berry responded with the chirping of a cricket until B.D. said no, mourning the effect of the drumbeats on his hangover.

The bus took off hitting the border of the United States near the Turtle Mountain Reservation in North Dakota. The drumbeats softened while the Director talked to the customs agents whom she knew from other crossings there.

"You know my boys are clean. No drugs or alcohol on the bus or they get their asses kicked off." The customs agents were eating their lunch sandwiches and were quite bored with trying to catch putative terrorists who were unlikely to come their way.

The bus roared off and the drummers beat hard and wailed loudly as they entered the promised land which had been less than wonderful to the Lakota in recent centuries. A dozen miles south in a cottonwood grove the rooftop passengers climbed down the ladder and the Director returned Berry's tambourine which made her happy. B.D. was a little dizzy and nauseous thinking that seven shooters would have been adequate rather than ten, and slightly disappointed that North Dakota looked identical to Manitoba but it might have been due to the way one hangover resembles another. Nothing helped until he had pork liver and onions and two beers in Rugby which was supposedly the geographical center of North America. Out in the restaurant parking lot he lamely tried to figure out how they'd determined this. He also wondered how he would protect himself from his excesses if Berry went under the Director's care for a while. The answer was to live so far back in the woods that you only went to the tavern once a week. Maybe twice. When he got back on the bus the Director teased him in a whisper about his short "staying power" then punched him so hard in the arm it went numb. He reflected from experience that you never quite knew if an Indian woman would make love or beat the shit out of you.

At nightfall the tour bus was camped at the site of Wounded Knee. Charles Eats Horses went off and spent the night sitting up wrapped in a blanket. The crew started a fire to cook the steaks the Director had bought along with a case of beer to celebrate the end of the tour. B.D. was mournful that a single case only offered two apiece, scarcely enough to wet your whistle. As much as possible he avoided remembering when he was sixteen and Grandpa had given him a lecture on the dangers of liquor saying that it had killed B.D.'s mom and dad. No more information on them had ever been forthcoming from Grandpa though B.D. had heard that his mom, Grandpa's daughter, had danced for a while in a strip club in Escanaba. Since Grandpa was mostly Swede and Irish the skin blood had come through his dad who had taken off for Lac du Flambeau. Right now at Wounded Knee he surely didn't care if he was part Indian or in his private thicket on the edge of the Kingston Plains where he could watch breeding sandhill cranes. Uncle Delmore was always watching horror films on television. Berry liked them but B.D. had an aversion to being frightened. He had peeked in from the kitchen during a werewolf film and decided he would a lot rather be a werecoyote assuming they existed.

He was washing up in his compartment when he heard the Director enter. She looked out the window at Berry and two crew members dancing around the fire.

"I'm going to make that girl into a fancy dancer. She's real good."

"That's a wonderful idea," B.D. said patting the Director's ass and hoping to redeem the idea that he had no staying power.

"Back away, dickhead," she chortled at him and made for the door. "You remind me too much of my husband. He was drunk and the police clocked him at over a hundred miles per hour outside of Chadron before his pickup flipped about twenty times."

She had left in a virtuous huff and B.D. remembered a conversation when he and Berry and Delmore were eating Sunday dinner at Gretchen's. Delmore had taken Berry for a ride down to the harbor and B.D. had whimsically asked Gretchen why no woman had ever asked him to marry her.

"You're a biological question mark," she had said. "Women in general want some romance but when they look for a mate they most often estimate the man, at least subconsciously, as a provider. You present yourself as a fuckup but the reason you can get laid is that you intensely like women without irony."

B.D. had reminded himself to look up "subconscious" and "irony" in Delmore's dictionary. Gretchen had been wearing pale blue fairly tight shorts and when she vigorously mashed potatoes at the stove her butt cheeks jiggled so attractively that B.D. felt tears arising. He had stopped well short of persisting on the marriage issue because Gretchen could be a little cruel. Years before, she had used her authority to thoroughly review his school records and discovered that his intelligence was well above average which made her question him sharply.

"Why live like you do? You're smart enough to do otherwise."

"I just slid into it," he had answered nervously.

"Well, you flunked English literature but you aced geometry."

"Geometry was real pretty."

It occurred to him then that she would never understand the deep pleasure of spending a whole day in the company of a creek. If he could make a subsistence living repairing deer-hunting cabins, cutting firewood or pulp why should he do more? He spent the rest of his time wandering in the woods and following creeks to their source. When Gretchen had said that he was frozen in place at age twelve he had reflected that that had been a good year. He had caught his first brook trout over three pounds on a beaver pond north of Rapid River, he owned a little terrier that rode in his bicycle basket and could occasionally catch a flushing grouse, and he had gotten to screw a beered-up sixteen-year-old tourist girl down on the town beach. The accusation of being frozen at age twelve did not seem to be a serious charge. Once when he got winter work at about age twenty as a janitor at a bowling alley he didn't think these fully employed men at their weekly bowling league were having all that much fun trying to break 200. They mostly had fat asses and when they jumped up and down they didn't jump high.

Now out the tour bus window it was pleasant to watch Berry and Turnip dancing at top speed. Turnip always looked ungainly but turned out to be a fine dancer. B.D. left the bus and moved hot coals off to the side and arranged the grill face so that it was well balanced on rocks, electing himself as the steak cook. Not so far off in the moonlight he could see Charles Eats Horses sitting in the cemetery with his hands pointed up toward the sky. The Director sat on a lawn chair guarding the beer and B.D. decided to drink his share of two real fast to acquire a modestly good feeling. The meat was real fatty rib steaks, his favorite cut, and the bone made it possible to eat with your hands rather than struggling with plastic knives and forks. Everyone was so tired that they ate fast and went to bed. When he went into the dark to pee B.D. was thrilled to have Turnip pass him a pint of schnapps for a couple of deep swigs. Berry continued to dance in the firelight without drums, banging on her tambourine, until the Director led her off to bed. Up home Berry tended to avoid all strangers but B.D. admitted to himself that she was having a good time with these people. She seemed to love music just like she was enchanted with birds. The Director had said that there were a lot worse things than being mute.

They got an early start in the morning and B.D. was upset when saying good-bye to Charles Eats Horses who was still sitting out in the cemetery but seemed to be in some

sort of trance though he hugged Berry. The tour bus
stopped in Pine Ridge and dropped off three crew members including a very strong young man named Pork. B.D.
had learned that Pork had gotten his name when he had
run away to Pierre when he was twelve. He was very hungry and went in to the supermarket to steal a pound of
hamburger to eat raw but had grabbed a package of pork
sausage by mistake. Ever since then Pork had had an affection for raw pork. He seemed fairly smart and said at
one time raw pork could be dangerous but trichinosis was
a thing of the past. Out the window in Pine Ridge, which
was a dreamy place surrounded by beautiful country, B.D.
saw Pork embrace his wife and son and get into a fairly
new Chevy pickup.

On the way up toward Rapid City, B.D. sat up front
with Turnip who invited him to stay at the condo he had
inherited from an aunt who had been a school principal and
a successful horse trader. Turnip said the group of condos
shared a heated pool and when the weather was warm he
would sit by the pool in Vuarnet sunglasses with a hand-
tooled leather briefcase a rich white woman had given him
down in Santa Fe, New Mexico, when the band toured
there. Pretty girls and women would come up to him at the
pool and chat because he looked like a big shot. He would
tease his neighbors because the briefcase was full of R.
Crumb comic books. He showed one to B.D. who thought
it was the best comic book he had ever read.

They stopped at a country gas station for fuel and coffee and in an adjoining field two girls were practicing barrel racing with their quarter horses. B.D. was appalled at

the speed at which the horses were running and turned to the Director beside him.

"They could die if they fell off."

"They don't," she said but then she yelled at Berry who vaulted the fence and ran toward the girls who now were taking a break. Berry went past them doing a top-speed figure eight around the barrels and then she stopped by the girls and petted the horses while she cooed like a dove. B.D. told the Director that he didn't think that Berry had ever been near a horse. They crawled through the fence and made their way to the girls. Berry was rubbing her nose against the nose of one of the horses who seemed to like it.

"She ain't right in the head," the girl said to the approaching B.D. and Director.

"That's true but she's a sweetheart. How about giving her a ride? She's never been in the saddle before," the Director said.

The girl gestured to Berry who leapt on with one flowing move.

"That's quite a trick," the girl said leading the horse by the reins then handing the reins to Berry. "I bet she can handle it."

The horse took off for the far barrel and B.D. covered his face with his hands and peeked through his fingers. Berry was pasted to the saddle and neck of the horse like a decal but when the girl whistled and the horse ran back toward them abruptly stopping Berry slid forward and hung there with her arms around the horse's neck. She was all aglow and crooning. B.D. reached for her and she dropped into his arms.

"Now she's both a dancer and a cowgirl. All is not lost," the Director said.

B.D. paused halfway crawling under the fence watching Berry grab a post and vault over the top wire the same way he used to do when he was young. Way too much had been happening in this life and there under the bottom wire he was suddenly trying to focus.

"How am I supposed to get back home?" he asked almost plaintively.

"Well you can't fly because the computer at the airport might pick up the Michigan warrant. They might not still be looking for you but we can't take a chance. The jail in Rapid City is full of drunk Indians. Your uncle Delmore is sending someone out to pick you up. He says you'll owe him big."

"He always says that," B.D. said thinking he'd have to find a good hiding place back home. Delmore had plenty of money but like many old people he was fretful about it. "During the Great Depression I couldn't afford the hole in a doughnut," he would say.

B.D. pretty much sat for two full days on a cement park bench on the grounds of the Rapid City hospital. He packed along sardines, cheese, crackers, and Bull Durham. He was rolling his own cigarettes from Bull Durham and though there was a mysterious sign saying "Smoke-Free Zone" he couldn't imagine anyone would object on these warm windy days of early spring. He was wrong. A security man approached and said he could be arrested which caused a quiver of fear. B.D. played dumb when the security man pointed at the sign ten feet away.

"Can't you read?"

"Not too good," B.D. said as if trying to parse the sign.

The Director was running Berry through a battery of tests. B.D. had tried to give the Director the five-hundred-dollar gift from Dr. Krider but the Director had refused saying, "You can't give me all your money. Are you stupid?"

This seemed possible. He hadn't been able to reach Uncle Delmore or Gretchen on the phone and her answering machine said she would be away for a week. Turnip had dialed the numbers for him on his cell phone and when B.D. worried about the expense Turnip said that he got a deal for three thousand minutes. B.D. wondered how they could possibly keep track of such things at the same time thinking that Delmore rarely answered the phone because bad news always came over the phone. He didn't watch television news because he said he didn't need to know all of the bad news in the world in ten minutes. Delmore listened now and then to Canadian news on his big powerful radio because things didn't seem to be going so bad up that way.

B.D. hung out on the bench in front of the hospital because the medical tests made Berry so unhappy that she cried which she never did normally. She was so sad that when she and the Director came out for a break from the tests she didn't even make gull cries when she shared sardines with B.D.

"Sardines have gone up from nineteen cents to a dollar in my lifetime," B.D. reflected. He was remembering his youth when toward the end of the month Grandpa's pension money ran low and they would eat five tins of sardines and boiled garden potatoes from the root cellar. It was their "dollar meal," better in the summer with added onions, radishes, and tomatoes from the garden.

"Christianity might be bullshit but I heard a priest say that greed was the Antichrist." The Director hugged Berry who was trembling.

"Berry's mom used to throw her naked out in the snow when she peed the bed. Back then Berry was always trembling but she lucked out when her mom got sent to prison."

"I'd like to slit that cunt's throat," the Director said matter-of-factly.

Berry began to cry again when the Director led her back toward the hospital. B.D. wasn't feeling well having had one too many with Turnip and his anger over Berry's trials exacerbated his discomfort. He had stayed two nights in a sleazy motel because he hadn't wanted to stay at the Director's because she wouldn't allow alcohol in her home and Turnip's condo made him too nervous. Turnip had had some young lady neighbors in for drinks in the late afternoon when they got home from work. They were dressed slick and neat and were professional women working in real estate and one was a teacher "looking for something better." The problem was that B.D. couldn't get a fix on what they were talking about and Turnip had put on loud rock-and-roll music. They fawned over Turnip but let their eyes pass quickly over B.D. They were technically real pretty but he didn't feel a true-to-life nut itch over a single one of them. When they entered a tall one name Deedee had approached him.

"What do you do?"

"Cut logs. A little carpentry when I can find it."

"You Indians are so devil-may-care," she giggled chugging her Budweiser.

"I'm not a real Indian like Turnip. I'm just a mixed breed like most dogs." He was tempted to tell he was a wanted man on the run but she had quickly turned away.

Turnip had made them a batch of margaritas and winked at B.D. when he poured most of a bottle of tequila into the shaker. "I'm sending these bitches to the moon pronto. We're in for some C-minus fun," he whispered.

B.D. took a couple of gulps of tequila and then when the rest of them went out to see someone's new leased car he slipped out the back door and headed for the scrungiest side of town where he had a fry bread taco covered with hot sauce. After dinner he bought a pint of McGillicuddy's schnapps to settle his stomach, then headed back to his motel room where there was a big photo of Mount Rushmore. He tried to imagine Charles Eats Horses pouring a gallon of blood-red paint down along George Washington's nose. Every movie on cable TV seemed to involve people shooting each other and he wasn't up to being a witness to malice of any sort. Finally on the National Geo channel he found a documentary on Siberia which seemed a totally wonderful place, the kind of country he'd learn to love in three minutes flat. He sipped out of the 100 proof bottle disliking plastic glasses because years ago one had sprung a leak and left a last drink on his wet lap. There was an improbable surge of homesickness and he made do by reliving a long trek west of Germfask in search of a rumored beaver pond which was actually in a federal wildlife area where it was illegal to fish, the smallest of considerations because on the sparse two-tracks you could hear the rare federal vehicle a half mile away and merely step into the brush. At the beaver pond he hooked what he thought would be the largest brook trout of his life but after a prolonged struggle the fish turned out to be a pike of a half dozen pounds. He would have preferred it to be a brook trout but gracefully accepted its pikedom. It was June and pike are quite tasty from the cool waters of the early season. By the time he got back to the car it was nearly dark, after ten this far north in June. He drove over to near Au Train where an old Indian lady he knew lived far back in the woods in a tar-paper cabin. His grandpa and this woman were sweet on each other and when he was a boy he'd fish a nearby creek while the two had their monthly assignation. When he arrived just before midnight with the pike her cabin was dark and it scared the shit out of him when he heard a growl from a nearby thicket. She was playing a joke on him after she had been out night walking. She cooked up the pike and they ate it with bread, salt, and some elderberry wine she had made the autumn before. She sang along with the country station from Ishpeming and was particularly good at duets with George Jones and Merle Haggard.

The reverie put him in a fine mood though the Siberian program segued to heart surgery on a zoo elephant and he turned off the television not wanting to know if this elephant failed to make it through the operation. The heart was red and huge and its beating was tentative. B.D. recalled that once when Grandpa was telling his World War II stories there was one about a whale seen in the North Pacific that had a heart big enough for a man to sleep in.

He managed his second long day of vigil fairly well. The Weather Channel predicted a storm by evening but the day had a warm breeze from the south. The hardest part was when the Director and Berry came out and Berry closed down and became stonelike. Due to some blood test she wasn't even allowed to eat the Big Mac with extra onions he had bought her. Berry's only sign of life was to point straight up at the tiny specks of hawks making their spring migration.

"She's not looking too good for a normal life," the Director said.

"I already knew that," B.D. said, his gorge rising.

"So did I but they have to figure out what's possible. She won't ever be able to talk but she's physically coordinated, strong, and agile."

"I already knew that." The anger was a knot in B.D.'s throat so that he couldn't swallow.

"These are specialists in this infirmity, B.D., so you'll have to be patient. We'll be finished by three and then I'm going to take Berry out north of Sturgis toward Bear Butte to see some baby buffalo. You got a big surprise coming about that time."

A doctor walked by and Berry shoved her head into B.D.'s jacket. He patted her back and her muscles were tight as a drum.

"I don't want no surprise. I want to head home with my daughter."

"You can't. We're already processing with the state of Michigan for the change of guardianship. Her mother has consented. Eventually the state of Michigan will withdraw the charges against you. Her mother got another five years for biting off a guard's ear. You know this is best. What would you do when she got pregnant at age twelve by whomever?"

"Likely kill whomever."

"Then she would have no one. She's going to live with my cousin's family north of here. They got cows, horses, and dogs and she'll go to this special school part-time."

B.D. began to cry for the first time he could remember. The Director hugged him and dabbed his tears with a good-smelling handkerchief and Berry came alive enough to hold his hand. They left and he quickly finished the bottle of schnapps, reached into his pocket, and rolled a cigarette and lit it. Suddenly the security guard was in front of him.

"I'm going to have to call the police, I warned you."

"It would be the last number you ever dialed," B.D. said levelly.

"How come you're crying?" The security man shrugged, not wanting to get his ass kicked.

"They're taking my daughter away from me," B.D. said.

"That's an awful thing to have happen," the guard said and walked away.

B.D. saw a black dog out in the parking lot. He whistled and the dog trotted over with its long rabbit ears and ungainly body what with its front rather slender compared to its big back end. B.D. unwrapped Berry's Big Mac and was amazed when the dog ate the burger in polite bites rather than gulps. The brass collar said that her name was Ethyl, a fine match he thought between name and this peculiar beast. Here Ethyl was out on a stroll and lucked into

a burger. The basis of a friendship having been made Ethyl
hopped up onto the bench, circled a few times, and nestled
in for a snooze. From her somewhat distended teats it was
apparent that Ethyl was a mother and B.D. mentally bet that
she was good at it as he stroked her long floppy ears. Turnip had said that the Director had raised five kids, the last
being a member of the Thunderskins. How could I know
how to be a mother when I didn't even have one myself,
he thought. He knew he was better than Berry's criminal
mother Rose but that might be like comparing cat and dog
turds. He leaned forward trying to prop his elbows on his
knees for a little snooze. There was a chance of falling on
his face if he fell asleep but that might be fun compared to
the rest of what had been happening. He was not under the
illusion that most of us are that he was in control, that he
was in the driver's seat, as they say. And a wide streak of
the dour Lutheran ethos of the Great North said that it is
always darkest before it gets even darker. His last hope
was to get home and have a life that the ancient Confu-
cians thought was the best life, one in which nothing much
happened.

He did doze and he did fall over but only scraped one
palm on the cement. The Director and Berry came back out
for a few minutes and Berry was a tad cheerier, especially
with Ethyl to pet.

"Your surprise is getting closer. I just gave directions,"
the Director said grabbing Berry's hand and walking swiftly
back toward the hospital. Ethyl tried to follow but there was
a shrill whistle from a block away out beyond the parking
lot. Ethyl took off toward the whistle and B.D. had the

maudlin thought, Now I've lost my dog, but then he saw something that made his heart jump. Out in the parking lot a woman looking like Gretchen got out of a car that looked like Gretchen's. Unable to believe this B.D. swiveled around until he was looking back toward the hospital. His skin prickled.

"B.D., it's me," she called out. "I'm here to drive you home."

It was as if the sun had risen in the middle of a stormy night. He didn't dare turn around and then a kind of paralysis seeped into his system. She sat down beside him and took his limp hand.

"I know it's been a hard time for you."

"You could say that."

"Everything is for the best. We've got to haul ass. It's Friday afternoon and I have to be to work Monday."

They all had a good-bye lunch at a plastic picnic table outside a McDonald's. Gretchen and the Director sipped sodas and ate granola bars while shuffling papers. B.D. and Berry ate with Berry sitting on his lap. She was fairly happy having perceived that she didn't have to go back to the hospital. B.D. and Gretchen were quite overcome and plans were discussed to come back to South Dakota around the Fourth of July for a visit.

Gretchen drove B.D. to the sleazy motel to pick up his bag and he had this idea that they should rest up because he had already paid for that day and night.

"Just get your bag, you nitwit," she laughed. She was wearing a blue summer skirt that thrilled him to the core.

PART III

"I was hoping to take a look at this Corn Palace." B.D. had been dozing but it seemed like every time he opened his eyes there was a billboard for the Corn Palace, a building constructed out of ears of corn. Since he had worked often as a carpenter he couldn't imagine corn as a building material. It was probably like cheap brick facing. "Why would they put up a building made of corn?"

"So that geeks like you will stop in Mitchell, South Dakota, and spend money. The weather is shit anyway and I'm tired and hungry."

It was sleeting and the thermometer in her Honda Accord had dropped to freezing from forty in the last hour. She steered downtown encircling the Corn Palace which indeed was made of full corncobs though they were the only tourists and downtown was pretty much closed. Gretchen chose a higher-end motel back out by the interstate because there was a restaurant attached and she didn't want to drive any farther.

"We've been talking all afternoon but I can't stop thinking about intrauterine pollution."

"What's that?"

"Chemicals from the environment get into the womb and affect the baby's teeth. I live too close to that stinking paper mill."

While she checked them into the motel B.D. reflected on her endless monologue on possibly having a baby. Since he was to be the sperm donor he first had to have a physical checkup to make sure he wasn't diseased.

"I'm thirty-three. I have to come to a decision," she had said.

"That's the age Jesus was when he died," B.D. had said lamely.

"What's that supposed to mean?"

"Nothing. I'm confused about being a sperm donor."

"It's easy. I don't want to do it in a doctor's office so it will happen at my house. After your checkup you'll whack off into a syringe bulb and I'll inject it you know where."

"I have my dignity," he had said, copping the line from one of Delmore's *Perry Mason* reruns.

"You'll get over it."

"Why can't I just put it in for a few minutes?"

"The idea is repellent to me."

While she was in the motel office it occurred to him that he associated repellent with the insect repellent he smeared on himself, especially in June when blackflies and mosquitoes were active in the trillions when he was fishing.

"You could drink a bunch and take one of your tranquilizers," he suggested.

"I'm a victim of anhedonia which means my neutrality is probably an organic response to trauma."

"I don't get it."

"I'll explain it over dinner."

Their two rooms were adjoining but when B.D. opened his side he noted that hers was still locked.

"Your door is locked."

"Yes, it is."

She took a quick shower and he got a hard-on just listening to the water run. He would have perished from lust if he hadn't found a two-ounce shooter of Canadian whiskey at the bottom of his duffel.

At dinner her soapy smell made his tummy quiver. So did his Seafood Medley for $9.95 for different reasons. It was all deep-fried and tasted like it had spent a lot of time on the bottom of a boat in the hot sun. Gretchen was kind enough to give him one of her two very tough pork chops though there was no gravy, just a slice of apple dyed red. She had ordered a bottle of white wine but he had never thought of white wine as actual alcohol so he opted for a couple of double whiskeys.

"You could say that whiskey is my wine," he said raising his glass and she clicked it with her own.

"Apparently."

"I'll pay for it," he said drawing out a ten-spot.

"Delmore gave me enough to bring you home. He's getting sentimental. We met a number of times and even danced at the American Legion fish fry to a band called Marvin and His Polka Dots."

"It's true if you say so."

"He even asked how women make love to each other and I said, 'Mind your own beeswax,' and then I told him I had given up sex for the rest of my life. He said he gave it up at age seventy because women kept borrowing money from him."

"I can't believe you two being friendly."

"He has a motive. He's eighty-eight years old and he's worried about you and Berry. He's not worried about Red who Cranbrook wrote him about and said was the best young math student they've ever had. Anyway as his nephew you're his only close living relative. I had to tell Delmore that it's unlikely that Berry has any memory of her brother."

"He never admitted I was his nephew."

"Well, you are and we agreed you need a short rope so I'll likely end up as your guardian."

B.D.'s mind whirled and he signaled the waitress for a third whiskey. Most of everything was going over his head because he was not one to think of the future. Up until Berry had entered his life the future was limited to the next day at most. Nearly every day he cooked food when he was hungry and slept when he was tired.

"You were going to tell me why sex is repellent." B.D. could practically smell 6-12 and Muskol in the air though you had to be careful about getting it in your eyes or you couldn't tie a fly on your leader.

"I'm tired of being sunk in mental shit. I can't talk about it now. Besides, you don't look so physically repellent after three glasses of wine." She leaned back, yawned, and stretched revealing her belly button, that sacred nubbin that connected her to a thousand generations before her.

"I'm telling you that if you drink two bottles of wine you'd be on me like flies on a cow's ass." He knew his words weren't quite right but the sight of her belly button was a jolt to his inner and outer beings.

"You can do better than that."

"Like a monarch butterfly on a daisy."

"You're a daisy!" She shrieked with laughter.

"Like an old maid sitting on a warm cucumber in her garden."

She leaned forward smirking and parted her blouse so he could see her left braless titty.

"In high school I was known as Miss Prick Tease," she laughed.

B.D. felt he was bubbling inside as Gretchen walked toward the cash register. Her body mystified him as it was far too slender for his normal taste. She had told him she had taken dance classes for fifteen years to "burn off anger" and that likely accounted for her tight build. On the way back down the hall to their rooms she stumbled and he caught her. She gave him an almost hug at her door and he thought of breaking his plastic key so he could enter through her door but she grabbed it and opened the door for him when he fumbled.

"We could have a nice glass of water for a nightcap," he said through her adjoining door.

"Sorry, kiddo. Right now I'm undressing. The squeaking sound you hear is my butt rubbing against the door."

"You can't do that to me. I won't sleep. I got a hard-on like a toothache."

"Just whack off. Get in practice as a sperm donor. Say your prayers. Think about your mom."

"I don't have a mom."

"I'm sorry. I misspoke."

He lay down on the rug and squinted through the quarter-inch space under the door. He heard her lights turn off. Lucky for him that he had darted next door into a liquor store when they had stopped for gas in Chamberlain and she had gone to the toilet. He sipped at the first of three shooters staring up at the creamy void of the ceiling. He slept on the floor until five A.M. then rushed to the bed to get fair use of the room cost.

Mum was the word in the morning except when he couldn't work the coffee machine and called out to her.

"Is this a rapist trick?" She rushed in wearing a short robe and while she got the machine going he leaned far over from his position at the end of the bed to get a peek up the back of her robe. His vision reached midway up her thighs so the effort was worth it except that she turned around and caught him.

"You're incorrigible."

"I'm just curious."

B.D. paid for his sins with a long wait for breakfast. Gretchen's eyes were vaguely teary and she drove with concentration buffeted by a blustery wind out of the southwest. She pulled off the interstate in Sioux Falls for a large container of franchise coffee which he declined because he didn't see the point of being that awake.

"Grandpa used to say, 'I'm so hungry I could eat the raw pork around a sow's ass.'"

She glanced at him with horror but stopped at a diner just over the Minnesota line when she turned to take Route 23 diagonally northeast across the state.

"You're not very interested in reality," she said, getting out of the car with a coolish smile.

"Define your terms." This came from his civics class thirty-five years before.

"I'm not being mean. It's just that you're more mammalian than anyone I've met. My father and his friends were fake mammals. For instance I bet you didn't notice that Berry scarcely recognized me."

"Yes I did. Sometimes when I picked her up from the speech therapist in Toronto she didn't instantly recognize me. I could see her mind saying to itself, 'Oh, it's you.'"

"Of course she was your pal more than anything."

"I was a fairly good dad. She always had clean clothes. I cooked her food she liked. We went on walks and fishing. We played games and looked at books though she didn't like words, only pictures. I let her have her garter snake on the table except when we ate at Delmore's. What more could I do?"

"Nothing. That's far more than most kids get. I mean my two cousins raped me over and over when I was ten and they were twelve and thirteen. I told my mother and she said, 'No they didn't.'"

"That's pretty bad reality," B.D. said looking up at the clouds scudding swiftly above them. She was shivering in the forty-degree wind. He tried to put an arm around her but she slipped away entering the diner. To his surprise she laughed at his "country boy special" which he covered with Tabasco and ketchup while she settled for a dry English muffin.

It was never the state, he thought, but the terrain. Once they were out of solid farm country and he saw birch, cedar, pine, and hemlock, his spirits lifted through the top of his head. A sign said that there were ten thousand lakes in Minnesota which he doubted but then he was more interested in streams and rivers. He noted that Gretchen was drowsy by midafternoon when they hit the Wisconsin border and he offered to drive. She reminded him that if a cop stopped them and ran a check on his license he'd end up in jail. The idea that everything with the police was connected by computer distressed him, remembering as he did a time when the world seemed friendlier and more haphazard. Delmore was always carping about Homeland Security but B.D. with his aversion to the news kept himself ignorant. Despite his bluster Delmore was rather timid about authority and kept badgering B.D. for not having a Social Security number. Nowadays, Delmore insisted that even babies are obligated to have Social Security numbers, adding that people in Washington, D.C., knew all of the considerable bad moves B.D. had made in his life to which B.D. had responded, "Why would they give a shit?" Delmore pretended to be an authority on Arabs having known a few in Detroit fifty years before and had told B.D. that the Arabs were pissed off because we had treated them as badly as we do blacks and American Indians. B.D.'s frame of reference was limited to a late-night movie where this sheikh in a huge tent had a harem of thirty women wearing see-through gowns. The women were always dancing and servants brought huge platters of food. B.D. had thought that thirty women was being a bit too ambitious if any were as energetic as Brenda, his big dentist, who had screwed him into the carpet.

Gretchen was suffering from road exhaustion when they entered Wisconsin and began maniacally dithering about her future baby perhaps to keep herself alert. She spoke of day care, the legalities of sperm donorship, and once again the specter of intrauterine pollution. B.D. liked the sound of the word "intrauterine" but didn't care what it meant because he was betting on something confusing. B.D. thought of the outside of a woman's private parts as lovely as a woodland but knew that just inside things got pretty complicated. Way back in biology class the illustrated cross sections of a woman were stupefying whereas a man's pecker was as plain as day.

Near Rice Lake on Wisconsin Route 8 his attention was caught by the core of the legalities.

"You're saying that though I'm the dad of the kid I'm not actually the parent?" She had used the new word "parenting" which seemed slippery.

"Well, yes."

"I'm just a piece of meat that shot off into a gizmo that you squirt into yourself?"

"That's essentially it but I'm choosing you because you're interesting genetically. I'm not picking a white-bread, white-car, white-house American like my dad and his awful friends. Once when I was having a pajama party and they were playing poker his friend named Charley shone a flashlight under the sheets when he thought we were asleep."

"Can't say that I blame him."

"You're disgusting. We were only fourteen."

"They used to say that if a girl is big enough she's old enough."

The car swerved when she swatted at him. She had raised his ire and he was baiting her.

"In other words when I see this baby I'm not supposed to think or say that I'm his dad?"

"It's better that way since we're never going to be married. I also liked the idea that the baby would be one-quarter Chippewa."

"Oh bullshit. I was a fine dad to Berry."

There was silence for many miles and by the time they passed through Ladysmith she became a little jealous of the landscape which had him sitting on the edge of his seat. It was the same latitude as the southern tier of the Upper Peninsula and he was seeing his homeground flora for the first time in nearly six months. At his insistence she stopped the car at a little tourist park near a river outside of Catawba so he could wander around breathing in the pungent smell of cedar and alder along the water and look up at the green buds of birch and aspen. The flowing water made his brain jiggle and he fondled the thin branches of willow and dogwood. At the edge of the woods he lay down on his stomach to smoke a cigarette with a ground-level view. She had followed and stood over him with her arms wrapped across her chest, a defensive posture against the cool spring air and her own out-of-control feelings.

"You seem to think I'm marginalizing you." She stooped down beside him and scratched his head.

"What the fuck else?" he muttered, not quite knowing what "marginalizing" meant except that she was pushing him off to the side. On Grandpa's sofa back home there was an embroidered pillow that said "Love Conquers All." He thought, I'm not so sure. He could tell his huffiness was paying off because he had a clear view up her skirt and he would bet she was doing it on purpose to win him over.

"I'm so sorry. I'm just not explaining it in the best terms."

He buried his face in his hands but not so completely that he couldn't see up past her inner thighs to the delightful muffin captured by white panties.

"Got you." He suddenly reached out and grabbed her ankles.

She pitched over sideways twisting her legs to get loose. He had a quick fine view of her butt before he let go of her ankles. She ran laughing toward the car and he scrambled after her on his hands and knees like a dog barking and howling. She was thinking that her old shameless prick-tease moves had at least changed the mood and he was thinking that playing difficult had paid off.

They reached Ironwood by nightfall still happy though Gretchen was so tired she asked him to pick her up some takeout. Many copper and iron miners had arrived from northern Italy in the mid-nineteenth century and maintained their interest in their own food so the U.P. abounded in Italian restaurants. B.D. walked down the road a scant half mile and ate a large order of lasagna with a whole bottle of acrid red wine and waited for a pizza to take back to Gretchen. She wanted double anchovies and onions and he thought, Strong flavors for a strong woman. He'd drunk the bottle of red at warp speed and treated himself to a double whiskey thinking unpleasantly of the time he came home drunk from an evening with David Four Feet. His grandpa was angry and told him that his mother was a drunk and he didn't want B.D. to die from the same "curse." Grandpa said that his daughter still made his heart ache so that was the most that was ever said about B.D.'s mother. Grandpa had emerged from World War II with a number of bullet holes in his legs and ass but they made out okay on half disability from the government and Grandpa's ability as a part-time cabinetmaker. He couldn't stand up for long but tended a fine vegetable garden on his hands and knees.

When B.D. got back to the motel with the pizza he knocked at Gretchen's door.

"A peek at your beautiful ass for a pizza," he hollered.

"Of course, darling." She opened the door, flipped the back of her nightie up, took the pizza, and slammed the door, leaving him with burning skin.

"I wish to dine alone. Good night, love."

B.D. recalled that there was a smart-ass guy from near Traverse City who used to hang out in the Dunes Saloon in Grand Marais in the summer who had said, "How does a woman's butt crack capture our imaginations? It's only negative space, in essence, a vacuum." This was puzzling and really made you think it over.

They reached Delmore's at noon and were promptly attacked by the pup Teddy whom B.D. hadn't seen since leaving for Toronto. Teddy had grown much larger. B.D. asked about Teddy's mother and Delmore looked into the air while responding as if the mother had ascended.

"She got shot while eating sheep down the road. We saved the hindquarters of the sheep. You owe me a hundred bucks." Delmore was busy giving Gretchen an overfond hug so that she finally pushed him away.

They sat on the porch swing talking and drinking Delmore's poor man's lemonade — too little lemons and too much sugar. It was Sunday and even the landscape was snoozing in premature warmth. The peepers, tiny frogs, were trilling from the swamp down the road in an evident state of spring fever. B.D. had a lump in his throat about life itself and the sight of Delmore sitting in the ragged old easy chair at the end of the porch with the dog in his lap. Gretchen began to fall asleep on the porch swing, then got up and reminded B.D. that he was due at the doctor's at nine in the morning for his checkup.

"Who's paying?" Delmore barked.

"I am, sweetheart. I'm sending him to a vet." She kissed Delmore on the forehead and escaped his attempt to give her a pat.

"She's going to be your stepmother when I pass on," Delmore said as Gretchen drove off down the gravel road with stones tinkling under the fenders. "I'm hoping that you'll fix me some fried chicken and noodles for Sunday dinner?"

B.D. nodded staring at his favorite hill about three miles off to the north. Gretchen wanted him to teach her how to catch a fish and he was busy concocting a fantasy about a riverside seduction. Meanwhile he was going to head for the hill to breathe air where others weren't breathing it. About three-quarters of the way up the hill there was a fine thicket in the middle of which there was a white pine stump to sit on. So much of his life had been solitary that the crowded nature of the past six months had been confusing. He could be confused enough when alone and the addition of the company of others raised the ante exponentially. For instance he didn't really want to teach Gretchen how to catch a fish. Love was love and fishing was fishing, an almost religious obsession that had added grace to his life for more than forty of his nearly fifty years. Sitting in the car with Gretchen from Ironwood to Delmore's a dozen miles from Escanaba had been difficult. By count the highway had crossed eleven streams that he had fished and each stream held a reverie of the experiences on the stream: "Small bear crying at twilight meant get out of there ASAP as the mother would be irritated. Left two trout behind as peace offering." But with Gretchen in the car he would turn away from the bridges, look down at her when she uttered the word "baby." The hugeness of the idea of a baby filled the speeding car and the world around it and the clarity of trout fishing disappeared despite her strange assurances that the baby had "nothing" to do with him. He had long since accepted that she was by far the most hopeless love of his life, for practical purposes as remote as the princess of Spain or a creature from outer space. He was one of those very rare men who, for better or worse, knew exactly who he was.

He reached his thicket in a fast-paced hour wiping the sweat from his face with his shirt and was pleased to find that a female Cooper's hawk still returned to the area, probably recently, and was not disturbed by his familiar presence. Before he could fully relax he checked the contents of his wallet for what was left of Dr. Krider's gift and discovered three hundred and seven dollars, a virtual fortune. If he was careful and avoided too much time in bars he could possibly fish for a month. He would do a little of it locally because Delmore was bitter about his lack of home-cooked meals. He was too far out in the country to be reached by Meals on Wheels and his fridge's freezer compartment was full of Swanson chicken pot pies which were sometimes on sale three for a dollar, and in the pantry there was a long neat line of cans of Dinty Moore beef stew. When B.D. went to the doctor in the morning he would pick up a few things to cook and freeze before he took off on his fishing trip.

Sitting uncomfortably on his stump B.D. lapsed into a state much envied by the ancients. He thought of nothing for an hour and merely absorbed the landscape, the billions of green buds in thousands of acres of trees surrounding him. Here and there were dark patches of conifers amid the pale green hardwoods and far off to the south a thin blue strip of Lake Michigan. He had never thought a second of the word "meditation" and this made it all easier because he was additionally blessed with no sense of self-importance or personality which are preoccupations of upscale people. Within a minute he was an extension of the stump he sat upon. After about an hour he was aroused by the Cooper's hawk flying by a scant ten feet away after which B.D. reached into a hole at the base of the stump for a pint of schnapps he stored there and was delighted by the wintergreen berry taste.

He was the doctor's first patient on Monday morning and the doctor was in a pissy mood because he was a friend of Gretchen's and her choice of a sperm donor was inscrutable to him. He carelessly drew blood from B.D.'s large forearm as if wanting to punish the nitwit.

"Sperm donorship is a serious thing," the doctor said. "It's better if it's anonymous."

"Why?" B.D. knew that he was normally invisible to the doctor and had decided to play dumb in hopes of getting out of the office as soon as possible.

"Obviously there are emotional issues. Have you been sexually active?"

"Now and then whenever it's possible. You can't always get what you want. It's better not to aim too high."

"What's that supposed to mean?" The doctor was clearly irritated.

"If you go to the bar at the alley on women's bowling night you're not likely to score one of the top ten ladies out of thirty so you aim low."

"Have you ever had a sexually transmitted disease?"

"None other than crabs in Chicago thirty years ago."

"Stand up and drop your trousers. I need to check you for herpes and warts."

"No."

"I insist."

"I don't give a fuck if you insist. I'm familiar with my dick and I don't have any warts." B.D. had never been to a doctor in his life except the time when a tree he was cutting down bucked back and shattered his kneecap and then the orthopedic doctor hadn't been curious about his dick.

"I'm afraid I can't recommend you to Gretchen as a sperm donor."

"Fuck you and the train you rode in on."

B.D. left the office whistling a merry tune and headed for the supermarket. Delmore had given him fifty bucks and he figured he could cook up a half dozen dishes from *Dad's Own Cookbook*, put them in the freezer, and still get over to Grand Marais before dark assuming the old Studebaker pickup didn't break down. Delmore had kindly had the windshield replaced the evening before and B.D. had packed his meager camping equipment including a seventy-year-old heavy canvas pup tent from World War II. He had slept outside because the things of Berry's left behind gave him a severe lump in the throat.

Leaving the supermarket he sorted out his own cans of beans and Spam putting them in a wooden potato crate in the pickup bed. Delmore didn't like him driving the old Studebaker except when B.D. used to visit Brenda, the big dentist, the thought of whom agitated his loins. They both got some serious knee burns on her fluffy white carpet. He was supposed to stop by Gretchen's office and tell her how things had gone with the doctor but he was willing to bet top dollar that the doctor had already called Gretchen. The obvious solution was to leave a message on her home phone saying that he could be contacted at eleven-thirty any evening this week at the Dunes Saloon in Grand Marais. Gretchen's office made him dry-mouthed and nervous. It was the rows of file cabinets that put him off along with the many computers. Why keep records on everyone? How could the contents of so many lives be kept in the cabinets and computers? Way back when, a teacher would show them the contents of his "frozen zoo," all the marvelous dead songbirds he had found which he kept in the freezer. His own records began with when he and David Four Feet were caught at age thirteen throwing cherry bombs under squad cars in Escanaba, and went on to include every pissant scrape with the law since then.

He was soothed cooking Delmore's dinners for the week with Delmore sitting there at the kitchen table making uninformed suggestions while flipping through the satellite channels. Delmore talked back to the television. If a character, say in a spy movie, were imperiled Delmore might holler, "Watch out behind your back you fucking nitwit!"

After a couple of hours B.D. was finished making six stews, two each of pork, chicken, and beef, mindful to keep the bites small as Delmore's teeth were sparse among his gums. B.D. slid the Tupperware containers into the freezer, then called Mike in Grand Marais and was pleased to hear the area was currently shy of a constable or deputy though one might be hired in June for the summer when tourists arrived. Tourists were appalled when there were fights at the taverns and someone was needed to unsuccessfully keep the lid on tempers and extreme public drunkenness. B.D. was still legally enjoined from the area due to a past mud bath and the unfairness of the law.

Delmore was asleep in his chair so B.D. tiptoed off for his first actual freedom in six months. At the last minute he remembered to pack a couple of very large construction trash bags in case the weather turned bad so he could crawl into one when the tent began to leak. On the four-hour drive northeast he stopped at two creeks and caught a half dozen brook trout for supper. When he reached Seney with only twenty-five miles left to go to Grand Marais he relented and stopped to buy a fishing license on the off chance of getting stopped. It wouldn't do to have a game warden calling head-quarters for information. He also bought a cold six-pack reminding himself to keep the beer he was drinking out of sight when driving up a hill because there might be a cop coming the other way, an old survival trick of the North.

Feeling rather soothed by the beer B.D. still resisted stopping at either tavern while driving through Grand Marais. It certainly would be stupid to tie one on while it was still daylight. He greeted the lovely harbor and Lake Superior beyond and headed east for a few miles before turning south on a log road for seven miles to a place he loved not because it was the best fishing which it wasn't but be-cause of the gentle, unobtrusive beauty of the place. He was a little surprised about two-thirds of the way in when he felt an unexpected tremor of fear in his stomach. A mile off to the west was the location where years ago he had found a large wild cherry tree blasted by lightning, an object largely held to be magical by all Indians and a few whites. And not fifty yards away in a thicket of sugar plum and dogwood he had discovered a small ancient graveyard of seven graves. When he had told a very old Indian friend about the graveyard the man said, "Don't even tell me where it is. If it's found out college people will come with their evil shovels." Sad to say B.D. had met a graduate student in anthropology from the University of Michigan who had come north to the Upper Peninsula to study possible battle sites of the Chippewa, known to themselves as the Anishinabe, and the Iroquois in the early nineteenth century. It was all in the way Shelley's ample but well-formed butt handled the bar stool beneath it. He was smitten, not a rare thing, but this was a powerful smiting indeed. He almost prayed, "Please God, let it be me." Suffused in the mixture of lust and alcohol he had spilled the beans and showed her the graveyard. How could he do such a pathetic and obvious thing? It was easy, though he tried to convince himself later that he had been caught up in a "whirl" whatever that was. He and Shelley became temporary lovers and in the following summer, sure enough, the University of Michigan began their anthropological "dig." By then B.D. was involved with Lone Marten's ill-fated and short-lived project of a "Wild Wild Midwest" tourist attraction. Lone Marten was David Four Feet's brother but also a rotten-to-the-core scam artist and fake Indian activist. Their little Wild, Wild Midwest group attacked the dig one dawn with an improbably large amount of fireworks. Unfortunately the Michigan State Police got wind of the plot and in the ensuing melee Berry's mother Rose had bitten off a cop's thumb. Lone Marten and

B.D. escaped and went on the lam with Delmore eventu-
ally bailing B.D. out. Rose was the only one to do hard time.
B.D. was enjoined from entering Alger County west of
Munising, his favorite spot on earth.

But here he was encamped several years later convinced that no one remembered that long ago because he
rarely had reason to do so himself. These rehearsals of the
past were brutal so he quickly gathered wood and started a
fire. The concentration required to cook his trout properly
would help abolish the past but then while he was setting
up the pup tent and waiting for the fire to get right another
behavioral glitch struck him hard. About ten years before
in a bar in Sault Sainte Marie he had said something nice to
a woman of about thirty who was drinking with her friends
and she had responded by saying, "Beat it, creep," and he
had poured a big mug of beer down her neck and fled.
Unfortunately at the time he was well known around the
Soo and the cops quickly found him. Two nights in jail were
unpleasant. He and a buddy who ran the job were notori-
ous for illegally diving on old Lake Superior shipwrecks and
pillaging what could be removed. An antique brass binnacle
could bring a thousand dollars assuming that you didn't get
caught but they did get caught with the body of an Indian
in full regalia B.D. had found on the lake floor.

B.D. had set up camp and cooked his supper fish hundreds of times and now this simple act soothed him at least
temporarily. The beans were in a saucepan off to the side
and he scooped some bacon fat into his iron skillet and put
it on the coals. He took a handful of watercress and put it
on his tin plate which kept the trout from congealing against

the metal. He looked up to see the last of the sun's top dropping over the ridge to the west. He saw an evening gros-
beak land in a chokecherry and a group of cedar waxwings
were doing their twilight limb dance.

He ate quickly and was still hungry wishing he had
kept a portion of the pork chops and potato casserole he had
cooked for Delmore. Or the chicken and Italian sausage
stew. He took a swallow of the peppermint schnapps and
made his way down a gulley perhaps fifty yards to the river
hidden by alder and sweet-smelling cedar. He flopped down
on a grassy patch of bank, a slight groan on his lips, thinking, You may as well fully accept how awful you've been
and entertain good thoughts like the glimpse of Gretchen's
bare butt just before you handed her the fine-smelling pizza.
Finally he was released into the beauty of the river for the
last hour before dark. Through the trees on the other side
of the river there was still a patch of snow on a north-facing
hillside though it was May 5. The river was still high and
strong from the snowmelt runoff and he was amazed as ever
by how wonderful it sounded, perhaps the best sound in the
world this water noise. He heard the drawn-out sound of
a whip-poor-will which always made his skin prickle. He
hoped to hear a wolf in the five days he intended to camp
there as a den was less than a mile away.

The Dunes Saloon was far less idyllic. Taking care of Berry
had made him lose his touch at nighttime bars. You had to
pace yourself and too many acquaintances from years ago
bought him drinks. Three doubles in thirty minutes was too

fast and when Gretchen called at eleven-thirty he was less than lucid.

"How could you do this to me?"

"What did I do to you?"

"You were rude to the doctor."

"The dickhead treated me like mixed-blood trash. I've been through this before."

"You were supposed to let him examine your penis for possible herpes warts."

"My penis doesn't own any herpes warts. It's pure as the driven snow."

She hung up on him and he was sorrowful for a full minute but then Big Marcia snuck up behind him and grabbed his wanger. He turned with a smile to see that Big Marcia had gotten even bigger. B.D. thought she had maybe reached two fifty and lost some of her attractiveness. At two hundred she hadn't looked that bad. She wore the T-shirt of the girls' softball team, the Bayside Bitches, and now was perilously drunk and smelling of a cocktail called the Tootsie Roll which was a mixture of orange pop, Kahlúa liqueur, and whatever Dave the bartender might mischievously dump in. Dave was a fan of mayhem. Marcia wanted to go outside and "smooch" and since B.D.'s true love had hung up on him he felt justified in tagging along. However, outside in the yard in the shadow of the tavern she started to waver in his arms and gradually lost consciousness. Her back was sweaty and his hands were losing their grip. She had no belt to hold on to and his hands couldn't get a big enough piece of her capacious ass. He quickly thrust an arm under her crotch and as gently as possible lowered her to the ground. Now he was sweating and there was a twinge in his back. He looked out toward the harbor to the moon above the streetlight and decided to go back to his camp.

B.D. spent a wonderful night sleeping only intermittently in order to keep track of the moon through the open face of the pup tent. He had largely missed the moon in Toronto and since his inner and outer child were pretty much glued together he had been quite disappointed. All that ambient light in Toronto had also made the night sky short on stars. From childhood on he had been an addict of "moon walks" not of the tawdry NASA golf-club-swing type but wandering in field and forest in strong moonlight say from the three-quarter phase onward. Grandpa never minded when his seven-year-old grandson would head out in the dark because there was a fence around eighty acres of pasture, woods, and swamp and the tyke could always follow the fence home.

He fed the coals at the first glimpse of light and made his boiled coffee getting back into the sleeping bag to drink it and to study the fog that had dropped from the heavens. He wiggled like a caterpillar in his bag dropping a half pound of bacon in the iron skillet and opening a can of Mexican refried beans. He searched his mind for the remnants of a dream in which he was a baby sitting on a woman's lap looking up but he could only see the bottom of her chin. Could this be his mother? he wondered. Life was so fantastically inconclusive. The dream was so much more pleasant than the recurrent seminightmare of being painfully thirsty with a wet ass in a crib and looking up at a rough cabin ceiling at boards that varied from narrow to very wide. He'd asked Gretchen about this one and she said it was likely he had been abandoned.

He reserved his grease, pushed the bacon off to the side, and heated the refried beans. This magical combination allowed him to fish eight hours without hunger at which point a thick Spam-and-onion sandwich would fuel another six hours at which point twilight arrived.

Sad to say but in a flat hour he had ripped his cheap Japanese waders on a snag while trying to reach a late lake-run rainbow of a couple of pounds. The fish had snagged the leader on a deadfall across the river and he couldn't jerk the line free. His aim was brook trout but a spring rainbow made a nice chowder fish. When the waders ripped he expelled his air in a whoosh and floundered toward the bank falling forward in the swift waters. Both the air and the water temperature were about forty and he shed the waders and trotted toward camp a half mile away, shuddering with cold but still amused that when he reached the bank the fish had managed to free itself.

He stoked up his campfire to a roar, peeled off his wet clothes, and danced around the fire buck naked to warm up, rather unconcerned because he had dunked himself dozens of times during his fishing life and only irritated at himself because one durable pair of hundred-dollar waders would have lasted through the long chain of cheapies. He generally avoided powwows but danced some native steps he had learned, laughing at the memory of when he was about ten and told Grandpa that he wanted to be a wild Indian when he grew up and Grandpa had said, "You already are." B.D.

frankly didn't see much difference between Indians and the rural poor of the Great North except that the relatively pure bloods tended to hang together as if they were members of the same isolated church.

He bank-fished until about noon becoming pissed off because there were so many good riffle corners he couldn't fish without waders. He headed to town to buy another pair of the twenty-five-buck model. At a bridge on the main road he thought he recognized a very old man and stopped to say hello. The old man was trying to fish off the bridge in a hole behind a culvert and it turned out that the man was ninety-two and had been a friend of his Grandpa's before he had moved to Muskallonge Lake near Deer Park in the late fifties. The man said he had known B.D. when he was "knee-high to a grasshopper," the kind of thing old men said. He paused a moment looking at B.D. as if questioning whether what he had to say was appropriate.

"I was around that day that your dad came up from downstate all dressed up like an old-timey Indian. His car broke down in Newberry and he stole a pickup. The cops chased him up to Deer Park where he stole Clifford's canoe and went paddling straight out into Lake Superior on a stormy day. They found the canoe miles down toward Crisp Point but never him. I imagine you knew that?"

"Nope," B.D. said, "but thanks for the info." In a lifetime of hearing very slight and flimsy rumors this was the most concrete story yet. He wasn't exactly startled, just a little ruminative and melancholy imagining what it would be like to try to keep a canoe upright in a storm on Lake Superior. His grandpa was his true father. His mother was a whore of sorts but since she was a drunk nothing was probably better having known Berry's mother Rose too well. Who needs someone who could throw a naked kid into a snowbank?

At the hardware store he ran into Big Marcia who was buying some plumbing supplies. "B.D.! It's been years," she said, embracing him. "Maybe we can have a brewski tonight?" He watched out the window as Marcia got into her newish pickup. She always was a hard worker if a little forgetful.

He tossed the new waders into the pickup and walked across the street to call Gretchen thinking that if he fished until dark he might feel up to coming to town tonight. He caught her at lunch on her cell.

"B.D., darling, I'm sorry I hung up on you. I was having issues. Anyway, Thursday and Friday are prime times for conception. I thought I'd take two days off and come over. I'd need directions."

B.D.'s innards began a small spin which actually reminded him there at the phone booth of a big round childhood top where you pumped down on a knob and it began to spin at great speed and make a moaning sound that was supposedly musical. He told Gretchen that he would meet her at noon on Thursday and then walked over to the IGA grocery store to buy a bar of soap. He wished he had a better tent but when he'd checked tents out at a Marquette sporting goods store a good one cost the equivalent of seventy-five six-packs. Gretchen had slept in the pup tent the summer before with Berry when they camped out at Twelve Mile Beach east of town while B.D. had curled up by the fire in an old green army blanket. The very thought that he'd be in this severely confined space doing whatever with Gretchen caused his heart to jiggle.

He fished hard throughout the afternoon and evening and resisted the urge to go into town for a few drinks. He ate a mediocre pork steak and took a long moonlit walk and the next morning was ready to fish at first light. He headed off toward an area he hadn't seen in a decade past a hilly few hundred acres where the watersheds of three rivers began, the Fox, the Two-Hearted, and the Sucker. He got turned around for a couple of hours near the roots of the Two-Hearted because he had become inattentive in the middle of a pussy trance over Gretchen. It was inevitable that he would see parts of her nude body in the tent and maybe she would hear a bear and throw herself into his arms. Or better yet a big thunderstorm which she was afraid of would cause her to crawl into his sleeping bag. He got a boner while crossing a neck of a swamp which didn't help his sense of direction. Seven years of totally unrequited love and lust and you inevitably build up quite a head of steam. He cooled off and collected his thoughts while sitting on a hardwood knoll eating his squashed Spam-and-raw-onion sandwich. Spam is a decidedly nonsexual meal and he immediately received an insight on just where he was. He walked south about a mile and then traced a small creek that led to the Sucker stopping to catch two fair-sized brookies in a beaver pond. He was thankful to finally hit the Sucker and turned north for a mile until he reached his camp. When you're lost you avoid panic by not quite admitting it but when you finally reach camp you're relieved indeed.

He spruced up his camp and gathered an immense pile of wood because Gretchen liked campfires. He washed some clothes with his bar of Ivory in a river eddy saving his own cleansing until just before he left to pick her up in the morning. They would have to leave her Honda in Grand Marais because the log roads were too rough for its low-slung frame. He made a mental grocery list remembering her fondness for Sapphire gin, expensive but then it might turn the sacred trick.

On a rather timid evening hike to another beaver pond it occurred to him that Gretchen had made a shambles of his fishing trip and that after he had fulfilled his destiny as a sperm donor he'd have to take off on an old-time, full-blast jaunt. It was unthinkable to miss two nights in a row at the tavern but then Gretchen was difficult enough to manage without a hangover. He remembered the Valentines from a distant past where a fat, naked kid with wings would shoot an arrow through a heart which stood for love. The pain was certainly there and its emotional havoc colored everything. For example on his third cast of his fly rod with a No. 12 brown Woolly Bugger fly his backcast was snagged fairly high in an alder bush and it was a fucking chore to untangle it. Just before dark he hooked a fine fish, possibly a rare two-pounder, but the fish wound the leader around a protruding tamarack root and broke off. He howled. He had been visualizing Gretchen on her hands and knees in the tent and he was behind and under her watching the firelight shimmer off her tummy and breasts. If he had been keeping track of his line and fish rather than this the brook trout would have been in his hands. For a millisecond he thought he heard a distant wolf howl, not an infrequent night sound in the area, but it turned out to be the much more comforting coyote. It was a mildly spooky place. A few years back he had fled after hearing two bears fight back in the forest, likely over a female. Even bears are pussy-crazed, he thought, walking swiftly back toward camp so he wouldn't have to wait for moonlight to find his way.

Dawn came bright and clear and he spent a long desultory morning rather aimlessly gathering more wood than they could possibly use. Some puffy clouds moved in from the southwest and he quickly walked to the river to catch a half dozen trout for their dinner. He took off his clothes and soaped himself down in a shallow eddy and when he dunked to rinse himself the water was pecker-shrinking cold. All the tree birds were urging themselves forward into a pastel green mist. He was feeling ever so vaguely religious and remembered a friend from the sixth grade named Skinny who was the Baptist preacher's son. Skinny was always praying aloud for everyone at recess but was indulged because he was by far the fastest boy in class. He would say stuff like, "Who are we that God is mindful of us" which one day B.D. mixed up and said, "Who is God that we are mindful of him," and Skinny was shocked to tears. B.D. had tried to pray when Grandpa was dying but was unsure of the process. Now standing naked by the river he had vague thoughts of how the prayer of love is answered in coupling.

Before noon he was standing on the hillock overlooking the harbor with the gin in a paper sack and studying the weather which was discouraging. It was still warmish with the wind from the southwest but way out there hours and hours away there was a bank of darkness to the northwest above Lake Superior. As a student of weather he knew that it could be the last Alberta clipper until mid-October, wherein the temperature borne by howling winds could drop forty degrees in minutes. Two fishing boats were speeding back into the harbor having noted the oncoming weather.

Gretchen pulled her Honda up beside his pickup, all smiles in blue shorts and carrying a flowery suitcase. There was certainly no point in discussing the weather with her.

"This is the biggest step of my life," she said, cozying up to him on the seat of the pickup.

"It sure is." She likely knew that her blue shorts would prime the pump as it were.

She had brought along his favorite sandwich, liverwurst and onion with hot mustard, and a hummus-and-lettuce for herself. They ate while he drove and had a modest wrangle when he contended that when she became pregnant she should eat lots of meat to make the baby grow in her stomach.

"It will be in the womb, darling."

"I meant the general area," he said, backing away. "I just know that Rose took on the wrong fuel when she was carrying Berry."

"I'm charmed by your concern but I'm thought to be quite smart."

They pulled into the campsite and she floated around in a state of delight while he took her flowery little suitcase out of the pickup bed. He suspected that the contents wouldn't be on the money for the coming weather.

"Let's get the show on the road," she said, kneeling and crawling into the open tent.

"Maybe we should have a little drink first," he said, unscrewing the gin bottle. He felt butterflies and needed liquid courage.

"A small one. We don't want to subvert your motility."

He had no idea what she meant but knelt at the front of the tent and poured two drinks in paper cups. She waved the syringe drawn from her big purse.

"That's a bulb baster like I use for roasting a turkey." He backed into the tent beside her.

"It's not for cooking. It cost seventy bucks."

"Wonderful." He wanted to say, You paid the equivalent of thirty six-packs for that fucking thing, but held back.

"Just take out your penis and get started." She sounded a little floaty like she had taken a tranq.

"I thought this over. I've never whacked off in front of anyone. You're going to have to do it and also show me some skin for inspiration."

"Do you have a glove?" she laughed.

"I don't carry gloves in May."

"Well, anything for the cause. I did this for a boy after the junior prom and he shot all over the place." She opened her blouse and slid down her shorts revealing bikini panties. She grabbed his penis and paused.

"You don't shoot like you did in high school." His voice was quivery as he stared at her body and she began to pump his penis holding the bulb of the syringe near the head. It didn't take long and she caught most of the fluid.

"Turn around and close your eyes."

"Okay." But he didn't. He couldn't help but peek as she slid down her panties and injected the fluid. She caught him looking.

"You cheated, you fucker." She scrambled out of the tent giving him the rear view he so desired. "We'll wait an hour and try again."

He lay there in his depleted postcoital state thinking that this was almost as good as the real thing. Sort of kinky and fun.

They took a slow stroll and then walked down to the river where he gave her a first fishing lesson. She was well coordinated and after a little while could make a modest cast. She checked her watch.

"Let's get down to business." She hadn't noticed that the wind was picking up in the ridge across the river and that the sky was getting fuzzy. She crawled into the tent and stayed with her head and shoulders toward the back. "I need to be near the source."

This time it took longer and the view of her cocked legs and tiny undies so close to his nose beat the hell out of any Hawaiian sunset. He groaned but it certainly wasn't heartbreak.

"You didn't do as well this time," she chided.

"I can only do so much." Without asking permission he took a glug of gin. He was disappointed when she covered herself with her light summer sleeping bag to make the injection.

They napped for nearly two hours waking to the roar of wind and Gretchen had trouble locating herself.

"What the fuck is happening?" she pouted when she heard distant thunder.

"A little storm." He took a wake-up swig of gin and prepared the fire to cook supper before the strongest part of the squall was upon them. She poured herself a drink and

looked fearfully at the sky. It didn't take long to cook the
brook trout and a can of beans. She wolfed her food as if
already pregnant or, more likely, frightened at the rolling
thunder in the west. B.D. knew the rehearsal having been
caught by such storms a number of times in the Upper Peninsula in spring and fall. It could be real ugly if you were a
couple of miles from your car. First came a driving rain and
then the wind got colder and it would snow. It could go on
for three days in the fall but in the spring it was usually only
a matter of hours before it cleared.

They had barely finished their meal when there was a
slash of lightning on the ridge across the river and a mon-
sterous crash of thunder. She shrieked, dropped her plate,
and burrowed into the tent. B.D. piled an armload of wood
on the fire as the first sheets of rain hit.

When he got back in the wind was buffeting the tent
and Gretchen was sniveling. He hugged her while listening
to the rain pouring heavily onto the tent, knowing where
the main leaks would begin. As if on cue he felt water drip-
ping onto his face. Despite the closed flaps there was enough
twilight in the tent for him to see the leaks nearest them. He
shone the flashlight down the roof line and detected some
major problems just as lightning sizzled the air and there was
a hollow, raspy crash of thunder.

"I'm supposedly smart so why does this scare the piss
out of me?" she said clutching him closer. She craned her
neck up. "My feet are getting wet."

"Everybody gets a little scared. Delmore says it's the
'thunder beings.'" He could see in the flashlight glare that
they were fucked. The tent was leaking everywhere. Also

through the front tent flap he could feel the temperature dropping precipitously. "Just a minute."

B.D. burst out of the tent, trotted to the pickup, and grabbed a big trash bag from his catchall box in the pickup bed. He stooped and shoved the big pile of wood closer to the tent entrance. When he got back in the water was falling everywhere. He shook open the Visqueen bag.

"Get in here. You'll be dry and warm."

Gretchen got out of her wet summer bag and wiggled into the plastic container. Quite suddenly the rain let up but not the cold wind. In the remaining twilight he could see the driving snow through a crack in the tent flap.

"This is already working," she said, curled deep in the trash container.

B.D. leaned out and stirred the remaining fire coals and heaped on a pile of pine branches for quick kindling, then cross-piled bigger sticks of hardwood. He shed his soaked clothes.

"Got room for me?" He had left the other trash bag in the truck hoping for companionship.

"If you behave," she whispered peeking out of the container.

He slid in and grabbed the gin taking a couple of quick gulps. She took a few sips and rubbed his nude chest to warm him.

"We'll be snug as two bugs in a rug," he said.

"Of course, dear, if you say so."

They lay there and then the fire caught and the wind subsided. They were rubbing each other and she parted the flaps to watch the snow falling thickly on the fire. It was dark and the fire's eerie orange light in the falling snow looked lovely to her. Now that the thunder was gone she was feeling better with the help of the gin. She took another slug and passed him the bottle. She slid her hand down feeling the closeness of his erection.

"We could have a third session for insurance. We should stop on an odd number. Three not two."

"Fine by me." For the first time he was being allowed to run his hands closely over her body which was warm and damp.

She abruptly made a decision. She slid down her shorts and panties and turned her back to him, arching out her bottom and thinking wistfully that this was the way all mammals get their babies. He was thinking immediately that this was the grandest moment of his life. He attacked his job with affectionate energy. Afterward they dozed for a while and then he opened the flaps and studied the scene. The world was quiet but the snow was still falling thickly. These storms rarely brought more than half a foot of snow but he couldn't be absolutely sure they wouldn't get stuck there if the snow mounted to a foot.

"We best get the fuck out of here. Sit tight."

He pulled on his wet clothes and boots and walked to the pickup, starting it and wiping the wet snow from the windshield. He would come back the next day and pick up his gear. Despite his wet clothes he was still warm from his exertions. When he turned around she was shining the flashlight on him and half out of the bag.

"Stay inside. The pickup doesn't have heat."

He picked her up in the bag and carried her to the pickup. It took nearly an hour to make their way along the log road to the blacktop that led to town. Off to the east the blackish clouds opened and the moon shone through. She was snoring lightly within her cocoon. He had the absurd feeling of a reverse Christmas in May and remembered the holiday line, "The moon on the breast of the new-fallen snow."

The little village had never looked better and when he knocked on the motel office door he could see the bright lights and the snow-covered cars parked in front of the Dunes Saloon. The new owner of the motel looked at him askance but was pleased to take his cash. Early May was slow in the Great North. He carried her into the room like they were newlyweds. She sleepily got out of the bag and under the covers of the twin beds, getting out of her clothes under the sheets.

"You sleep there," she said, pointing at the other bed.

"It wasn't that bad, was it?" He smiled.

"It was bearable but I'm not intending to do it again. I got this feeling I'm going to be pregnant."

"I did my best. I'm heading down the street for a few drinks."

"Suit yourself, darling."

His heart was light with pleasure as he walked toward the tavern, turning around once to look at his tracks then flopping down in a vacant lot to make a snow angel. It was a fine one and he smelled Gretchen's sweet-smelling sweat on his hands. Somehow the big trash bag had been the perfect place.

The Games of Night

PART I

I am Afflicted

There was a bit much of me to stay in one locale for very long. I was too heavy a rock to sit on any shelf as country people used to say about especially difficult individuals, no matter that my problem was systemic before it was behavioral. However, I do not favor the posture of a victim.

My parents were both unsuccessful academics, my mother with a master's in classics and my father a doctorate in ornithology which he finally acquired in his early forties from Cornell after a twenty-year struggle with his colleagues and superiors. My mother was of Quaker inclination and grew up on a small farm near Fitchburg, Massachusetts, and my father was raised by Unitarian parents in Dowagiac, a small city in southern Michigan near the Indiana border. They shared the reality of their parents being disappointed in them and tended to be remote from their families. Both of my parents as academics tended to think that life was in the effort to understand it. Given this background it is peculiar that I became a hunter though only on two nights a month and I went unarmed.

If you are hard-hearted and hard-boned enough my father's problems were all in all comic. Simply enough he couldn't see well enough to be a competent ornithologist. I mean he could read but birds as objects of study are rarely within reading distance. His sight wasn't disastrously poor but if you're only right 90 percent of the time you'll suffer the ridicule of your peers. Poor-sighted birders can be amazingly accurate when they know the songs but my father's obsessive subject of study was hummingbirds and they don't sing. They're too busy eating to feed their furious energy. My father's main character faults were a free-floating dreaminess and perpetual ill-directed anger. When I was ten years old Cornell let him go from his marginal position as an instructor because of a nasty public fistfight he had with a colleague over a drawer full of sixty-eight Mexican hummingbirds he had hidden in his office from the prying of an up-and-coming hummingbird expert who was an assistant professor and who used his superior rank to bully my father. My mother never forgave him for their expulsion from Cornell which had offered her the only opportunity in her career to teach an actual course in classics literature. She had graduated summa cum laude from Radcliffe and taken a master's in classics from Harvard but had truncated her studies to marry my father. She told me later when I was in my teens that she had loved my father for a scant two years and after that their marriage was fueled by their intricate quarrels. Such quarrels of academic nature take place on the head of a pin what with both classics and ornithology being of severely limited use in our society.

I've always taken delight in the accidental nature of their meeting and my consequent arrival on earth. She was reading on an old wooden chair near a fine pond on her family's farmette near Fitchburg when down the gravel country road came a van full of birders (it's hard not to think of them as twitchers, the British name) led by my father who could see fairly well back then. He spotted the fetching girl but, more important, a relatively rare Hudsonian godwit wading near the pond's edge. He asked permission to enter the property for a closer look at the bird and my mother said no, that she didn't want to be disturbed while reading. My mother continued this habit of outside reading even when she had to bundle up against the cold. That afternoon while she was working a shift at her father's fusty hardware store my father entered to replace a broken thermos. They began to talk and the fatal tie was made though she wasn't the least bit interested in birds except those unique to Greece and Italy mentioned in classical literature.

It is pleasantly awkward to think of how close we come to not existing. Without the Hudsonian godwit on the pond's edge my father might have slowed down but certainly wouldn't have stopped. And without a broken thermos he wouldn't have visited Grandfather's hardware store. I'm only nominally interested in birds and a thermos is a trifling thing but I owe my life to them. If I ever bothered to design a personal escutcheon there would have to be a needlepointed Hudsonian godwit and thermos.

Enough of my parents. A few days before I left for Northwestern University in Evanston near Chicago at age seventeen, I noticed that my mother was packing several trunks and suitcases with books and clothing and a sparse number of bibelots and mementos in a spare room of our rented house in Cincinnati where my father's academic career had descended to his teaching life sciences at a junior college. This room was at the back of the second story of our house and I'd go in there on warm, sunny afternoons in hopes of seeing the girl next door rubbing lotion on herself and sunbathing. She was homely but her lush, almost tubby body was attractive.

Mother was startled when I entered the room and could not look at me directly.

"I'm leaving when you do," she said in a whisper.

"I don't blame you," I said, surprised that I'd said it, watching her pack her small, green Loeb classics.

"I met a man who's going to take me to Greece and Italy." She smiled at the thought of the trip.

And that was that. She taught a Latin course in adult education, her pay depended on the number of students which was never more than five, and she had met an Italian widower, a retired civil servant in his midsixties who loved Ovid and Virgil as much as she did. At my age it was hard to imagine that a romance had blossomed but I knew little of such matters. The day before we both left I met the man in a park. He was small, courtly, well-dressed, and had a fine sense of humor, the latter a quality totally missing in my father. It was a hot, early-September day and the air stank of auto exhaust and the fetid river. My mother and this man,

Armandino by name, walked hand in hand which embarrassed me but I managed to say, "I wish you well." She was forty at the time and I had no idea what she expected of this man beyond plane fare though they lived in Modena, Italy, with infrequent trips back to the States until he died at eighty at which point she moved to Greece for a number of years before returning to Massachusetts to take care of her ailing parents.

I suppose my mother was an odd duck indeed but then I had no meaningful base of comparison. She certainly wasn't what we think of as motherly but was a far step up from my father who tended to ignore me. From my childhood on she always spoke to me as if I were an adult.

My most peculiar memory of my mother came from a spring afternoon when I was fifteen. I was morbidly distraught over my love for an upper-crust girl who utterly ignored me. I was in the backyard digging my mother a perennial bed while she sat there reading aloud to me from the Rolfe Humphries translation of Ovid's *Metamorphoses*. I was too self-sunken to listen. We were, at the time, in Cincinnati, Ohio. Curiously she was never to see any of her perennial beds come to full flower. She knew slightly of my hopeless love having caught me weeping in the lilacs. I was digging with too much energy and she stopped me with a short lecture: "Samuel, try to imagine you are inside the house looking at yourself out the back window. Loving someone who doesn't love you is one of the world's oldest and dreariest stories. Loving someone who thinks they love you can be worse. There's no guarantees but if you don't love you're a coward. So now you're inside looking out here at yourself. Just who do you think you are? That's the point you have to work on."

This struck home. I have found it helpful at any given moment to know who I am, not to speak of where I am geographically, historically, botanically, geologically. I was amused in a beginning anthropology course at Northwestern to hear a junior professor say that the Navajo bow to the four directions on waking to remind themselves where they are within the nature of life. I spoke briefly to him after class and he advised me to read Clyde Kluckhohn's *Navaho Witchcraft,* surely the eeriest scholarly text in Christendom. Of course you can shellac Catholicism onto these people but it's a mere patina.

Well, we moved from place to place every year or two in tow to my nitwit father, dragging a U-Haul trailer behind an old Dodge. My two favorites were Bozeman, Montana, and Alpine, Texas, between my years of eight and twelve. I exercised a weak religion in both places in hopes that we could stay in each but it was a vain hope indeed. This was in the sixties but both places were conservative bulwarks against the social upheavals of the time. When we made the long slow drive from Tallahassee in Florida to Montana we were amazed to see actual cowboys doing cowboy things in Wyoming and Montana. I had never been interested in the usual cowboy-Indian myth but this quickly changed. In the parking lot of a shabby country cafe near Hardin, Montana, with an eight-year-old's occasional boldness I introduced myself to two preposterously tall Crow Indians who were drinking morning wine leaning against their decrepit Studebaker. They told me that their grandfather killed

Custer which proved to be untrue because it was the Lakota. My mother interrupted the usual quarrel with my father, apologizing to the Indians for my "cheekiness." The drunker of the Crows said to my mother, "You're quite a piece of ass," and she said, "Thank you," and curtsied. I noticed at lunch that my mother was particularly cheery.

We lived in a modernized bunkhouse on a small ranch about a dozen miles from Bozeman where my father taught. The rent was free on the condition that my mother look after the old rancher who showed occasional signs of dementia. This was all arranged by the rancher's obnoxious son who ran an auto dealership in town. The old man was a dream grandfather for me teaching me how to trout fish on a spring creek that ran through the property, ride a horse of which he had several, and drive the ancient Ford tractor. Here I was an eight-year-old driving a tractor like other ranch kids. My father questioned the legality of this but the old rancher said, "I'm the law of the land," which I learned was a typical Montana attitude, also true in our next stop two years later in Alpine, Texas. My father was forever complaining about the paucity of songbirds in Montana but my mother was generally delighted because the rancher's deceased wife had left ample perennial beds and a good vegetable and herb garden spot. My parents were always squeamish about eating much meat but the rancher had to have it three times a day and I joined in. He was easier to cook for because Mother had only to fry his homegrown beef, spuds, and to a lesser extent pork which he only ate for breakfast. I can still see her sitting beside the luminous peony blooms reading Virgil's *Georgics*, the text brought to vivid life by her surroundings. When we left Montana after two years I wept for days. When we said good-bye old Duane's voice was quivery and he gave me his spurs saying, "I wish you were my son." A couple years later when we left Alpine for Cincinnati which I immediately hated I called Duane and got no answer, and then his auto dealer son who said he was dead. I had intended to run away back to where I was happy.

After Bozeman our move to Alpine in west Texas was puzzling. There is a clarity to childhood because the attention you pay to what you are doing is total. Whether you're currycombing a horse or trying to catch a brown trout in a spring creek or teasing a rattlesnake to its exhaustion that's all you're doing. You're also a good listener because you're unsure of what to say except to disagree on principle with your parents. When I sat on the porch one day with old Duane having a summer lemonade he told me that in his own childhood back at the turn of the century there were still a few wolves in the surrounding mountain ranges, the Bridgers and Gallatins, and the huge Spanish Peaks to the south. His talk was intensely vivid as wolves along with grizzly bears were mythologized creatures to me. It was hard to connect anything in my schoolbooks to the world I daily witnessed on that ranch.

It was even harder when we drove south from Montana to the soaring heat of west Texas that August, a region that seems a country of its own. I didn't mind the extreme heat because it reduced my parents' nattering quarrels. My mother would lean forward in the front seat vainly trying to find classical music on the radio as we chugged slowly up the mountains of western Colorado with the Dodge laboring in exhaustion pulling the U-Haul full of Father's books and our odds and ends of battered furniture.

Looking back at my early life from age six I'm amazed at what trifling things determine our future. Being ignored by the rich girl in Cincinnati made me vow never to be as poor as my parents even though in my twenties I realized she was from a distinctly middle-class family albeit still far from our threadbare existence. And on the second day after our arrival in Alpine I was roundly pummeled by two neighbor brothers which caused me to begin a lifelong somewhat obsessive program of physical fitness that has lasted to this day. The brothers were aged ten and twelve and named Dicky and Lawrence Gagnon. I was saved by their sister Emelia who was eleven, not out of kindness but her view that she was destined to direct all activities. She whacked them with an old Mexican riding crop that concealed an actual dagger that no one knew existed except us kids. Emelia had had an early growth spurt and was taller than her brothers. Perhaps from reading a comic book she fashioned herself an Amazon princess and we had to call her "Princess." She was rather pretty and I felt a yearning toward her that I didn't recognize but began to understand in the two years of our companionship. Their family had only been there a year from Lafayette, Louisiana, and the father worked on pipelines. Their mother, Mina, was corpulent and mostly sat on the shaded porch, drank beer, read mysteries, and thought about what she would eat next. They were an odd pair but she and my mother became friends probably because Mina was knowledgeable about wildflowers.

Our shabby little stucco house was on the outskirts of the
poor side of town. I was lucky to be taken under the wing
of Emelia, Dicky, and Lawrence because they were the
toughest kids at the grade school. Their rarely seen father
must have made good money because they all had newish
bikes while mine was a pinkish girl's bike my father had
picked up at a yard sale. My tears over this indignity were
brief because I had already come to understand that in practical matters he was a nitwit. To comfort me he said, "At least
no one will steal it."

We rode far and wide into the mountainous countryside that first fall, hiding our bikes and hiking up canyons,
killing rattlesnakes with Lawrence's single-shot Remington
.22. Lawrence bought shells containing BBs and potted quail
which Emelia expertly cooked on a flat rock surrounded by
coals. Little Dicky carried salt in a belt pouch. He was quite
outspoken and announced one day in a semimutiny that there
were no princesses in Texas and that he was plumb tired of
calling Emelia "Princess." She slapped him several times
though the next day she announced that her new name was
Zora of the Amazons but that we only had to use the first
part. Lawrence told me that she had power over him because
she had caught him playing with himself and threatened to
tell her parents unless he was obedient.

And so it went for nearly two years. Our clubhouse was
in a shed behind our place where I did my exercises. We
had a small woodstove for the cold winter days when we
had to sit attentively while Zora sang country songs not very
well. Her favorite was Patsy Cline's "The Last Word in
Lonesome Is Me." We had a plan that once we could afford

horses we would rob a bank and escape south into Mexico and lead a free life.

Curiously, my father was known as "Professor" in the neighborhood though he was only an instructor at Sul Ross State University. We were respected for this and what with my mother so fluent in Greek and Latin she picked up Spanish quickly which delighted all of our Mexican neighbors. I think that my mother thrived because Alpine had a feeling of a foreign country to her.

Our second year together was more awkward because of Emelia's early puberty. At twelve and a half she had become a very attractive young woman with her light olive skin and coal-black hair. Her physical changes seemed to make her unhappy and she dressed as sloppily as possible to hide them, becoming an even more pronounced tomboy if that was possible. One day I caught my father standing at our kitchen window watching Emelia bounce up and down on the small trampoline in their backyard. He blushed in a way I didn't quite understand though I attributed it to his recent horrible mistake of having flown to Fayetteville, North Carolina, for an ornithological conference that was being held in Fayetteville, Arkansas. He was properly mortified and I felt very sorry for him though he rejected sympathy of any kind. Both he and my mother were distressed at the time because I was imitating the Cajun accents of Dicky, Lawrence, and Emelia. When their father had come home for Christmas that year I could barely understand his speech. The mother, Mina, who was from Mississippi, translated for me.

My own body changes began to fill me with anxiety as I was no more interested in joining the adult world than

Emelia. I suspected that they were accelerated by the hour of violent calisthenics I did in the shed before school each morning. Emelia was the fastest girl in the seventh grade and I was the fastest boy. We'd ride our bikes down toward Cathedral Mountain, then take off into the backcountry running and leaving Lawrence and Dicky far behind. Texas has strict trespass laws but no one seemed to mind kids. A rancher even gave us a dollar once for locating a sick calf. One warm spring day Emelia and I took a dip in a stock tank to cool off. Far in the distance we could see Lawrence and Dicky plodding toward us. Emelia was wearing a blue T-shirt and soft cotton shorts and the water made her clothes transparent. "If you look at my titties I'll slap your face," she said. I swiveled around in the water because her slaps truly hurt. She came up behind me and tugged me saying, "You can look a little but don't concentrate on my body. You're my blood brother." We had done the usual rite of making small cuts on our arms and exchanging smears of blood. She slid her hand down under my shorts and grabbed my erect penis. "Zora's great powers have given you a boner," she laughed. She massaged me with predictable results and when my sperm rose to the surface of the water she shrieked and laughed while I sweated with shame despite the coolness of the water. "That's your future as a dickhead," she said pointing at the floating effluent and continuing to laugh. "An eighth-grade girl told me how to do that. If a boy comes at you with a hard dick you do that and he becomes nice as pie." I continued to burn with shame though it was leavened by her laughter as if she had told a joke and the joke was me. Since Emelia was a blood sister I had restricted my lust to a photo of Janet Leigh clipped from a *Life* magazine that I'd stare at in a mood of concern. When she expertly flipped herself out of the stock tank the very visible crack of her butt in the wet shorts gave me another hot twinge. At my age of twelve sexuality didn't have a real aim or target but was a warm itchy feeling starting in the abdomen.

Emelia and I were to have two more collisions that melancholy May when our world began to disintegrate. Her family was moving to Albuquerque, New Mexico, in July to follow a pipeline's construction and once more my father had failed to have his contract renewed though another low-grade teaching job was in the offing in Alpine after which we moved to Cincinnati. He said that there were more warblers in Ohio and when I in tears said, "Fuck warblers," he tried to slap me but I ducked and ran out the back door.

Emelia and I found ourselves in the shed when her family went out to dinner and she had refused to go. She actually dominated her parents in the same way she did the rest of us. It was early evening and Emelia had brought over her mother's *Cosmopolitan* which had an article on "effective kissing." She was back in her soft blue cotton shorts and a white T-shirt that showed her braless titties. We sat on a dilapidated easy chair that smelled like motor oil. We kissed mightily and it shocked me when she stuck her tongue in my mouth. She tasted like peanut butter and grape jelly and let me rub her breasts but when my hands lowered she punched me in the Adam's apple so that I choked. She apologized saying she had meant to hit my chin. She took out my peter from my trousers and jerked it then said, "Wipe it up dickhead" with a laugh, grabbed her magazine, and left.

Early June was murky with sorrow except for my mother who fairly glowed having won a grant to return to Radcliffe for six weeks. My father and I were to drive the Dodge down into Mexico to look for a very rare humming-bird that was said to be semicarnivorous. There were said to be thirty-eight species of hummingbirds in the area we were headed for, the idea of which did not enthuse me.

The gods are not kind to young people in love and I was hauntingly in love with Emelia that June. I had an ex-plicit foreshadowing of the doom of our love. Our Mexico trip was only to comprise two weeks but I was sure she would be gone when I returned. My pillow would liter-ally become wet with tears though she shed none in my presence.

After we took my mother to her dawn plane my dad went back to bed and I went out to the shed to exercise myself into a tranquil frazzle. I had barely begun when Emelia showed up on her bicycle saying that we were going to take a ride out toward our stock tank before it got too hot. She always ordered rather than suggested. Off we went on our bikes both silent at the oncoming unfairness of our lives. We tried to sprint toward the tank a mile distant but slowed our pace in the gathering morning heat. Far to the south there were ominous thunderclouds but I judged that they would move to the east of us. It was years later at the university that I recognized the true meaning of that liter-ary term "foreshadowing." There was a large rattler on the shaded west side of the tank that buzzed at us as we arrived. Instead of letting a man do the job Emelia in her Zora guise pitched a large rock onto its head and it shivered in its death

throes. Rather than going into the tank in her shorts and
T-shirt like the other time Emelia quickly shed to her skin.
I felt squirmy in my innards at my first clear look at her sex.
She folded her arms across her chest and challenged me with
a stare. I slipped down my shorts and she said, "Your pecker
looks dumb," and then flipped into the tank. The water was
cool that early in the morning and we shivered into an embrace. She ordered me to suckle her small breasts which
were semiconical and told me to rub myself against her
buttocks which were clenched. She said that if my "stuff"
even got close to her pussy it could impregnate her through
the water. Afterward she tried to drown me by holding my
head underwater. I had become fairly strong and pitched
her by running an arm through her crotch. My arm seemed
hot where it rubbed against her chubby little pussy. She
stared at me blankly and told me to touch her "one single
minute." I did so and she shivered. I was dumbfounded by
touching her and looking off over her shoulder at a mountain and the thunderstorm that seemed to be approaching.
My hand seemed to be thinking about what it was touching and coming to no conclusions.

A lightning bolt hit but a quarter of a mile away and
there was a ripping crackle of thunder. We dressed and ran
to the Emory oak about a mile away where we had left our
bikes. We had only run a hundred yards or so when the
downpour hit stinging our faces. It was a rough and rocky
terrain so we ran with heads down and weathered eyes out
for rattlers which were a fact of life in the area rather than
something to be particularly frightened about. The rain was
coolish and we rubbed each other briskly under the tree to

warm ourselves. The oak gave us some protection from the driving rain. We began French-kissing and I told her I would love her forever and she said, "Why?" which has always puzzled me. I became hopelessly erect and we repeated our bare-butt grinding with Emelia pressed laughing against the tree. Afterward she went out into the rain past the tree's shelter and let the downpour clean my sperm off her bare bottom, her high clear laughter mixing with the thunder. It was one of those few rare images the brain stores flawlessly.

Early the next morning, I recall it was dawn, we packed our crummy camping equipment and a carton of cans of my father's favorite pork and beans and were off, passing the darkened Gagnon home at five-thirty A.M. with me swiveling in the seat for a last look. Her whole family had gone to a movie the night before and I had waited patiently on their porch for their return. I shook hands with Dicky and Lawrence and Emelia walked me out to their sidewalk gate. She said she was tired and had got her "monthlies" during the movie which was *Butterfield 8*. She said it was about rich people and that she was going to marry a rich man and live in a very high building in New York City. Our good-bye kiss tasted like Dentyne, a gum I didn't like. It was to be almost twenty years before I saw her again.

We drove south toward Mexico, a scant ninety miles south on our fatal trip, fatal for me at least so that in later years I could see the slender, attenuated line of my destiny as Route 67 heading toward the border crossing of Presidio and Ojinaga. I was chief navigator, normally my mother's job. Added to my father's other difficulties he was a dyslexic so I couldn't say "turn left" or "turn right" but had to point in the correct direction. On the other side of Marfa the Dodge had a flat tire which set my father to wailing. He was amazed when I expertly jacked up the car and put on the spare. Lawrence helped out at the corner gas station, changing and rotating tires, and had taught me the ropes. Lawrence got a dollar for changing a tire and when I helped I'd get a quarter. My father sat in the shade of the car reading Alexander Skutch's *Life Histories of Central American Birds*. I knew the book because I had to read it aloud while he drove. When I finished the tire chores he asked me where I'd gotten my muscles. This surprised me as his tiny study had a window that looked into the backyard and he must have seen me go out to the shed hundreds of times to exercise but then he probably had never looked in through the shed door. He was without curiosity except for birds and their predators.

This kind of journey is inevitably a stomach churner for a boy of twelve and a half. He's aware of how far he is from his friends who are more family than his own, his mother in distant Massachusetts which he saw once when he was young but the memory is truncated beyond bits and pieces, and the inscrutable dodo father beside him swerving the car ineptly to look at any passing bird, yelling "Aplomado" in personal triumph. On the outskirts of Ojinaga I saw two women necking passionately outside a cement-block bar and Father said, "Disgusting." I knew better having looked into my mother's volume containing the fragments of Sappho. Mother had told me in regard to Sappho that it wasn't for us to quarrel with the nature of nature. After my inconclusive good-bye the night before I had even read the fragment, "Eros shook my mind like a mountain wind falling on oak trees," and thought this was on the money for Emelia at the water tank and under the oak tree. Love was messy to be sure. Before we swam we'd have to step gingerly around all of the nasty cow plots.

I decided that Mexico so far didn't look very foreign when we turned onto Route 49 after an uneventful border crossing. This was the 1960s well before the media was full of the dangers of Mexico. Back then it was considered a serene alternative to our overpowering busyness, our grotesque squabbles in Vietnam. Emelia could sing what she called "Mexican country songs," really *corridos*, which were even sadder than our own and comprehensible with the rudimentary Spanish I'd learned at school which was a multilingual babbling ground.

Meanwhile I had the gut feeling that we were going in the wrong direction because I had just read my mother's copy of *Drums Along the Mohawk*, one of her favorite early books. In my then-literal imagination I wanted to be an Indian in the northern forests, perhaps capture a white girl from a settlement and live with her near a waterfall. Prophetically enough I intended to wear a suit of wolf pelts. Mexico was also the wrong direction for another recent reading experience, mother's copy of *Little Women* where I had the somewhat unpleasant perception that girls were only big women in miniature and consequently quite dangerous. Lawrence had told me how a nun had broken one of his fingers for "tinkering" with a girl.

We reached our campsite near La Poquito de Conchos by suppertime. No one had told me but it was grand indeed to see that we weren't camping alone. There were three other men my father's age, all former graduate school ornithology pals from Cornell. The dominant male apparently was George, already an associate professor at Yale. He evidently had some money because as a "treat" he had hired a Mexican outfitter and his wife, Nestor and Celia, who had set up our floor tents. George had brought along his wife, Laurel, a sullen woman interested in the primitive art of the Sierra Madre. She was lovely and the beginning woman in the very long line of attractive creatures who seemed quite unhappy to me, but then she was married to the kind of man described by Emelia's little brother Dicky as "just another asshole."

"I thought we agreed that no one was bringing kids," George said, looking at me with distaste.

My father explained that my mother had received a last-minute grant for Radcliffe and he hadn't wanted to leave me with "low-rent neighbors" which angered me. He added that I was handy and would help out around camp and wouldn't be going on their expeditions.

"She better watch out. We all know how those Radcliffe women like to cozy up to each other," George guffawed.

"You pig," George's wife said, sitting down in a camp chair with a book.

Off they went with their birding paraphernalia: spotting scopes, binoculars, cameras. I must have looked forlorn because Celia who was fixing supper at a big camp stove came over and hugged me and kissed me on the cheek. She must have troweled on her ruby-red lipstick because she left a smear though I liked its scent.

Nestor gestured and we took off in his ancient pickup. Nestor spoke English with a German accent and explained that he was half German Mennonite and half Mexican but the Mexican part won over when he ran away from the Mennonite farm colony at age twelve. I mentally seized on this, thinking of what courage it must have taken to leave his family at my own age, but also the possible fear and hunger. Nestor sensed my thinking and said his liberation from the Mennonites was wonderful. Anything was better than hoeing corn and the interminable praying. He ran up into the mountains and lived with a cousin of his Mexican mother's. While his father was constructed of stone this cousin was a hunter and trapper and made mescal. "There is no freer life than that of a hunter," Nestor said. Now he earned a living guiding rich men from Chihuahua, Hermosillo, and Mexico City on their hunts and sometimes American naturalists and anthropologists. He swigged from a flask of mescal and offered me a drink which I took out of politeness and which made me half-gag and choke from its rawness.

He parked the truck and we hiked up a creek for a half mile to a lovely little glade where the creek formed a rock pool. It was hot so I shed my clothes and paddled around quite stunned by the hundreds of hummingbirds in the flowering bushes, one of which rammed his beak into the smear of red lipstick left by Nestor's wife Celia. I yelped at my wound and Nestor laughed saying the wound was good luck which I doubted. He said that the local Indians, nearly all of which had been murdered by Mexican cowboys, believed that hummingbirds contained the soul of thunder in their bodies.

Not oddly my memory is blurred about these days nearly twenty years ago, perhaps because my unwittingly violent hummingbird was a mere peck on the cheek compared to what followed in a scant few days. It was as if Nestor telling me about his life blinded me to my surroundings for at least a few days. He said he had to leave the casita of his mother's cousin after the first winter because they were too poor for another mouth plus the local priest at the nearby village was always trying to fuck him. He had slept all winter in the goat shed under a pile of goat skins. The goats had to be herded into the shed late every afternoon because there was a jaguar in the area that would kill and eat goats. The local men were too cowardly to hunt the jaguar so Nestor went to the largest landowner of the area and said he could kill the jaguar if the landowner would loan him a rifle. The landowner was very amused that this mere boy intended to kill a jaguar and loaned him a single-shot .22 rifle and a few shells. Nestor hunted the jaguar for five months and finally killed it when it was sleeping in a tree. At the last possible moment the jaguar awoke and snarled and Nestor pissed his pants. He managed a lucky shot to the beast's head and it fell from the limb. It took Nestor two days to drag the beast to the landowner's finca and on the way an *hombre* tried to take the jaguar from Nestor for its valuable pelt. Nestor shot him in the head and he also fell dead. (Here I was talking to a murderer!) The landowner gave him twenty dollars which was a fortune in the mountains at the time though Nestor soon found out that the landowner had sold the pelt for five hundred dollars. Nestor was acclaimed as a boy who hunted jaguars and began to get occasional jobs guiding rich hunters but he was still often hungry. One of his hunters killed a female black bear and Nestor fed a remaining cub goat's milk but one winter day when he was cold and hungry he killed the cub and roasted it. When Nestor told me this he began weeping and we walked back to his pickup. On the ride back to camp he said that by the time he was eighteen he knew he was himself becoming a wild animal so he married Celia. He said that he had feared someone would mistake him for a lobo and shoot him.

At dinner I tried to tell my father about the hundreds of hummingbirds I had seen but he ignored me. The four ornithologists hadn't done very well and were disgruntled. The blowhard George overheard me and was angry that Nestor hadn't directed them to the place. Nestor said he would take them in the morning. George continued fuming and his wife said, "Shut up," and he did. I learned later it was Laurel who had the money. She was upset at my swollen cheek and doctored me with a medicine kit. The men seemed distracted by Laurel's shorts and brief halter and so was I when she rubbed iodine on my cheek, her breasts were grand and I got an uncomfortable hard-on in my camping shorts which she noticed and laughed. Later in the evening just after nightfall while the men drank beer and waxed sentimental about Cornell she was looking at a book about Goya in the light of a Coleman lantern. I told her shyly that my mother owned the same book and as a child I had been frightened by the drawing of the gathering of *brujas*, or witches.

"You're no longer a child?" she teased.

"Not at all, madame," I said rather archly.

This started a friendship that continued until last year in Madrid. O Laurel, what grace and protection you occasionally offered my life!

Early the next morning my cheek was further swollen and Laurel insisted I be taken to a doctor. Nestor dropped off the four men whom Laurel referred to as "birdbrains" at the hummingbird rock pool.

Nestor drove us north on the main road toward the doctor's. I sat between Nestor and Laurel who were talking rapid-fire Spanish. Laurel had lived in Madrid for two years studying folk art and I could tell with my own minimal Spanish that hers was formal and educated. Nestor stopped the truck and got out to talk to a man who was coming down an arroyo from the Diablo Mountains leading a packhorse. Laurel whispered to me that Nestor had been talking "dirty" to her. This upset me because naturally I was infatuated with her and consequently jealous. She was flushed and her nipples were obviously more erect under the halter. Lawrence or Emelia would have described the halter as that of a *puta,* or whore. I sat there in the hot cab of the pickup wondering at the inscrutable nature of adults. It was dawning on me that Nestor and Laurel were "sweet" on each other and I couldn't comprehend why. She was lovely and sophisticated and he was a weather-beaten Mexican about fifty years old whose features reminded me of the Catahoula wild hog dogs owned by a rancher near Alpine.

Nestor gestured us out of the truck and when we approached there was a terrible stench. On the packhorse were the gutted bodies of a wolf and her two pups. The man was animated and happy because he would collect a bounty for the animals from a local rancher. Laurel screeched, "Disgusting," and I backed away from the odor.

Back in the pickup I asked about the huge claws on the man's necklace and Nestor said that the man had killed the last grizzly bear in the central Sierra Madre right after World War II. Nestor also said there had been a third pup that got away and we would go looking for it in the next few days.

Laurel was upset when the doctor we stopped to see turned out not to be a real doctor but a very old lady with a bulging left eye that looked like it was full of milk. She lived in a tiny adobe hut and at first I was frightened but she quickly soothed me. She made a poultice out of clay and herbal plant leaves and taped it to my cheek. The old lady thought Laurel was my mother and told her to be careful because I had "vulnerable" blood. Laurel was pleased to be mistaken for my mother and ever afterward even when I was suckling at her breasts she would laughingly call me son.

Within minutes of driving back toward our camp my previously hot cheek felt cooler and my jaw less sore. Nestor teased me about having hummingbird thunder in my blood and Laurel began singing a song about love being strange. I was shocked when Nestor stopped the truck and told me to stay still while he and Laurel took a walk. I sat there thinking that life isn't as I wish. Nestor and Laurel were likely up behind the boulder and bushes fucking like dogs as my friend Lawrence used to say. Emelia had told me that she was never going to blow a man or fuck on her hands and knees. I kept thinking of the female wolf's huge teeth and purple deliquescent tongue. The dead pups were unbearable to me sitting there being treated like a pup myself. I slipped out of the truck and the radiating heat coming through the windshield. I heard Laurel yelping from the bushes and tears of embarrassment formed. As a young romantic I was getting my nose rubbed in the animality of people. I was so distressed I wished I had the copy of Virgil's *Georgics* my mother had bribed me five dollars to read. I wanted to be a noble farmer in a green and leafy land not waiting there in the immense hellhole of Mexico while the engine heat ticked off the truck hood. When they returned Nestor was soaked with sweat and brushing the dirt, grass, and leaves from his clothes. Laurel was merely smiling as if she had been reading from the little stack of *New Yorker*s she had packed into camp.

Before suppertime I had the mature thought that there are aspects of humans that make us barely governable. After returning both Laurel and Nestor had to take naps from their hard sexual work but not before Celia and Nestor had a nasty quarrel. I had barely enough Spanish to understand that Celia had smelled another woman on her husband. Laurel speedily retreated to her tent. I sat at a camp table in the shade leafing through my father's nature guidebooks wishing that I had brought along something more interesting to read. Disappointingly my father always gave me such nature guidebooks for Christmas and they bored me though in truth a lot of their information was helpful later. I sat there finally amused when Nestor woke up from his nap and remembered that he had forgotten to pick up his four ornithologist clients from the rock pool and roared off. I treated

myself to a beer from the cooler suddenly quite lonely for my
true love Emelia and our sessions in the cattle water tank.
Laurel got up from her nap and went into the camp shower
under a tree which was only a canvas shroud with gravity-
fed water from up the hill. By moving over to Celia's cooking area I could see Laurel soaping herself through a parting
in the canvas. Boys are natural voyeurs. While Laurel was
rinsing off she glanced out, grinned, and waved at me. I was
bold enough to wave back. After all I knew the secret. Laurel was my first full-blown naked adult woman and I felt
nearly ill, quite overwhelmed by what I was seeing. My
pecker felt like it was leaking and my face glowed hot as if
my whole head was a hummingbird.

When Nestor brought back the bird-watchers rather
than being angry they were effusive and babbling about
their great day though also teasing my father about a few
misidentifications. Nestor suggested a longer expedition the
next day that would involve several hours of hiking in steep
terrain but the men all wanted to go back to the rock pool.
Nestor then asked their permission to take me on a long hike
to look for the stray wolf pup and they agreed in the light-
ness of the moment. Unlike the other men Nestor was rather
burly but could scamper up a mountain like a goat.

I was sitting there eating my posole, a hominy-and-pork
stew, and listening to the quarrelsome men. I wondered why
educated people always seemed to be arguing. I noticed that
Laurel wasn't listening. She made a silly face at me and I
smiled. This reminded me of my mother who remained calm
about everything while my father moment by moment tried
to readjust reality to his wishes. Just then George noted

thunderheads far to the southeast and started complaining
that the monsoons weren't supposed to begin until early
July and here it was the day before the solstice and there
were already signs of the dreaded summer thunderstorms
and their flash floods. He demanded an explanation from
Nestor who only said that since he wasn't God he had
learned to enjoy the weather that arrived. Laurel quipped,
"Imagine that," and laughed. My father looked at her oddly
as if it was the first time he had noticed her. I was counting
and knew he was at his three-beer limit after which he would
snivel in the most maudlin way. A few weeks before at an
academic picnic to celebrate the end of the school year he
had had extra beers and on the ride home said, "People are
so evil they shoot their own dogs." I asked if that was the
reason that I couldn't have a dog because he was afraid he'd
shoot it. He leaned over the front seat and tried to slap me.
My mother swerved the car and shrieked, "Don't you hit
him, you lamebrain fuckhead," and I felt thrilled that she
was coming to my defense.

Everyone turned in when darkness fell or, it seemed
to me, rose up from the burnt earth. In this clime the earth
was the color of burnt toast until the monsoons took effect
except for greenish arroyos and, farther up the mountains,
the green conifers. I sat up for a while at the camp table
looking with Laurel at a Velázquez art book in the gas
lantern's light. It was too dry for mosquitoes but large, lovely
moths appeared. Of course I didn't admit to Laurel that my
pillaging of my mother's art books was because I was looking for paintings of nude women and inevitably picked up
a little knowledge along the way. I did admit that I liked

Modigliani and she teased that it was because Modigliani painted beautiful women. I blushed visibly in the dim light and she smiled and said, "I'm an awful person. You remind me of my first boyfriend when I was about your age. He was always trying to play with me." Then she asked if I had a girlfriend I played with and I said, "A little bit." She probed further asking what we did but I couldn't say anything except that we "rubbed" against each other. I was staring at her slight halter top and she released a nipple. She said, "Touch it," and I touched it with a forefinger which was trembling. She touched my erection through my shorts then said, "I'm being stupid," and walked off to her tent with the lantern, leaving me in the dark.

I left with Nestor soon after dawn with the birdbrains just getting up, muttering and looking for their gear. Far to the east there was thunder with the first of the rising sun casting its broad yellow light through black clouds. I felt weird and restless having slept poorly from my father's snoring and the vividness of the incident with Laurel, a euphemism at best.

We drove a half dozen miles on a logging road through a canyon road up into the mountains and then parked in a little glade under some oaks. I realized I had dreamt about that Goya drawing that Laurel said was called *La Cocina de las Brujas* and that had furthered my unrest. I wasn't listening too carefully to Nestor who by coincidence was describing Laurel as a possible witch. He insisted that some women were more than women and you had to avoid those who were too close to the animal world. "Of course I never have," he added.

Nestor gave me a canteen to attach to my belt and a sturdy walking stick to help me up steep places. He showed me how he would rig a noose at the end of his walking stick to pull the remaining pup from the den. "What will you do with it?" I asked, worried that if caught the pup would have the same destiny as its sisters. Nestor said that in his own private religion it was okay to kill a mountain lion or jaguar or deer but unthinkable to kill a wolf. In his day pack he showed me a bag of *machaca* for our lunch and a jar of goat milk, explaining that the pup wasn't weaned and at this moment was probably starving. He looked off to the southeast and shrugged at the storm clouds which were obviously coming closer in the vast landscape.

It was a rigorous two-hour hike to the lobo den fraught with those mood changes that victimize a boy of twelve. At one moment you presume to be a full-grown man climbing the rough mountain trail into your first true wilderness, and the next moment you are an academic waif, really the same as an army brat, and you are lonely for your mother and wish to be with her listening to the Texaco Saturday afternoon opera in the kitchen while she makes you both a hot Mexican chocolate and when your father comes out of his study complaining about the noise Mother says, "Please go away."

Near a tiny spring or seep coming out of a crack in solid rock Nestor showed me a set of jaguar tracks. I was frightened and he patted the big *pistola* he wore on his belt, saying that all the jaguars within a hundred miles knew his scent and avoided him. I was unsure of the truth of this but then I knew that even house cats avoided certain people for undetermined reasons. Nestor said that we soon would reach the den and my stomach growled in foreboding, perhaps because the dark clouds split by yellow lightning were approaching ever closer from the southeast and I could feel the thunder on the boulders I grabbed for handholds on the steep trail. Finally we reached a small plateau and Nestor rigged the noose on his walking stick and crawled through the bushes to a small cave. There were bones and pieces of deer hide here and there. I crawled after Nestor and we could hear puppy weeping noises. Nestor had a small flashlight which he shone into the hole then quickly dragged the pup out with the noose around its neck.

The pup looked woebegone, near death and did not resist as Nestor made a slurry of goat milk and *machaca* rubbing and mashing it into the pup's mouth, then as I held its jaws open Nestor poured it into the pup's mouth and down its throat. Nestor explained that canines processed protein very quickly. We sat there staring out at the impending storm and at the end of perhaps a half hour the pup struggled to its wobbly feet and Nestor pronounced that it would live. I took the pup onto my lap and scratched its tummy as I had little piglets on the Bozeman ranch. Nestor said we had to get out of there before the coming rain had a chance to cause a flash flood on our trail. He tied a piece of rope on the back of his belt for me to hold on to during the descent. I cuddled the pup against my neck and we started down the trail but barely had traversed a hundred yards when lightning struck a tall pine near us. It was shattering, deafening, and the top of the tree burst into flame. My legs went dead and I sat down hard on my butt and the pup sank its teeth into the soft flesh of my neck. I yowled and Nestor tried to detach the pup who wouldn't let go and Nestor's strong hand finally broke its neck. Nestor stuffed the dead pup into his day pack saying they would have to determine if the pup had *rabia* which meant rabies.

PART II

I am at Large

Looking back nearly twenty years or so at a few scraps of paper my first diagnosis was "congenital erythropoietic porphyria," or Gunther's disease, determined by a subtropical hematologist named Alfredo Guevara in a hospital in Chihuahua, a disease leading to scarring and disfigurement but so rare that only two hundred or so people on earth at any time endure it. After death, under a black light the bones of the victims glow. But enough of such pathetic details. The important thing was that I wasn't a victim of *rabia,* fearsome because a kid in our Alpine neighborhood had gone through the long series of hypodermics in the stomach to prevent death by rabies.

When we reached the camp in midafternoon after having to wait out the plunging rivers of water on our mountain trail, a virtual flash flood, the camp was in disarray. It had become sunny and hot with the storm heading north toward the distant Rio Grande. The four birdbrains had managed to get their vehicle stuck and had to walk "two miles" back to camp though their vehicle was clearly visible about a half mile to the south. The problem was what they referred to back in Montana as "gumbo," a substantial rain making a dirt road impassable what with the clay and sand turning into goo.

Meanwhile on our arrival Laurel had me sit in a camp chair and stretch my head over the back so she could doctor my wounds with a basic medicine kit. She couldn't get anyone's attention except for Nestor and Celia what with the four birdbrains still buried in their perilous experience. Laurel actually had to shake my father by the shoulders to get his attention. He looked over my wounds with his usual "why have you done this to me" attitude. He was all for getting in touch with my mother and having her retrieve me because he had important work. I had told Laurel about my pride and pleasure in my mother getting the Radcliffe grant so she merely stared at my father as if he were a maggot and announced that she would drive me up to Chihuahua as soon as the roads dried a bit. Her husband George was upset with the plan but she merely glared at him.

Off we went in the late afternoon with the air fresh and golden from the rain. I was laid out in the back seat of Laurel's Land Cruiser in a blanket because despite the hot weather I was already shivering from a high fever. My wounds pulsed with a life of their own which indeed they did have. The wolf pup was on the floor and I petted its dead body having so much wanted a dog since I could remember, and now that I'd owned a dog creature for so short a time my young heart swelled mournfully at its death.

I was a full week in a hospital in the city of Chihuahua lapsing in and out of consciousness with my extreme fever. I did have a few of my senses about me on the second day when I asked Laurel and Dr. Guevara who were in my room to please give the pup a proper burial, say under a cairn of rocks outside the city. Later I doubted that they did so but it seemed right at the time.

After the week in Chihuahua we drove to El Paso for three days of outpatient work with an old hematologist who had been Dr. Guevara's mentor in his medical school days. When they had parted I'd noted that Laurel and Dr. Guevara lingered on their kiss good-bye and I had natural suspicions. It is completely impossible for some to resist sexual temptation. Laurel had told me that she and her husband George had been grade school sweethearts but by the time they married after college they were not much more than spare parts for each other's convenience. George was pleasant enough alone with her but around other men he preened and pouted and became the falsely hearty blowhard. I described my parents' marriage and she said that it's puzzling what we become when love has fled.

This chat took place in El Paso where I had a small connecting room to her hotel suite. I was still too weak to have rejoined my absurd and perpetual desire, but then the second night I dreamt of Emelia and how sometimes on weekends we'd wander by the schoolyard and teeter-totter, a form of play usually limited to those younger than us but we seemed to like the metronomic almost autistic feeling.

Then the dream continued with Lawrence and Dicky
window-peeking in the neighborhood with me in tow. It was
slim pickings and we resorted to spying through Emelia's
mostly closed venetian blinds. It pissed off Lawrence and
Dicky that Emelia had her own room and the door was
always locked. There she was on the bed naked from the
waist down listening to the Beach Boys rolling back and
forth with a large teddy bear between her legs. Dicky
whispered, "What the fuck is she doing?" and I fled.

After three nonconclusive days in El Paso the medical people sent us on to Houston where help in a complete
diagnosis supposedly would be available. Laurel was now
speaking to my mother in Cambridge, Massachusetts, every
evening with a report on our progress. When I picked up
the phone I always quickly assured my mother that I was
doing well and certainly did not mention my imponderable
nightmares and full-body cramps. Mother and Laurel had
known each other only slightly at Cornell because graduate students with extra money were in a higher social set.
To be frank, other than my sometimes stupefying infirmi-
ties about which I had no significant comprehension I was
enjoying leading the high life. My life with my parents had
been close to the bone and good beefsteak was unknown to
us. In Houston we stayed at an incredible hotel called the
Alden though I spent at least three days and nights a week
at the hospital being probed, punctured, and tested by the
tropical-medicine doctors. Laurel explained to me that much
of medicine is pro forma and slightly banal so that when
doctors find an interesting case they become obsessive about
it. Early every morning we would take a fast walk for an

hour and then exercise in the hotel's gym though my system was frequently too upset by the drugs I'd been prescribed for me to be strenuous. Still I was regaining my strength and with it my hopeless, nearly berserk romanticism. Of course Laurel noted my mooniness over her and was chastely remote which wasn't really part of her nature. Early one morning when I thought we were going to be late for an appointment I went into her room which had a separate living and sitting space. I heard her snoring lightly and looked into the open door where she lay on the bed with her bare bottom exposed. I stood there memorizing her ass for my bank of fantasies. Her breathing changed and she said, "Your eyes are burning holes in my ass," and laughed. I knew that several times when I overnighted at the hospital she had gentlemen visitors. I met one who was a hideous snot from New York City who had lived near the Frick museum in Laurel's old neighborhood. Laurel had told me that her obsession with art history came about when as a girl she used the Frick as a daily escape from her "wicked" parents.

We were into our fourth week of my problem and it was mid-July. We took a three-day outing down to Corpus Christi's Mustang Island while waiting for a final diagnosis that was never to arrive. Laurel thought that swimming in the gulf might relax my tortured musculature whereas the chlorine in the hotel pool had made me nauseous. There was only a single room available at the nicest beachfront motel and my heart jumped at the idea of contiguity though there were two beds. Laurel teased me saying, "Just behave and I will too." We sat on a veranda the first evening and watched the big moon rising in the east. I was feeling swollen in my head and quite agitated. Laurel allowed me to have a beer which I had often had with Dicky, Lawrence, and Emelia, stealing from their mother's ample stash.

The surf was quite heavy because a modest hurricane had struck the day before to the south beyond Matamoros. Laurel often drank too much and was fixing herself large tequilas over ice. I went down the steps, shed my clothes to my underpants, and ran into the surf while she screamed, "Don't!" The rising yellow moon was glittering off the white-capped wave foam and I swam toward the moon. I felt unnaturally strong and hypnotized by the glory of the sea and the moon. I finally turned around and someone was with Laurel shining a strong flashlight toward me so I swam back. The last huge wave near shore flipped me through the air but I landed on my feet. The motel employee with the flashlight said, "Quite a trick, asshole," and walked away. I embraced Laurel who was weeping drunkenly. I took a breast out of her halter and suckled it. She stiffened, pushed me away, and walked up the steps and back into the room, pausing at the table to pour another drink. She slipped out of her skirt and sat on the edge of the bed looking down into her drink, then swallowed it all and let the glass tumble to the rug. I stood in front of her and pulled down my underpants, then hugged my chest which was sticky with the salt water. "This should help," she said massaging my penis. I immediately shot all over her chest and she laughed. Of course it didn't help. A boy just short of thirteen is an overflowing fountain. She stretched to turn off the bed lamp and I was on her. She struggled then gave up. I made love to her many times whether she was asleep or awake. I don't know what I was thinking because I wasn't thinking.

This was the first of hundreds of seizures in my life. I've often wondered if we metamorphose or only stand more revealed? Memory, or portions of it, so condenses the past that we struggle to reproduce the essence of it in the present. The sliding doors were open to the slow drumming surf and the moonlight. I fed on her vulva with my mouth with the moon shining off her bottom. We hadn't eaten dinner and I was mounting her like a dog when she vomited up some tequila off the edge of the bed. Before dawn she violently pushed me off the end of the bed and I knocked my head against the coffee table bringing on blessed unconsciousness. At dawn I remember her covering me with a blanket where I lay shivering in the coolish morning air. When I woke at midmorning I was shaking convulsively and she led me to a full hot tub in the bathroom after feeding me tranquilizers and muscle relaxants. Within an hour I was calm enough to go to a restaurant, where I ate an improbable amount of menudo, a tripe stew the texture of which reminded me of her vulva.

We spent the afternoon sleeping and swimming in the gentle surf, and in the evening drove south to Riviera Beach where I ate a prodigious amount of fresh seafood. It was still light on the way home and she pulled off on a deserted road and began weeping. She was so sorry about the terrible thing we had done. It was her fault and must forever be our secret. It hadn't been mentioned all day and I was surprised that I hadn't thought about it that much in my fatigue as if it had happened in another life.

It was Thursday and there was a vacancy and she had managed to get me a room down the way from her own. She loaned me a Goya book about the horrors of war with drawings of battles and dismembered bodies hanging from trees. At the seafood restaurant I had watched a group of businessmen enter all puffed up as if they were much larger than they were. My mother owned a book of Mathew Brady's photos of the Civil War and I recalled my incomprehension about the way men rend each other. I walked down the beach until it was dark and the top of the moon began to rise above the surface of the Gulf of Mexico. In the darkness I pulled down my trousers and tried to fuck the wet sand but it hurt. I walked up to the deck in front of Laurel's room but the sliding doors were locked and her drapes were drawn though I could hear music from her radio and an announcer say, "Scarlatti." I sat there with my brain seeming to bubble and my muscles clench and unclench. I wondered at my inability to think. A group of seabirds flew across the moon and my skin prickled at the beauty of it. It occurred to me that I could sense beauty even if I couldn't think other than to be sure I scented Laurel. I whispered through the crack in the door and finally she opened it. She said that we must never see each other again as if in a language I couldn't understand. We lay down on the bed and she sucked at me several times saying she was too sore. She put lotion on her anus and I made love to her there. She gave me several tranquilizers with a water glass of tequila. She looked at my raw penis with horror. She helped me on with my trousers and pushed me out the door.

At dawn a ranger from the Padre Island National Seashore found me lying facedown at the edge of the surf and thought I was dead. I was so weak and shaky that he gave me a ride the fifteen miles back to the motel. I certainly didn't remember wandering that far. We passed two policemen talking to a group of campers and the ranger said someone had tried to chase the "weird" stranger away from their campfire. One man had a broken arm and the stranger had tried to drown the other man in the surf. I remembered the incident very well and was amused when the ranger said the attacker had been described as a "great big guy."

Needless to say Laurel was relieved to see me. We packed up and drove to Houston. At the hospital they said I had an "acute blood virus" and gave us a big bottle of antiviral pills. We went to the airport and flew to El Paso where we picked up Laurel's vehicle and then drove to Alpine where my mother was overjoyed to see us. I was relieved to hear my father was down in Big Bend birding but was saddened to learn that Emelia and her family had moved to Albuquerque that morning. Laurel quickly excused herself as if in a slight panic to be rid of my company. Nevertheless I walked her out to her car and said, "I love you," which brought tears to her eyes. "God help you whoever he is," she said.

Back in the house my mother said she couldn't believe how changed I was in a month. She looked at my ugly throat scar and then the prescription on the big bottle of pills and then a page of the doctor's instructions which were beyond my immediate interest. My own aim was to stay free of doctors after a grueling month of them. We talked for an hour

about her grand time at Radcliffe. I wanted to tell her to
leave Father but I didn't have the courage. I felt utterly
depleted and went to bed early, quite relieved that the moon
through the east bedroom window had no effect on me.
Early in the morning I walked over to Emelia's and looked
into the windows of her empty house.

In the ensuing months I was to discover the awful side
effects of the antiviral drugs I only took a few days before
the moon was at its largest. I was a bright lad and it didn't
take much energy in terms of reading and study to perceive
that if the moon had such a mighty effect on the tides of the
world's oceans it could have at least a minor effect on the
closed system of our blood.

Late in August we moved to Cincinnati dragging the
usual budget U-Haul. I sat in the back seat not exactly
savoring our boloney sandwiches and making mental notes
on which landscapes I might want to visit when I was finally
liberated from my parents, especially the Black Jack Hills
of northern Oklahoma, and the tallgrass prairie in southern Kansas.

Of course this is a cursory view looking back at my raw
youth from the vantage of thirty-two years. In your early
teens your perceptions are incapable of providing any reassuring conclusion. That's why I used the word "raw" to mean
abraded, sore, the metaphoric tongue always probing life's
sore truth. I remember kneeling in the water tank and nuz-
zling Emelia's tailbone. Why should a pretty girl have a tailbone? I was disturbed daily because I had overheard in
Houston a doctor saying to Laurel, "This boy has enough
testosterone to fuel a football team." I wished not to be the

stranger I was. Why did I love a rich girl who totally ignored
me? My relative salvation in Cincinnati was hard study and
exercise to improve myself and making friends with a mu-
latto boy who lived two blocks away in the Tenderloin. His
name was Cedric and he was being raised by his grandfather who was a retired railroad employee who spent his
days playing the piano and reading history books from
Cincinnati's splendid library. Their little house was immaculate except for the kitchen which was a jumble. The
grandfather was a tad obese and obsessed by the idea that
man had eaten wild meat for a couple million years and
should continue doing so. Cedric taught me to hunt and
snare along the Ohio River and in whatever farm woodlots
we could manage to poach. We'd ride our bikes east, west,
south at least twenty miles from the city once or twice a week
and come back with squirrels, rabbits, raccoons, muskrats,
opossum, and occasionally ducks which were a prize. We
ignored hunting seasons and no one cared or noticed. Cedric
had a Stevens single-shot .22 which I carried strapped across
my bike's handlebars because it was a time of racial unrest
and it looked better for a white boy to have a rifle than a
black. Early on a cop stopped us but when we explained
what we were doing he gave us his phone number in case
we got an extra muskrat which he favored fried up in pork
fat. Over the next few years we brought him a lot of game
and sometimes he'd come over and eat at Cedric's house. He
was a great big man and would always bring a poorly made
cake and a pint of whiskey. Cedric's grandfather was the
finest rudimentary cook in my life and far later in the bis-
tros of Lyon I recognized him in the divinity of the ordinary

food that springs unbidden from the earth. Most would make light of a possum pie but they are fools indeed. When you're roasting, a young female raccoon is best and I preferred muskrat and cottontail simply fried after marinating it in buttermilk and Tabasco.

Meanwhile my parents were appalled that I had become a hunter. My father was speechless with disgust while my mother's dismay turned into curiosity but then she let it drop. My answer to them was the anthropological fact that people have always hunted. They would have been more upset if they had known that by age fourteen I was visiting this big black single mother named Charlene once a month, always near the big moon when despite the antiviral pills I was highly agitated. Charlene was amused by my energies. Cedric caught on to my strangeness one afternoon while we were hunting and were too far from our bikes to reach them by dark unless we cut across a marsh which he dreaded. I weighed only one hundred sixty at the time and he one hundred eighty but I carried him over my shoulder across the wide bog and still visited Charlene that evening with my ten-dollar bill.

Of course at odd moments we wonder who we truly are beneath the layers of paint the culture has applied to us. I was struggling to do no harm within the human construct of a permanent stranger. I read widely in all of the historical nonsense considering lycanthropy arriving at the conclusion that all of the cases, including those from thirteenth-century France, might resemble my own a bit but I was ultimately a child and I didn't resemble those subjects. The only magic was in the infinite varieties of blood chemistry and the viral interlopers that could not totally be extinguished any more than they later could with HIV. By my late teens I had been so winnowed and withered by the medical profession that I shuddered when passing by any medical facility. My father was without much curiosity about my condition and my classicist mother only thought I had a blood condition and valued the palliative of pills. It was Laurel who kept me before the Stone Age fire, Stone Age because for all the vast knowledge in medical research there were equally vast lacunae in blood diseases. This fact came into play because of Laurel with whom I had an intermittent correspondence that made no mention of our two sexual nights. She had left George and her letters were either from Seville or Granada in Spain. Through her Cornell University contacts she had been in touch with a young hematologist in Chicago. When I wrote that I was off to Northwestern University the die was cast. I arrived in Evanston near Chicago quite happy because my mother had fled my irascible nitwit father. I was starting a new life in which the only people I'd miss were Mother, Cedric, and big Charlene for whom I felt a great deal of affection.

I met with Laurel at a medical center in Chicago early one morning after taking a bus in from Evanston and my instantly dreary dormitory room. Laurel was worn from jet lag but still lovely and I was palpably excited when we embraced. The young doctor was at the same time cold and goofy, a pure scientist of the body who didn't want to recognize the human within it. I immediately had blood drawn into the different vials and then a disgustingly unpleasant spinal tap. This was on a Thursday and I spent a long weekend with Laurel at the Drake. I was curiously intimidated by the immense vase of flowers in the lobby. Back to the rawness of an eighteen-year-old's perceptions, and a relatively poor young man at that. Chicago seemed so grand compared to Cincinnati mostly because Chicago is a grand city. I was near my monthly frenzy and had cut back on my antivirals to have the energies that I could sense Laurel was expecting. It was all reminiscent of Padre Island because during our spells of rest we could look out at the moon glistening on Lake Michigan's wave caps.

On Saturday Laurel bought me some clothes because that evening we were to have dinner with her father. He was an arch and cynical New Englander who split his time between Beverly, Massachusetts, and New York City. He had a peculiar accent and teased his daughter about "robbing the cradle" with me. She blushed and denied that we were lovers and he said, "Oh, nonsense," and laughed. He gave me some investment advice which in itself was laughable because though I was on a full scholarship my main problem would be affording enough to eat, especially in the time surrounding the efflorescence of my infirmity. That evening I ate five dozen oysters and a very large porterhouse which amused him. They were the first oysters of my life and I was ever after an addict.

On Monday morning we returned to the hospital and Laurel's hotshot young doctor said I had both avian and canine viruses that were apparently incurable and had become neural. He referred to the diseases as "zoonotic." He knew about the wolf pup and I explained about the hummingbird wound adding that on the way down the mountain several hummingbirds had been attached to my bloody throat. I told him that my father and his ornithologist friends were forever looking for a rare semicarnivorous humming-bird that lived in southern Chihuahua. He was clearly fas-cinated and said he would do further pro bono research on my problem and see me again. I joked that it was unlikely because dogs hate to go to the vet's.

That early afternoon I rode out to the airport with Lau-rel who was on her way back to Spain to study art. She had her driver drop me off in Evanston in a wonderful thunder-storm. Our leave-taking had been melancholy and I refused to accept any money from her. At the time money was quite confusing to me and I felt better living on the edge on the minimal budget I would be earning as a busboy in an Ital-ian restaurant. I had resolved that because of my physical problems I had to run what people call a "tight ship." Ulti-mately the nature of viruses is far more interesting, compli-cated, and mysterious than the nature of superstition which is only an amalgam of ignorance and the predictable conse-quences of fear. My problem demanded that I become an ardent student of natural causes. The direct meaning of "zoonotic" is that I have been invaded by invisible creatures. There was simply not a moment available for the very human emotion of fear or the disastrous effects of self-pity.

Here's what I mean: after returning to Evanston from saying good-bye to Laurel I took a long walk in hopes of burning off my excess energies. By nightfall I was twenty miles north up near Lake Forest with my feet hurting from my cheap shoes. It was then I remembered the lesson of the stray dogs I used to walk with on the outskirts of Alpine.

Such dogs have a level of attention unknown to us. They
are worthy of imitation. They know they are strays so they
don't go "astray" as it were. Sitting on a park bench near
Lake Michigan far from my pathetically ugly dorm room I
resolved that I must always be able to locate myself geographically down to a millimeter, also historically, botanically, and
sociologically if I were to survive with my problem. To maintain a level of attention I also had to ignore my moods which
were only the content of billions of neurons at play.

There is a great deal that is wretchedly tentative about
living within the confines of an institution. A university is a
process that is always trying to interfere with its contents.
Despite the institutional interruptions I was an obsessive
student though I would have been well ahead if I had devoted my time to libraries and the splendid museums of the
arts and sciences in Chicago. I was a speed reader like my
mother who could finish an English mystery in an hour.
There is a grueling punishment to nearly all academic prose
which encourages speed reading. Naturally one slowed
down in literature and the humanities where the aesthetic
component offers reason to pause. When I became bleary
from reading in my major, economics (again, I didn't want
to be poor like my parents), I would return for a half hour
to Ovid or Virgil, Walt Whitman or Chaucer. Also to beginning Spanish, French, and Italian because foreign languages are playful. I took botany and zoology for the same
reason. Simply enough, I could see the spirit of random play
in all living creatures.

Looking back I see that at the time I felt envious of
those who could afford to follow their curiosity outside an

institution. Of course part of my modest repulsion came from the struggles of my father which had set me to brooding early on with my childish antennae wavering to pick up life's perverse signals that find expression in parents.

Part of my entertainment came from my half-English, half-Chinese physics-major roommate. He was brilliant in his subject and had an enormous sense of humor, and could answer any question I had in the sciences. He left at the end of his freshman year for Caltech but his gift to me was eventually enormous. What happened was that my mother's maiden sister, a librarian in Boston who had visited us only once because she loathed my father, had set up an education fund for me of a thousand dollars. In the spring of my freshman year I had bought a junky old Chevrolet and a good bicycle. I loaned my roommate five hundred dollars to move to California which in his mind constituted an investment in the inventions he was always diddling with on paper. One of them dealt with measuring solar winds (steady at a million miles per hour, but gusting to two million). This small investment eventually supported me for my entire life as my roommate was to become a pioneer in the computer field.

I had to have a car because I was exhausted with taking the Greyhound bus north to upper Wisconsin or Minnesota during my monthly difficulties. I couldn't very well endanger my university career with my inevitable energetic behavior. During December's big moon before Christmas I had fucked my Spanish instructor nearly to death and I was fearful for both of us. She was in her early fifties and had carelessly seduced me after cooking dinner for us. Luckily it was during the mutual loneliness of Christmas vacation so she didn't miss any of her teaching duties. The staff at Emergency at the hospital were sure she had been gang-raped. I brought flowers and read to her during her three days in the hospital. She had taken her PhD at Columbia writing her dissertation on Antonio Machado. After our unforgettable experience she quoted a Machado passage to me from her hospital bed:

> Look in your mirror for the other one,
> the one who accompanies you.

We remained friends but naturally not lovers and this fearsome experience taught me to seek out the big tavern tarts of the North in Duluth, Minnesota, or Superior, Wisconsin, and occasionally vigorous black women in Chicago, one of whose pimps I had to throttle perhaps fatally though I found nothing in the *Tribune* about it.

The Great North brought me back to hunting with open arms but more so as a retreat from areas where I might do damage. My life began to take firm shape around the principle of finding a relatively safe place for my seizures, and then I would have to move on for the next month's two-day period because my memory of what I'd done during the seizures was somewhat short-circuited so that I only remembered in visual jolts. For instance I was camped near Cayuga in northern Wisconsin in the Chequamegon-Nicolet National Forest and on a late-afternoon hike on a bitterly cold and snowy late November day I came upon a vacant deer-hunting camp of three floor tents. There was a hindquarter of venison hanging from a cache pole. I maneuvered the meat to the ground and was making off with it when a burly man emerged from one of the tents and began shouting at me. I ran with the hindquarter under an arm and he gave chase on a snowmobile. Rather than backtracking toward my own camp I entered a swampy delta near a small river thinking that the thick brush would prevent him from following. Unfortunately he knew the landscape better than I did and was waiting on a tract downstream. When he rushed at me I swung the frozen venison quarter which likely weighed thirty pounds striking him on the head. I lifted his body onto his snowmobile and ran it into the river hoping to make it look like an accident.

Frankly I doubted if he survived. The hunter was hunted. The next morning I remembered this in the briefest visual images and recalled the feelings especially in my hands when the meat slammed into his head. I moved camp a half dozen miles and spent the night thawing, cooking, and eating the meat, a grand feast indeed. I heard wolves howl in the distance and responded.

And so life went. I graduated from Northwestern on an accelerated program in a little more than two years and moved to Minneapolis where I took courses on property management. I was able to set myself up overseeing remote properties for wealthy men in Minneapolis and Chicago. I rarely ever met the men themselves but dealt with their money managers who at first were suspicious of my peerless academic credentials. I explained that I was the son of a naturalist and had always suffered from acute claustrophobia.

I further offered that man had spent a couple of million years out of doors and had only recently moved indoors. I was likely less evolved except intellectually and preferred the outside. A couple of them said, "Oh, the lone wolf type" and I jokingly responded, "More like a lone dog."

In successive years I took care of properties in the western Dakotas, Wyoming, northern Minnesota, and several places in Montana. I thrived especially in winter when for weeks, sometimes a month, I'd never see another soul except when traveling out for supplies. It's a comfort for wealthy men to own such properties even though they rarely visit them except for a short time in the summer. I stayed away from keeping an eye on working ranches for the obvious reason of my monthly infirmity. To counter the emotional starvation of keeping my personal lid on so tight I read poetry, the best of world fiction, and listened to classical music and also rhythm and blues the passion of which intrigued me. I also began a lifelong project of studying the languages of the nonhuman creatures, quite amazed to find myself fallen into my father's obsession with birds. With most mammalian species the language is in the nose which was equally fascinating. I did a great deal of hunting for meat, and to avoid the curiosity of game wardens I rarely used a rifle. I followed the path of the great anthropologist Louis Leakey by hunting in trees. Elk were too large but deer were manageable. You baited an area beneath a tree with fruit or grain and waited up there on a branch, falling on the creature with a knife in hand. Your weight usually broke the animal's back, especially the young females who were the tastiest eating.

Sadly I spent a great deal of time in a state of sexual deprivation in these years. My best outlet was in the company of large Indian women who abound in the many reservation areas of the American West. I was making decent money and could afford to be generous in terms of food, alcohol, and outright cash. In our long occasionally grotesque history we have treated these people with a hygienic savagery they could never imagine. It seems that the most civilized and mechanized countries are the best at meting out slow torture and prolonged and sophisticated punishment. In the wake of World War II we treated the Japanese and Germans far better than our resident natives.

My body had begun to bring me down to my very sore knees after a half dozen years in the West. I had continued eating mountainous amounts of meat and because of that along with the extreme physical exertion my joints had become occasionally cripplingly painful. At the time I was looking after a large property near the Washakie Wilderness Area in Wyoming and one spring morning no longer able to bear the pain I drove fifty miles over to Meeteetse to visit a very old doctor who, after elementary lab work, determined that I had enough purines in my blood to kill any human who wasn't part dog. I liked his humor. He said ranch hands who lived in remote line shacks and ate only meat and beans had modest versions of my blood problem. While looking at my body he said it resembled that of a bulldogger (a rodeo cowboy who leaps on a steer from a horse and wrestles it to the ground). I joked that I only wrestled deer for dinner. He advised that I go the tropics

and eat fruit, rice, and fish for a decade or my goutish blood
would permanently cripple me.

A few days later by sheer luck I was liberated. I occasionally corresponded with my Chinese-English roommate
from Northwestern and I heard from him that he had sold
his small company in Palo Alto and wanted to know what
to do with my share. I called and was somewhat stunned at
the amount. I asked him to wire it to the bank in Chicago
that had held my original college fund and my small savings
over the years. Since it was necessary for me to be mobile I
had to live simply which anyway was my preference. Any
money more than the minimum for my needs would blind
me to the actual world I had come to love. My continuing
motto was that nothing is what it appears to be. I had the
advantage of being a permanent stranger on earth which
gave me quite a different point of view. True, my character
was occasionally violent but it seemed to me that most men
have an itchy trigger finger in the womb. My own life would
always be a barely containable arc but it now needed an
adjustment in direction.

I packed up and drove east with vague intentions of
going to Madrid which could be settled at an airport. I thought
of my mother and Laurel both of whom I corresponded with
every month or two. My mother was amused when I told her
that when I read certain passages in Ovid's *Metamorphoses* or
in Virgil's *Georgics* I would recall the visual ambience where I
first read the passages near Bozeman, or in Alpine, or in Cincinnati. Location is everything when we are young animals
and our survival depends on our attentiveness to where we

are. The young are always walking on thin ice. I was jolted when Mother wrote that she thought my friendship with Emelia was wonderful because every boy should have a sister. When I wrote back teasingly that my friendship with Emelia was rather more physically intense than a sister could offer she answered that by far the best sex of her life had been at fourteen when she and the neighbor boy had spent a long summer necking and "petting" out in the far corner of the orchard. This news curiously made me wonder about the nature of language I had been observing in the creature world. An emotion arises and you express it with a noise. Or you smell something and recite the nature of the smell to yourself in a wordless language. If on a rare occasion I wrote to Mother and Laurel the same evening I was amazed by the difference in language I used on the two. To a certain extent my language was a defense, an apologia for my nature, but then I was duplicitous because I couldn't very well express my true nature could I? As a boy I had been fascinated with "secret codes" so I devised a simple alphabetical code to at least express my nature to myself. This helped alleviate the essential loneliness of being a true stranger and the disadvantage of a single child not born among a human litter. Were I to die and someone find my journal the contents would look like gibberish except to a cryptographer to whom my code would be simpleminded. Here is a decoded sample:

Aug. 4
    Encamped along the Bois de Sioux River between Wahpeton and Sisseton in far eastern Dakotas. Would

have preferred a motel for my aching bones but my monthly fit is upon me. Awoke after dawn and noted with despair the severed head and feet of a piglet near me and the still warm coals of a fire on which I made coffee. Obviously I had feasted on a piglet and some night images returned in my brain's light show. A moonlit barnyard. Grabbing a piglet from a pen while the sow cowered at my scent. Crushed piglet's neck to still its squeal. Very large farm dog jumped at me. Plunged thumb and forefinger into dog's eye sockets and drowned it in water trough. Ran as yard light came on.

Took early walk to ease full stomach and cramped body. Heard chattering on small gravel road. Two girls bird-watching on their old bikes. They looked Indian or at least half-breed, from local Chippewa reserve. Said their names were Lise and Louise. I said I heard a larkspur and they said more likely a horned lark. I was sideways to them and when I turned they screamed, "Rougarou rougarou rougarou" and raced off on their bikes. I looked down and my shirt was covered with piglet blood. I felt my face which was caked with grease and blood. I hastily washed up in river, changed clothes, and fled in my pickup.

A few hours south I stopped at the public library in Sioux Falls and determined in a section devoted to local Native Americans that *rougarou* was a métis term for a lycanthrope, French-sounding as Natives intermarried with French trappers.

I passed the inevitable second night of my fit camped north of La Crosse, Wisconsin. Still full of pig meat I spent the night swimming in the Mississippi. Dawn found me well downriver and some kindly fishermen gave me a ride in their motorboat back to my campsite about a dozen miles north. They seemed uncomfortable in my naked and overmuscled presence and were glad to get rid of me.

Other than for the infernal traffic it was grand to revisit Chicago. Oddly, traffic jams remind me of overflowing public toilets, in short, our condensed excrescences, and those religious stampedes that kill so many in the Middle East and India. After buying some nice clothes I checked into the Drake what with my newfound financial luck. I had been without a television for seven years in the West and turned it on seeing something that was also strangely reminiscent of a traffic jam. It was a minute or so of the audience at a rock concert. They were howling and jumping up and down, their faces contorted in pleasure that resembled subdued rage.

I had time for a brief visit to Northern Trust to straighten out my financial matters. The bank officer was surprised that I planned on living on so little per year. I explained that I had been working for very wealthy men the past seven years and disapproved of the way their money sterilized their lives. I preferred a simpler life on the edge to continue my studies in nonhuman language. Perhaps down the road I would draw out more funds to build myself a cabin someplace remote or to take a fishing trip to some foreign place. The officer was a little melancholy and said, "I suppose my life is a bit sterile."

On the way back to the hotel in the late afternoon I questioned my unrest. It was the third night of a big moon by which time I was normally okay but I felt fearful of having even a modest spell in the city. The steak restaurant where I had eaten a decade ago with Laurel and her father was just opening. They were fully booked but I begged and they allowed me to eat a porterhouse and three dozen oysters at the bar while drinking a bottle of French wine. The bartender was a little troubled with my speed eating and I explained I had been in the mountains for a long time without a first-rate meal.

I returned to my room tentatively happy that the wine had calmed me down. I sat at the window for an hour looking out at Lake Michigan and thinking I might need a swim but then rejected the idea remembering my swim of the night before. It occurred to me that if one bottle of wine had helped my disposition two bottles might be a good idea. I recalled seeing a sign in the foyer for the hotel's Cape Cod Room, a seafood restaurant. I went down and ate the first lobster of my life and three dozen oysters, accompanying the meal with a bottle of white wine. Back in my room my joints were shrieking at my wolfish behavior with me knowing how quickly a canine can process protein compared to a human. I had a shower thinking I might take a stroll and find a prostitute but when I got out of the shower I was appalled at my semicrouched, hypermuscular figure in the mirror. My brain flooded with depression and I impulsively called the geeky doctor I had visited with Laurel so many years before. Naturally I only reached his message machine but he called back within a restless hour in which I drank a couple of shooters from the minibar. Normally I drink rarely but alcohol seemed to help. I told the doctor all of my problems and symptoms in a mad rush and he offered to meet me in Emergency at his local hospital which wasn't that far away. He said he had often thought of me in the transpired years and had come up with some possible remedies.

I walked swiftly the dozen blocks to the hospital and he was waiting. In one of those small rooms with the walls plastered with grotesque posters of cross sections of bodies I let down my guard and poured out all the worst of my behavior leaving out the few possible deaths at my hands. I admitted my wild meat eating and my two-day-a-month seizures which occasionally lapsed into three.

He listened to my forlorn babbling while closely inspecting my body which he without humor pronounced perfectly suited for prehistoric life. When I fell silent I began to study him closely and sensed a mildly deranged aspect to his character as if he were a doctor in one of those "creature features," horror movies I used to watch with Emelia, Lawrence, and Dicky with all of us huddled in fear close together on the sofa. He drew a number of vials of blood and admitted that my first visit eight years before had deeply troubled him, especially his pride as he had graduated at the top of his class at both his university and medical school. Now he was involved in the first studies of HIV which was slowly making its appearance in 1979. He said he would have to meet me the following evening in his small private laboratory because the treatment he expected to make was "extralegal." He trusted me only because of my desperation for a cure. He called me a cab and gave me a strong sedative telling me with a crazy grin to "behave" myself. I was struck by the feeling in his demeanor that he had lost the hubris I first sensed so many years before. He walked me out to a street corner talking in little more than a whisper about how much in the human body wasn't correctable but that it could be temporarily steered. As I was getting into the cab I stared at two passing young women who were obviously prostitutes. He took my arm in his weak grip and said, "No," adding that I was in grave danger of dying within a few years unless my seizures could be contained. I was properly terrified and eager for the safety of my room though on the elevator I exchanged looks with a rather dumpy middle-aged woman who appeared to be up for anything.

I had been exchanging calls with my mother in Italy and early in the morning I was awakened by her with a request that I see her first rather than flying to Madrid to spend time with Laurel. Mother's elderly husband was ill and she needed help for a few days guiding an older Cincinnati couple around northern Italy. My mother had always been a phenomenally bad driver mostly because, or so she said, driving was boring and she couldn't concentrate on little things like staying within the lines. I told her I was waiting for a diagnosis and she suggested that I call my father in Dowagiac which was only a couple of hours from Chicago. This was already on my mind more out of curiosity than affection. I hadn't seen him in ten years so I called and we made plans, it being Saturday morning and he wouldn't be teaching. I ate a boringly meatless break-

fast to help my joints and their overload of purines and then
called the travel agent in the hotel and changed my flight
from Madrid to Milan. I was chafing with claustrophobia
because for years my mornings had included at least a two-
hour walk and run in a peopleless landscape. A change in
routine as we all know can come bearing more than a hint
of vertigo. At my room service breakfast I had watched a
TV documentary dealing with the enormous anacondas in
the swamps of Venezuela and I had an urge to wrestle with
one of these beasts to see if I could subdue it, admittedly
a strange idea. I had a stroke of luck downstairs when a
bellhop retrieved my pickup truck. I had chatted with him
before about his plan to drive to Alaska with a friend and
now I made a generous offer to sell him the pickup. Looking at the truck my routineless vertigo gave me a glimmer of nausea because the truck seemed to represent my
life as a stranger enduring all of those seizures in the re-
motest landscapes. I had to try something else for a while
though I felt doomed to end my life in the Centennial Valley, a nearly empty place of 350,000 acres down on the
border between southwest Montana and Idaho. Absolutely
no one is there in the winter which would suit me fine.
When your body is slowly immolating itself extreme cold
is attractive.

To my surprise my father was happy, absurdly so. He
was looking after his infirm mother with the help of a black
practical nurse and teaching science at a middle school,
sixth, seventh, and eighth grades, over west of Dowagiac
in Benton Harbor. My father said giddily that it gave him

such pleasure to teach science to those so eager to learn unlike the usual whining college students. Even now in the summer he was teaching gratis to students who had fallen behind out of poverty. He said his first two years after we had "abandoned" him were difficult but now he was thriving. I detected that he and the practical nurse were sleeping together and was mildly jealous of this domesticity. We had a nice roast chicken for lunch then pushed my father's infirm mother around Dowagiac in her wheelchair. The small town was full of the kind of well-built old homes rarely seen in the sparser areas west of the Mississippi. I enjoyed my daffy grandmother who was confident that her eccentric perceptions represented the real world. For instance, she greeted certain trees she had known since her childhood. I regretted leaving in the late afternoon to ensure that I'd make my doctor's appointment.

In the doctor's minimalist laboratory he poured us a vodka saying that he had been quite distressed of late because he and his colleagues in the field expected that HIV would kill tens of millions. This was difficult to believe in 1979 but of course proved to be true. He repeated that in my present state my uncontrollable diet and seizures would certainly kill me. He had prepared a drug mixture of a unique nature and I'd have to return every year for a refill. Chemistry is certainly my weakest point but he said the bottle of spansules he gave me included ketamine, an animal tranquilizer, plus Xylazine and atropine to calm the effects of the ketamine, plus a small amount of Thorazine which is normally used for schizophrenics. He could think of no other way to preserve my life. I was to find the safest possible place for taking the drugs for seventy-two hours. I thanked him and left. I spent a long evening reading tourist guidebooks, eating a piece of fish, and drinking a bottle of pallid white wine in my room rather than going out for the longed for porterhouse and oysters.

PART III

I Look for a Home

By age thirty most of us have found, and are perhaps confined by, the arc of our lives. We wander in the sphere of our idiosyncrasies usually unmindful of what a poet said: "Beware, O wanderer, the road is walking too."

I gave up on my obsession with the language of living creatures other than human while staying the usual twenty-seven days in Reggio, in Italy. I had rented a bicycle and taken a long ride north to see the ruins of the eleventh-century castle of Matilda (I think it is called the Castle of Canossa and was owned by Matilda of Tuscany) who once owned northern Italy and saved the Catholic Church from the powerful Germans, a matter of minimal interest to me. I was intrigued by Matilda because she wrote poetry, practiced falconry, and hunted with hounds, in short, an ideal woman.

It was a cold day, wet and nasty, with the last mile up the mountain, which was enveloped in a cloud, quite arduous. As I've said I need to know the history, among other things, of any area I inhabit and in Europe it was quite a job compared to America where in many areas west of the Mississippi the history is of nominal content if it exists at all beyond the history of Native tribes and the unheroic efforts of those who stole their land to raise a limitless number of cows.

Anyway, in the cold foggy rain I was remarking to myself what discomfort my curiosity brought upon me, in short, what the fuck was I doing? The caretaker of the property was so obviously appalled by the weather that he didn't come out of his attractive, tiny house. I made my way upward on a slippery, stone trail and hadn't gone that far when I turned to discover that five of the gatekeeper's chickens were closely following me. I stopped. They stopped, looking up at my face, the apparent seat of my being. Why follow me in the hideous weather up into a nonconclusive immense pile of rocks? In an almost flashing moment I perceived the vanity of my study of nonhuman communication. I wasn't a scientist satisfied with drilling holes in a thin piece of board. Only that morning two ants had crossed the decrepit table in my little room in Reggio and had met in the middle, conversed, turned, and gone off in random directions. I decided looking down at my wet but friendly chickens that I'd never have a meaningful clue what they were clucking to each other, or what two tiny brown birds were saying to each other in the tree above me.

Riding back south toward Reggio in the intense rain I reflected on my first clue to a change the full nature of which I hadn't yet comprehended. The day before on a pleasant,

sunny October morning I had been sitting against a tree
reading a book (Alberto Moravia) when a minuscule lizard
crept down the tree trunk close to my head and I thought
the contents of the novel were within my reach but the lizard wasn't from its forked tongue testing the air to the tail
that diminished itself into nothing. I thought it would be easy
enough to identify the lizard but I would never understand
its lizardness. After a few moments studying me the lizard
followed its path back up the tree. What about my own path,
I thought. It was only informed by chaotic unrest.

Three months before, I had landed in Milano but its
large size unnerved me. I mean that while I had learned
Chicago, Milano was a last-minute change of plans and I
hadn't studied its skeletal map. I was there a day and a half
before I met my mother back at the airport when we picked
up her clients, an elderly couple from Cincinnati I'll call
Robert and Sylvia. Robert was morbidly obese and only
interested in eating, drinking, and sleeping. Sylvia was interested in Etruscan culture and medieval art though she
was distressingly simpleminded about both. In the four
days of driving them around they were never ready to go
before eleven in the morning when the July weather was
already overwarm. Robert barely looked out the car window so intently was he studying his briefcase full of food
guidebooks.

Mother was pleasant but not overly warm, feeling bad
as she was over the ill health of her elderly husband who was
left behind in Milano when we drove south to Parma. Robert smelled poor despite his wealth which came from a well-
known Cincinnati company that makes soap and toothpaste.

In Parma we had a few free hours after dropping Robert and Sylvia off at a grand hotel and checking into a simple *pensione*. While we were sharing a bottle of *prosecco* Mother said, "What horrid miserable fuckers," referring to her clients. We laughed and she dug into her purse coming up with a letter from my first love Emelia which had been forwarded but which she had misplaced for several months.

"There's something terribly wrong with you," she shyly observed.

"Of course," I said, adding a few details about complicated viruses.

"Do you have AIDS, dear?" she asked taking my hand.

"No, this is more complicated if possible." I desperately wanted to read the letter from Emelia the thought of whom made my heart thump.

The point was, I would never be able to share my secret except with the doctor and even with him leaving out the core of the violence. My mother sat there puzzled and then I rushed up to my room to read Emelia's letter, really just a note, which except in two small patches was banal. It was mostly a litany of unsuccess: marriage at nineteen to a country singer whose one small recognizable hit carried them for half a dozen years in small venues. They had no permanent home other than a traveling van, ending up as a house band in Reno where her husband had become a heroin addict. She tried to help him for a year then abandoned him to his drug. She returned home when her brother Lawrence died in a stock car accident. Her mother had collapsed mentally and she and her father tended her mother except he was gone a lot building pipelines. One day a letter from her father came from Falstaff, Arizona, saying he had "found another." The bright spot was that Dicky had become an electrical engineer for Sandia and helped financially while she made her way through nursing school at the University of New Mexico from which she would graduate by Christmas. She still had dreams about our beautiful times at the water tank south of Alpine. She ended, "Your first girlfriend, Emelia," adding as a P.S.:"I still haven't lived in a tall building in New York City."

I immediately became excited thinking about the water tank and Emelia's bare bottom and ejaculating as I stared off across her shoulder at a group of shy Corriente cattle waiting to drink. I immediately moved my mother and myself to a fine hotel with reliable phone service though it was a full day before I reached Emelia at dawn in Albuquerque. She was petulant at being wakened but quickly became friendly. I wanted to send her a ticket immediately but she said it would have to wait until December when she graduated with her nursing degree which was five months distant and nearly unbearable. The point though was that I suddenly had hope of some sort. Here I was only a few days in Italy and something marvelous had happened. Now it didn't repel me to take meals with wealthy Bob while Mother and Sylvia in disgust would eat lightly and take a walk. At a fine restaurant, Checci, in Parma Bob had three orders of *zampone,* a stuffed pig's leg, and three bottles of wine. Other diners and the staff cheered as I managed to carry three-hundred-pound-plus Bob out the door and into a waiting cab. My own extreme hungers were centered around the periods when the infirmity in my blood would arise suddenly like fungi.

Now as I rode through the rain south from Matilda's castle I was a scant forty days away from Emelia's arrival in Bologna, forty more days of loneliness for her. The trouble was that a big moon was due in twelve days, and another for Emelia's arrival. I had taken the drug three times and it had turned me into a vomiting zombie, two days of complete stasis wherein I could barely manage to reach the toilet. It was death-in-life which made me value pure unmitigated consciousness. Here I was pumping along the highway on my bike and now thinking of a literature-appreciation course for science majors at Northwestern. The course was normally taught by a kindly old man but then he fell ill in the middle of the semester and his substitute was a firebrand who had us read Dostoevsky's *Notes from Underground,* surely the most mind-scorching piece of fiction extant. We science majors, perhaps less so me, were quite disturbed when we were asked to write a short paper on the sentence "I maintain that to be acutely conscious is to be diseased." I was amused by this collegiate memory but then a large diesel truck beeped right behind me and I slid off the road tipping over into a huge mud puddle. There was a decided advantage to the canine in my system because I merely shook myself off like a dog and proceeded down the highway with my interesting burden of thoughts. I had long been resolved not to let my illness unduly affect my perceptions of reality. I had years ago learned to seek out stillness in wild settings and allow everything to be as it is. I had overstepped my boundaries in thinking I could ever understand the details of the language of creatures though their sense of reality must be added to our own for a complete picture of life on earth. I mean I could closely study their otherness and then let it go.

By sheer luck I swerved into a country restaurant parking lot where a few cars were parked. Near the entry two French girls were straddling their bikes reading the menu and arguing. Their bikes were laden with sodden camping equipment and they looked utterly woebegone. The shorter, pudgy one was counting the change in her small rubber purse and the taller, prettier one was crying. They were arguing about their lack of money. I made out that though it was Saturday morning more money was being wired to them on Monday.

"Allow me to buy you lunch," I said impulsively.

They turned to me scowling as if I were the most repulsive dickhead on earth.

"I'm not a beast. I'm alone and it's my birthday." I lied on both counts.

"Fine by us, American pig," the pudgy one laughed, determining the nationality behind my pidgin French.

My luck further intensified when the manager turned out to be a man who lived only a few doors down the street in Reggio and we had spoken several times about birds during early-morning coffee at a café. He set us up a table in front of the fireplace and we ate like hounds. I had three orders of pork braised with figs and the girls ate both fish soup and game hens. We drank three bottles of wine, laughed about nonsense, and became drowsy before the fire. One of them was studying art history and the other an ancient poetess named Gaspara Stampa and they were on a month-long trip through northern Italy, camping as they went, a clear impossibility in the weather of the day. They hoped to reach Modena, the neighboring city, by evening. I talked to the manager and he called a friend with a van taxi. I bought a bottle of wine and a bottle of grappa and we were off. My landlady at the *pensione* wasn't happy with my visitors but I gave her twenty bucks in lire and begged her to be nice. I gave them dry T-shirts to wear after soaking in a hot tub. I went to sleep in my cozy sleeping bag on the floor and the pudgy one, Mireille, joined me in the late afternoon, enveloping me in her wonderful vise. When the tall, prettier one, Kristabelle, was wakened by our activity she hissed, "I would never fuck an American," and I said, "Then don't," and they laughed hysterically. They drank the wine and I had several snorts of the grappa. We went out in the evening for more wine and pizza with them enjoying my baggy clothes and old western cowboy shirts. Kristabelle was rather sullen as pretty girls often are but we coupled briefly at dawn with all of us in bed in the coolish room. They were off for Modena on Sunday morning. I gave them some money and said I might see them on Monday as I had intended to visit Modena.

What a happy time it was. I had had scant love since helping out my mother in late July after which I'd visited Laurel in Madrid. We had a fine reunion with nights of love but then five days into my visit her father appeared and was definitely not happy to see me. Laurel became disconsolate because her father had been badgering her to have a baby. Laurel was the last of their particular family line. He was now in his early seventies and had none of the charm left that I had witnessed twelve years before. I asked late one night why he didn't father another child and she said that he had tried but a doctor had told him after a test that his sperm count was too low. "What about you?" she suddenly asked. I was startled. It had never occurred to me that a man in my condition should father a child. The next morning I called the doctor in Chicago and he said, "Definitely not," and that I shouldn't even make love he now believed without my wearing a couple of layers of protection. Laurel took this poorly and it was the effective end of our love morning. She had kindly identified three areas in France that were relatively empty, what cartographers call "sleeping beauties," and might give me refuge for the arrival of my seizures: the Morvan in western Burgundy, the Massif Central, and the Pays Basque. Galicia in western Spain was also possible. Not oddly I felt too much of the weight of Spain's past which had been very alive for my Spanish-teacher lover back at Northwestern whose grandfather had been tortured to death by Falangists in Granada. Much of my basic orientation is in the sciences, especially in zoology and botany, and there is no real space for superstition but I curiously felt what the hippies called "bad vibrations" in Spain. Even a cursory examination of the Spanish Civil War reminds one deeply of the prolonged horrors of our own. The predominant shock waves in world history are the capacity of humans to kill each other for political or religious reasons, most often a combination of both.

Laurel and I decided to take a brief train trip to Seville, thence to Granada, and then back to Madrid but then her father had left early on the morning of our departure and

he had utterly exhausted her with his badgering about her
having a baby. She sat on a packed suitcase in her elegant
apartment and sobbed for a full hour and I could do nothing to help. I couldn't make a dent in her uncomfortable
relationship with her father and what's more I couldn't offer
her a baby for medical reasons. Consequently she asked me
to leave and I made a brief tour to Granada and Seville and
then to Barcelona, all by rather slow local trains which I love.
Why be in a hurry with such a questionable future? I see in
my journal later on that I was overwhelmed by the physical
beauty of Spain but at the same time drowning in the melancholy of its history. As I've said I like to become intensely
familiar with any country I visit by reading and study including the literature, which indicates the nature of a
country's soul life. With Spain this was a disaster because I
was reading volumes of the poetry of Lorca, Machado, and
Hernández in whose bleached bones you see Spain's historical torment. Two days in the grandeur of Barcelona gave
me modest relief but not quite enough for survival. I went
to a ratty and smallish Gypsy club (the Gypsies are called
gitanos) and an old lady began to scream, evidently sensing my true nature, and I fled. I took a slow train along
the Costa Brava to Collioure in France where I stopped
to visit Machado's grave. I proceeded then along the Mediterranean coast all the way back to Italy, again by slow
local trains. What is more pleasant than reading a book
on a train and lifting your eyes so as not to miss the landscape? It was immediately pleasant to escape Spain's
spirit of murder and between Narbonne and Montpellier
a girl student was curled up on the seat across from me

revealing her miniskirted butt which I studied as if it were the true origin of the universe. The conductor took note, reddened, and shrugged as if put upon by gratuitous lust. I made notes to revisit the area especially the mountainous area north of the coast where I might seek the usual refuge.

Now in Modena in early November with Emelia's visit thirty-five days away I am restless despite a fine room and minuscule kitchenette not far from the city square, cathedral, and the immense gorgeous market from which I buy food for meals. Yesterday I made a pasta sauce from three kinds of wild fungi and this morning I bought myself a middling-sized octopus. My Chicago doctor's spansules have killed the wildness of my appetite for which I am grateful but then at least once a day I briefly miss that edgy fire in the blood which is as pure as sexual desire. The girl on the train with the exposed bottom near Montpellier grinned at her spectators on waking. *That is us* in our wild play.

This morning in a café before I went to the market the sound system was playing a group of arias by the Modena native son Pavarotti. My hair rose and my skin prickled at this voice of a god. I looked around and noticed that people had ceased reading their morning papers. I was reading a volume of poems by Ungaretti and the type blurred with my tears. Some music apparently returns us to the core of our being and this despite my unrest over finding a location for my seizure which was due in five days.

On the way back from the market I bought a battery-operated tape player and several tapes of Pavarotti thinking that I must study the voice. I even thought it might be best to study this voice in the city from which it had emerged.

In my room I listened while laying out my maps and found myself drawn to the Morvan region of Burgundy. I had idly looked at a volume about this area of Burgundy while at Laurel's apartment in Madrid but now rather than its Celtic or Roman origins I felt compelled by the dimensions of its forested areas. I had noticed that in the few days leading up to a seizure I felt an inevitable loneliness for forests, the odor of hardwoods in late fall. This was a kind of physiological sentimentality I had read in Proust in college. There were a few patches of fine hardwoods near Cincinnati that I could visualize from my earliest hunting experiences. I clearly needed a forest for my oncoming trauma.

I quickly ate my octopus and then went off and bought a small delivery van from a man who was giving up his produce stall at the market. After I paid him in cash he advised me that it would take days to get it properly licensed. I said, "Fuck 'em," as they do out west. He was amused by this and for an extra twenty bucks left his plates on the van. He was on his way to Seattle in the U.S. to visit his daughter who was a chef there and felt rather carefree. Within an hour I was headed northwest toward France via Torino.

Nov. 7–Nov. 10. I reached a campsite west of Autun in three days in my pathetic putt-putt van that could barely reach 65 kilometers per hr. (40 mph). I was tempted by Mt. Beuvray as a campsite but there were too many visitors thereabouts due to its fame from Julius Caesar being there about 60 B.C. I was unnerved in Vézelay to see above the main door of the cathedral the sculpted figures of men with the heads of dogs. Startled at lunch in a bistro when a local man told me the Celts were here in about 4000 B.C. This man was goofy rather than the ordinarily cynical Frenchman and told me to be wary of forest spirits after I said I was camping. He went into a rant as a lover of horses as the mountain people used to kill and eat wild horses. Later in the afternoon as my vehicle was struggling up a mountain trail I indeed felt strange and it was an effort to resist the silly feeling. It had begun in Vézelay and Autun. In both places when I'd wandered around as a garden-variety sightseer stray dogs, shy and deferential, had followed me and I suspected my scent was changing more radically than it had in the past with the oncoming big moon. Three girls near the cathedral in Autun teased me about being part dog and I gave a mock but convincing growl. They screeched and ran. I thought it would be fine if they could camp with me tonight but then my conscience cautioned me into its "do no harm" mode. How culture struggles to make us think we aren't what we are. I knew the Nazis had executed whole villages in the area. How could anyone kill a child? The other evening at a rest stop near Grenoble I'd tried to nap curled up in my cold van and a thief's hand had reached in the back door which I hadn't locked. I crushed the hand in my own feeling the thief's bones grind and shatter in my grip. He howled. I stopped short of jerking out a few fingers. On the long drive I felt strongly the strange burden of my early life. I thought I had rejected my parents but I never went anywhere without my volumes of Virgil and Ovid and often Sappho, and also the patrimony of bird books. The most overwhelming memories during the trip were of Emelia. I was often more than a little frightened of her but after eighteen years the merest slip of an image of her body would engorge my cock. How can memory do this to the body? An idle question because it does. Emelia flipping out of the water tank, her bare butt in the air with the small hairs sprouting in her miniature crevasse, the chubby lips of her pussy and her tiny pink asshole, the conflicting odors of her Dentyne gum and Camay soap. Or sitting on the musty couch in my shed with knees drawn up so that the undersides of her thighs drew one down to her puffy pussy under the white cotton panties, and her face saying, "Go ahead and look, fool." When I found a campsite in a thicket surrounded by shaggy and gnarled oaks I fucked a small patch of cold moss in desperation, then in the firelight I cut a spansule in half thinking that a partial dose would be enough in this remote place. I folded the rest of the spansule of powder in a square of notebook paper in the manner of the way I once bought a gram of cocaine in college and put it in my pocket. Well, the half dose wasn't enough and eleven hours later dawn found me in a flatland forest that turned out to be thirty miles west with a dog laying a dozen feet away. I immediately vomited thinking I might have eaten part of it but then it awoke and I was happy that I hadn't been cannibalistic. The dog approached and I petted it and then it trotted off as if it had accomplished its mission of protecting me, a joke indeed when I might have eaten it. I curled back up to sleep a little more then bounded to my feet when I saw a deer in the dawn mist through the trees perhaps a hundred yards in the distance. I was able to caution myself and quickly snorted the other half of the drug in its paper wrapper. I began to walk east toward the rising sun pausing now and then to fill my capacious jacket with the many boletus mushrooms I saw on the dense forest floor. I soon had found so many that I had to construct a makeshift sack out of my overshirt. I kept thinking of Professor Hamric back in college quoting Heidegger in my only philosophy course: "Living life is somewhat unfamiliar to us all." I was quite tired from my long night's run when the forest had seemed a broad river of moonlight. My fatigue was also from the soporific effect of the drug which at least controlled the savagery of appetite. I sat down against a tree to rest and not long after two men and a dog were standing before me. Their approach would have been impossible if I hadn't taken the drug. Since he was at eye level I greeted the dog first. One of the men was very large and exclaimed, "Jesus Christ!" when he saw my big shirt-sack of boletus. The other man was tall and slender and looked at me with concern. He said, "You are ill," quite accurately. I lamely explained that I used to run marathons and had run all night. I offered to give them my sack of mushrooms if they would give me a ride back to my campsite. The big man virtually yelled, "Yes," and we were soon on our way in their large comfortable car, stopping at a village butcher's where I bought a baguette and a kilo of *fromage de tête*, a large chunk of rough pâté made from the fat, cheek meat, and tongue of a pig. I literally wolfed down the whole two pounds in minutes. I could tell they were pleased when we reached the two-track to my camp-site. I hugged and kissed their dog Eliot who had slept on my lap and with whom I had shared some of my snack. I was relieved to reach my campsite and unpacked the remaining mushrooms from my jacket pocket. I found a large human finger and its bloody stump which I tossed off into the trees. The finger jogged my pitiful memory and I recalled that early in my night run I had stopped at a country tavern and had drunk several glasses of both red wine and water. The owner of the tavern and a big farmer yelled at me to leave, obviously uncomfortable with my com-pany. I was slow as if unable to understand human language. They grabbed me and hauled me out the front door. The farmer twisted my arm painfully and I overreacted, throwing them around the parking lot and coming up with a finger. I had hoped to cook my mushrooms with a skillet and olive oil over a camp-fire but quickly decided that I should leave the area.

I drove south to Lyon where hunger stopped me in the late afternoon. I met two sizable whores in a workingmen's district and took them to dinner in a bistro. I was manic and barely aware that this was the second night of my seizure. The confluence of the rivers in Lyon was eating the moon so I ate a great deal at the bistro, including several portions of beef snout in vinaigrette and three portions of beef stew. I like the tough, chewy texture of the beef snout and recalled Liz, a Catahoula cow dog on a ranch I took care of in Wyoming who would sink her teeth into the nose of a recalcitrant bull and drop it on the spot. I don't remember much about the whores except sensations of pleasure. At dawn the police fished me out of the Rhône River where I had been taking a swim. They assumed I was drunk and only said, "Go home."

I headed back toward Torino sinking ever deeper by the mile in a fresh sort of melancholy, a hypothermia of the soul. I was bone weary and stopped now and then in the fierce mistral winds from the north to nap in any available forest in my sleeping bag. I was frankly suicidal to a degree I had never experienced before and it was only the arrival of Emelia in a few weeks that held me back. Not oddly I began to think of religion. Was Emelia my religion, a female I hadn't seen since age twelve? In my current state she made as much sense as the thousands of bleeding Jesuses I had seen in the museums and churches of Italy. Who was I but a diseased soul who knew no one as well as the books he packed along? My mother's religion were books and my father's birds. As a child I was totally without any religious training. Perhaps my perceptual muse was the nature of nature but the more I studied it the more inscrutable it became. Was I built to truly understand a rat or a galaxy? For eighteen years I had been trying to run ahead of my disease, an act that might be called a will to live. If Emelia was keeping me on earth, how did I know I'd still care for her or she would care for me? This was a slight string to climb rather than a sturdy rope. My exhaustion was a vacuum the landscape couldn't fill. All of this sheer beauty in Europe, manmade and natural, but perhaps only wildness could keep me engrossed between moons. I couldn't bring myself to think that Emelia would want to live with me. There wouldn't be a point in not telling her absolutely everything. I had no unknown God to pray to and the hundreds in mythology were no more reassuring than a rattlesnake or grizzly bear.

I turned south in Torino toward Savona and continued on down the coast thinking that the Mediterranean might console me, or at least absorb my poisonous mind. It did so only because the strong mistral winds made the water so implacable with their offshore power so that far out the dark water was rumpled. I suddenly wished I had packed an anthology of Chinese poetry called *The White Pony* which I had owned since my junior year in high school. There are no reassurances in Wang Wei, Li Po, Tu Fu, or Su Tung-Po which ends up being reassuring. You end up accepting that you live and die at ground zero but you also learn that your possible unhappiness or melancholy are only self-indulgent. I recalled that on the wall of the small adobe house of the woman, the *curandera,* who put a poultice on my cheek where the hummingbird had pierced the flesh, there was a black mask of a wolf with the figure of a nude woman draped across its nose. I'd pointed it out to Nestor who'd laughed and said it was just "part of life." When I reached Modena late in the evening of my third day of the return trip in my wretched van I made a pot of coffee and stayed up all night reading about European trees, the Second World War in

Italy, and a volume of poems Laurel had given me by a contemporary French poet, René Char. She had said rather lamely and ambiguously that Char "preferred the outside like you." I read and read and thought it would be grand to know such a man but then I knew scarcely anyone on earth and my own story was scarcely tellable. I couldn't very well mention that just the other day I'd found a finger in my pocket. It was altogether natural to try to compensate in my reading for the evident fact that I belonged as convincingly to the animal world as I did to the human. It has amused me that the other morning while I was napping on a cold Mediterranean beach two Bouviers which are normally guard dogs had curled up beside me perhaps thinking that I was their long-lost pack leader who would protect them in this vale of woe. Their owner, a florid Englishman, called them without success and came huffing up demanding to know my "trick" and I jokingly told him that I was part dog.

I made myself busy researching this and that while waiting the following weeks for Emelia. I took the train to Bologna and then to Florence to visit bookstores. This period of waiting for Emelia I absorbed as a purgatory prefatory to heaven or hell. I had no idea which it would be but cautioned myself against thinking in terms of polar opposites which are invariably moderated by reality. I only talked to her once a week at the most because she was studying for her final exams for her nursing degree. In her voice I caught again how difficult she could be. She said that because of her "dickhead" ex-husband she had certainly learned never again to be dependent on a man. She had always referred to her father as "the asshole bully." I didn't see it but heard about it later when on a December morning we had a rare half foot of fluffy snow and she had run out in her bra and panties and rolled in the snow. Lawrence told me, "Dad tanned her butt" and she hadn't spoken to him for weeks until she got the new bicycle she desired as his penance. In a very real way she controlled her family. She had already warned me not to "jump her" when she arrived in Italy. She had taken several years of martial arts courses and I would be sorry indeed. If her arrival was to be my deliverance, almost a religious event, it certainly had the captious quality of what I had learned of organized religion.

My trip to Bologna, a beautiful city, was a flop because it was jam-packed with businesspeople at trade meetings. One has every right in our time to develop suspicions about those who wear suits and ties. My room was too small and it was right next to a bump shop so that while I was reading a history of World War II there was an incessant sound of sanders and hammers. I gave up and took the train to Florence chiding myself for my frugality. I had never spent more than half of my monthly check that came through the American Express office so in Florence I rented a room in a hotel facing the Piazza della Repubblica. I found a bookstore where there were many titles in English so that I could stop struggling with the slowness in my use of French and Italian dictionaries. I even bought a nonsense book of world facts to read at lunch and dinner when strenuous reading can ruin a meal. I learned while eating a huge Florentine steak (for two) three evenings in a row at Sostanza that we Americans had extirpated our buffalo to the tune of seventy

million beasts in the nineteenth century while Chairman
Mao had engineered the deaths of seventy million Chinese.
What was I to make of this? I abandoned history of any sort.
The bookstores didn't have the Chinese anthology *The White
Pony* but they ordered it for me and would send it on to
Modena. I did, however, find Chinese translations by Bur-
ton Watson and Willis Barnstone wherein famine and war
were only to be expected.

My nights were haunted to a manic degree by Emelia.
I dozed off and on then got up and took longish walks in
the nighttime city. I kept catching myself trapped in the
abstraction of the future. Did I expect her to throw herself
into my arms and stay with me forever? In our last phone
call she had said she had accepted a job in a small hospital
in Dillon, Montana, to start in January. She hoped to meet
a rancher who would buy her horses. I was immediately
jealous and said I could do that and in my years of overseeing ranches I had become knowledgeable about horses. This
wasn't quite true because I preferred walking but it wasn't
part of my love campaign to admit the truth. She grilled me
on where I'd gotten the money and I said I had made a wise
investment of five hundred bucks back in college. She said,
"Oh bullshit, that's not fair," and I said nothing in world
economics is fair. Our talk became inane because we only
knew each other in eighteen-year-old memories.

Meanwhile it had become unseasonably warm so I took
the train back north to Modena, really not that far in American terms, where it was also unseasonably warm. Suddenly
I was homesick for cold as if in my circadian rhythms there
was a craving for the cold in the northern parts of the West,

or the violent cold of far northern Minnesota, Wisconsin, and Michigan when I hunted up there when I was in college. It was just after Thanksgiving week back home and I was swatting flies in an overwarm room in Italy, imagining my snowshoes and cross-country skis in storage back in Chicago.

I became a severe insomniac walking Modena on cool nights in a thin shirt so I could become cold and then the iron shoe dropped on December first, a week from her arrival. My landlady woke me at five A.M. to say a woman was calling from New Mexico. Of course it was Emelia intermittently crying because she and her brother Dicky had been out riding near Mountainair and Dicky's horse had thrown him crushing a hip bone and even now he was in surgery having a metal rod put in his hip. He'd be in the hospital for a week and she'd nurse him until she went to Montana in late January when he'd be back on his feet. She was both grief-stricken and pissed because she dearly wanted to come see me. "Are there water tanks over there?" she joked in her sniffling. I stood there stunned into silence until she asked, "Are you still there?" She pronounced Europe "Yerp."

"If you can't come here I'm coming there," I finally said.

"Okay. See you when you get here," was all she said and without a trace of romanticism. My mother used to say when we first moved to Alpine that Emelia's was a very nice "white trash" family. I asked Mother to stop saying that and she eventually got along with Emelia's mother talking about their perennial beds and drinking beer on the porch.

I moved at warp speed arriving in Dallas in thirty-six hours via Milano and Paris. Emelia's plan had been for me to take her to Paris and up the Eiffel Tower, the singular thing she seemed to know about Paris. What with my bookish nature I was counting on the idea that opposites attract. The flight from Milano to Paris made me giddy but the very long section from Paris to Dallas was cast in somber guilt. The idea that my life was being changed radically by Dicky being pitched off a horse was confusing, I mean the sheer randomness. The fact that I had merged with Emelia in our hormonal puberty wasn't a reassuring principle for seeing her eighteen years later. I was trying to read a book by Primo Levi when I wasn't thinking about Emelia and the both of them gave me an unending lump in the throat. I recalled Professor Hamric telling us that ideas of ethnic virtue were inevitably destructive to whites, blacks, Jews, and American Indians. Who else? I had read that in the genetic defect of two-headed turtles the heads invariably fought over food. The plane held a lot of noisy exchange students so I went into the toilet and took a tiny pinch of my zombie dust which allowed me to sleep the last seven hours of the flight. Luckily it was Saturday afternoon so I didn't have to deal with traffic jams in the hellhole of urban sprawl of Dallas. I angled up to Amarillo then over to Santa Rosa in New Mexico on Route 40 short of midnight. I called Emelia and she said not to expect too much company on Sunday because her biggest final exam was on Monday and between studying and visiting Dicky, which I should do also, she wouldn't have much time.

In Santa Rosa I left the motel before dawn and drove up to the Variadero area where I once briefly took care of a property until the summer heat drove me back to Montana.

I walked a half dozen miles along a ranch road in the very cold first daylight reveling in the vast juniper landscape. The jump from northern Italy to this emptiness was startling. Italy was as far as you could go toward beauty in a man-dominated landscape. I tried to imagine what those grasslands looked like before the juniper invaded which you could still see up north between Mountainair and Vaughn.

By the time I got back to the car I was beside myself looking at my body wondering just what this body was doing. I reached Albuquerque and Emelia's apartment in a remodeled motel at noon. I was so remote I couldn't feel my knuckles knock on the door and when she opened it I couldn't visually put her all together at once but had to do it in sections. She was taller than I expected but my expectations were meaningless. I'd say about my height which was five-ten. Not surprisingly she still had an olive complexion and black hair from her father's side which was named Gagnon out of Louisiana. I was having trouble putting her together but then I'd had so little solid contact with other people in my thirty years. I stupidly offered a hand rather than trying to hug her but then I was confused by the idea that she was handsome rather than pretty.

"You look like you haven't had an easy life," she said, massaging my hand.

"Not exactly," I said, catching her slight lilac odor.

"I was up until five studying and now I've got to go see Dicky. You can stay here after I finish this exam tomorrow morning. Be a dear and make me scrambled eggs and grits so I can take a shower."

She went through her bedroom and into the toilet and I could hear the shower running before I finally started to breathe. I began to make her breakfast with my heart still thumping. I had never had an actual all-out lover. I wouldn't know what to call Laurel or Emelia for that matter when we were twelve. I had made love to dozens of prostitutes and the stray tavern tarts of the West in the vicinity of my property and ranch jobs but ultimately because of medical problems I kept distant. I had even kept distant from the idea of belief except in the details of aspects of the natural world. I could scarcely indulge my mind in anything the least bit mushy. Now making grits and eggs which I had done since childhood what with my mother being a late sleeper all I wanted truly on earth was a girlfriend. Whether we proceeded far enough that I would be obligated to fully admit my condition was another matter.

She came out of the bedroom about three-quarters dressed, barefoot in a green skirt and half-opened blouse. She stared at me a moment, doused her breakfast with Tabasco, and quickly ate it. She lit a cigarette and stared at me again then took my forearm coming out of my short-sleeved shirt.

"I've had a fair amount of training and I'm not stupid. I need to know what's wrong with you. You look at least forty not thirty. You're burning up and wearing out."

I hadn't thought of rehearsing but I had hoped to slowly work into this. I went for broke for want of any options and told her everything except for a few violent experiences I could barely admit to myself.

"Jesus H. Christ," she fairly screamed. "Get out of here until noon tomorrow. I've got a thirty-eight but I hope I won't have to shoot your sorry ass. I never was afraid of anything."

"I remember that," I said with a quaver in my voice. At the door she gave me a full kiss and she was amused that I was shaking.

I broke down in the car and wept, an alien act because I simply couldn't remember ever having wept before. She must have been watching from her apartment because suddenly there was a knock at the car window. I opened the door and she drew me tightly to her breast saying, "Maybe I can take care of you."

I drove south because I had to find a location for my oncoming seizure in two days. I turned right in Socorro and drove west far into an area called the Plains of San Agustin, again a place on the map cartographers would call a "sleeping beauty" relatively without the blemishes with which we have permanently scarred the earth. I decided to spend the night so had to drive farther to the edge of the Gila Wilderness Area to find firewood because I could see it would be bitterly cold, the kind of temperature I craved in Italy, and I doubted my sleeping bag would be adequate. I had bought a couple of burritos in Socorro which I could warm by the fire. What I most looked forward to was the full sweep of stars as ambient light tends to blind us to them in our populated areas and Europe.

I made camp at the mouth of a canyon not daring to go farther on the two-track in my rental car. I stacked quite a pile of firewood, mostly juniper, and started three good fires so I could sleep in the triangle's middle, an effective ritual. There was about an hour of daylight left so I climbed the steepest slope I could find to try to exhaust myself.

It was a glorious night with the stars drawing almost too closely, or so I thought, stretched there in the cold air within the coals of three fires. The stars helped me slow my mind before the moon rose with its inevitable enervating power. Emelia's last embrace had lightened my mind to a degree I couldn't remember. I suppose that my emotional response to the stars that were nearly creamy in their density came close to what others felt was their religion. It was interesting lying there that my mother as a classicist had given me the gods rather than a more theistic God and perhaps the errant and antic ancient gods offered a better explanation for our life on the planet. In the earth's turning the sky became an endless river and even when the moon rose rather than be disturbed I thought of myself as only a child of gravity. I kept thinking of a poem my Spanish teacher had quoted to me several times when we were sitting on a park bench on a May evening looking out at a dulcet Lake Michigan. The poem was by a Portuguese named Pessoa:

> *The gods by their example*
> *Help only those*
> *Who seek to go nowhere*
> *But in the river of things.*

Before I finally slept well after midnight, and while listening to coyotes in chase, it occurred to me that Emelia might accept me despite what I'd told her because we were

lovers so early in life. Embracing nude in the water tank
with our tongues and limbs intertwined was a baptism that
couldn't be erased by dire language. The adolescent ache of
two bodies for each other never failed to reenter my mind
and body. It was the overwhelming rule of what was supposed to *be*.

I did a rare thing and slept through dawn as if I were
part of the ground. The weather had changed and there was
a slight warmish wind from the south. I made coffee from
the small pot in my knapsack and the remnants of a bag of
coffee from Modena so that as I drank there was the jar-
ring feeling from the scent and taste that I was still at my
breakfast café down the street. I was curious about a canyon far to the west and walked there rapidly, stopping to
watch a huge flock of doves circling a water tank. This made
me hungry. When I began hunting with my friend Cedric
south of Cincinnati we'd shoot ten or so doves, start a fire,
and pluck and grill them in the wire basket he'd detach from
his bicycle. I had nothing to eat and hunger turned me back
to the car. Something nagged at me and I remembered a
short nightmare I'd had about the cluster of hummingbirds
flitting around the raw wound on my throat in the rain. I
stopped in Socorro and had two bowls of menudo, Mexican tripe stew, and headed north toward Emelia and Albuquerque stopping to pick up some decent wine as I had seen
an empty bottle of wretched plonk on her counter, also a
bottle of fine Herradura tequila.

When I reached her apartment she had just gotten
home from her final exam. She was a pink-eyed, frazzled
mess. I poured her a shot of tequila watching through the

bedroom door as she stripped to her panties. I put a washcloth under the hot tap and wrung it out. She drank the
tequila in a gulp and I knelt and put the washcloth over
her eyes. I kissed a nipple with my heart in my mouth.

"I'm too tired to fuck but I will," she said with a pained
smile.

Afterward she asked me to go see Dicky, also to buy
her a steak, barely getting out the words before she lapsed
into a soft snore. On a desk mostly covered with medical
textbooks and cosmetics there was a photo of her, Dicky,
Lawrence, and me dressed up for Halloween so long ago.
She was in a turban and I was in a cheap, loose-fitting Super-
man costume, a yard-sale special.

At the butcher shop I thought how strange it was to
make love to someone you loved. I visited Dicky who was
happy to see me, half-suspended in a hip cast. "Too bad
Lawrence isn't here," he said, and then we were silent for a
few minutes looking at the Jemez Mountains far to the
north. I wondered if Emelia had told him anything about
my condition but he gave no indication that she had.

"I'm glad you're here for Emelia. She was a fucking
mess four years ago. I think she was even taking heroin like
her husband. I told that shitsucker that if he ever showed
up in New Mexico again I'd have his throat cut."

We talked for an easy hour and I told him I'd move
Emelia out to his place in Sandia Park once I bought a
pickup in the morning. She could take care of him and I'd
drive up to Dillon and find a place to live. I didn't presume
to say "find us" a place to live.

When I got back to the apartment she had largely

recovered. She didn't have a grill for the steak but assured me she could do fine with an iron skillet. I had forgotten to take the price tag off the wine.

"I'm not going to tell you that you've had all the luck," she laughed.

We had the best evening of my life and in the morning we shopped for a pickup. I told her that it was time for me to leave town for two days. She wanted to go too and take care of me but I said that maybe in the future we could do so once we created a "safe" situation. She was tremulous when she said, "You sure you're coming back?" The world has created so many waifs.

I went back to the Plains of San Agustin and exhausted myself for two nights but had the minimal sense to move in a wide circle since I finally had a destination though I took a little more of the drug than usual in hopes of staying safe. When I got back I moved her out to Dicky's house then headed north to Montana to find a place for us to live.

I looked around Dillon in wider and wider circles for nearly a week, constantly on pay phones with Emelia who always reminded me that we'd need enough space for a horse. She liked the idea of keeping up with me on my monthly jaunts. I finally found a place only a few miles south of Melrose which was about thirty miles north of Dillon. It was an old but spacious trout fisherman's cabin that had ten acres on the Big Hole River and a shed I could convert into a stable. I'd have liked something a little more remote but the surrounding territory redefined the modern concept of remote. The local bar and restaurant already had a hitching post along the front for horses. I bought a pair of hip boots from the local fly-fishing shop and made my way across the river from the cabin to look at a triangular flat of pasture surrounded by fairly steep cliffs, one stained copiously by bird dung and far up you could make out a golden eagles' nest. At the back corner of the flat there were sage bushes ten feet high, a phenomenon I had never seen before despite my years working in ranch country in the West. When you lifted the lid a bit the natural world, including ourselves, offered as much darkness in human terms as light. To look at it with any clarity you certainly had to attempt to look at it through the perceptions of a million-plus other species.

EPILOGUE

I drove back to Albuquerque and we moved north not really like newlyweds after having Christmas with Dicky. I did the cooking, clearly seeing this as part of my future as Emelia's attention span was ill-suited to it ("Let's put the lamb chops in the oven and take a walk"). During Christmas dinner with lots of wine we argued about which set of parents were worse but lightened up in the forgiving nature of the season. Their mother had gone back home, had had a questionable second marriage, and was starting on a third with a neighbor in the alligator business, whatever that is.

Emelia liked her job in Dillon and more importantly the place I had bought near Melrose. I took a month during a very cold January to convert the shed into a stable and tightly mend ten acres of fence. We ended up buying two reasonably priced horses because Emelia insisted that "one gets lonely."

Our life together fell well short of an idyll but then idylls by definition are short. I had one truly bad seizure in April ten miles west in the Pioneer Mountains and was arrested for possessing an illegal deer. The charges were dropped when the game warden couldn't figure out how the animal had been killed. After that Emelia dropped me off in the largely vacant high-altitude Centennial Valley with an acreage of 400,000. I had to be well prepared because the temperatures reached forty below zero in the winter.

The relatively bad news came in June when we were nearly a week in Chicago. I spent much of three days with the doctor while Emelia went up the elevator in every tall building in which she was permitted plus various museums. She was quite frightened flying out of Bozeman because she had never had the occasion to fly before. She loved having room service breakfast looking out at Lake Michigan. Those from the Southwest can't conceive of that much water and she kept saying, "Just look at that water."

The bad news came in the form of the doctor telling me that I showed signs of having a form of canine progeria, a malady of accelerating aging that would include inevitable kidney and joint failure. I was thirty-one and he doubted I'd reach forty. I refrained from telling Emelia this not wanting to diminish her pleasure in Chicago. I told the doctor I had found a place where I could endure my seizures without the stultifying drugs which took a week to get over. He was happy for me. I must say that my death sentence vastly intensified the pleasure I took in my remaining time. So there is an end to all of this, I thought stupidly. Emelia noticed the lightening in my spirit after Chicago.

On the long flight back to Montana Emelia mostly slept with her head against my shoulder somehow cracking her gum once in her sleep. I thought how curious it was to see the outline of the girl in the woman. It is so difficult to wrap certain sets of feelings in language. Naturally we're all afraid of the suffering in our future and in the middle of the suffering we just as naturally wonder, How long can this go on? When there is some relief the most ordinary aspects of the world can look quite beautiful. There on the plane crossing the improbable Mississippi and the verdancy we never see in the West I recalled a harsh morning a half dozen years before up near Choteau in northern Montana south of the Blackfeet Reservation. A neighbor had called needing help with a bear. His small ranch backed up to the Sun River coming out of the Bob Marshall Wilderness. I drove over stopping in the yard to say hello to his wife who was a mixed-blood Blackfeet and to look at her gorgeous row of peonies. The trouble with the bear was that he had shot it in the act of killing a calf. My neighbor had pulled his front-end loader around to behind the shed where the bear lay, an old female grizzly, and he said her two-year-old cub had taken off for the mountains. I looked down at the massive sow and then over about thirty yards to the dead calf with quite a chunk taken out of the back of its neck right through the upper spine. My neighbor said, "Poor old girl," then went into the shed to look for a wrench to tighten the nuts on the loader. He was going to bury the animal to avoid dealing with the game officials. While he was gone I stooped down to examine the bear's teeth determining that she was old indeed and that the escaped cub was anyway her last. At age two the cub would likely not survive but maybe. On impulse I lay down beside her and looked into her dead eyes a scant foot from my own. I put a hand on her massive head as if she were a lover. I had a disturbing thought, saying to myself, "It's not you or me but us," including the dead calf off to the side and the bright blue sky above us. Though her head was the size of a bushel basket and her claws as long as my fingers at least for a moment I felt as if we were cousins.